A.C. HACHEM

DAWN OF LEGAIA

3RD MILLENNIA ENTERTAINMENT

I have studied the past;

my eyes have grown tired of the present,

and so I dream of the future.

DAWN OF LEGAIA

Los Angeles, 2083

1

An Android With An Agenda

Although the Port of Long Beach was still bustling well after the sun had set, its operations manager had snuck away, taking refuge in his office trailer. His reflective vest, hard hat, and tablet computer, had been placed neatly onto the sofa near his desk. The trickle of his automated coffee pot was a welcomed change, relative to the traffic outside.

As he deleted emails from his inbox, a knock at the trailer's door brought a sudden end to his tranquility. He turned to look at a 3-D security monitor, rather than immediately opening the door. In the rendering, he saw what appeared to be a port worker, accompanied by a dark android.

He sighed as he placed his hands upon his knees and got up, before making his way toward the door, hard hat in hand.

"Gerald Meyers?" asked the visitor.

"You must be Tony…" replied Gerry, before noticing Tony's ring.

The android silently surveyed the room as well as his

1

surroundings as the men spoke. A few moments into their conversation, the operations manager used a vocal command to turn out the lights, before closing the door behind him and joining his guests for a walk.

However, along the way, the visitor's robot companion deviated from their path. After veering off to the right, it dove quietly into the dark bay.

The men continued walking, unfazed. They reached their destination and shook the hand of another port employee, without addressing the fact that the android robot the guest had shown up with decided to go for an untimely late night swim. As the gentlemen walked away, engrossed in their conversation, the mysterious android swam deeper and farther, eventually making its way to a small, dark, and stealthy submarine vessel.

With a look of determination upon its face, it muscled open an external door and made its way into the sub. The exterior door shut slowly, as the water in the sub's entryway was pumped out. The android with an agenda was now in the vessel's control room, where it wasted no time getting to work.

It powered up the submarine and activated all of its various components with innate ease, feverishly pressing buttons and flipping switches. The whites of the android's eyes flickered with a bluish hue, signaling that it was transmitting communications, as it released the submarine from the rubberized docking arm that held it in place and departed.

The android piloted the stealth sub farther and farther from land. Its virtual telemetry system gave the robot precise guidance, as it spotted its target along the edge of one of the onboard monitors. The sub continued directly toward a large freight vessel headed for the port. In an awkward maneuver, the android captain flipped the submarine upside down, as it went deeper underwater. As cautiously as it could, the 'droid approached the ship's hull, magnetically attaching itself to the huge cargo ship's underbelly. Realizing it had reached its objective, the android pressed several more buttons on the sub's control panel. A red switch, protected by a thermoplastic cover, lit up. The robot stared at the see-through housing for several seconds, as if it were second guessing its own prerogatives.

With sudden conviction, it lifted the housing, wrapped its finger around the illuminated trigger, and squeezed.

The cargo ship shook violently, as crew members ducked, dodged, and covered their ears in an attempt to ease the effects of the violent eruption. Some workers helped fallen staff members up off the ship's main floor while others ran for stairs leading to higher decks.

This kamikaze sub had created a gaping hole in the left underside of the vessel. The ship began to creek louder and tilt toward its port side. Crew members fell off the upper decks in life vests, flailing their arms and legs as they descended toward the intimidating waters.

Lost and damaged supplies would cost hundreds of millions of California dollars to replace, causing months of delays.

It was late into their shift, which meant the guards were either oblivious with fatigue or nodding off at their posts, but the air horns coming from the ship would soon put an end to their midnight haze. The explosion was both visible and audible from the port, and workers back on dry land couldn't believe what was happening, looking on in horror at the fiery glow of the ship's remains.

Coast Guard rescue teams reached the disaster site quickly and plucked frightened crew members from the chilly waters. Pieces of flaming debris floated just feet away from port police speedboats, as firefighters doused the wreckage with flame-retardant foam. It was a nightmare of a scene, and it was all the work of one treacherous robot.

The next morning, Monte Cizek laid in bed and browsed

applications on his mobile device—the first thing he did each morning after silencing his alarm clock. It was during this morning routine that he learned of the port disaster and immediately called his nanotechnology professor, Doctor Randal Porter.

Dr. Porter was an early riser. He'd already had two cups of tea and skimmed an entire holographic Sunday paper by the time he received Monte's phone call.

"I'm sure you've heard the news by now. We don't ever just get to work in peace, do we?" asked Monte, skipping the hello's and how are you's.

"Un-fucking-believable…" responded the blunt professor.

"Are we screwed?"

"No, we're not screwed…Just inconvenienced…That was a pretty sizeable shipment that bastard blew to bits, but I have vendors on every piece of land on this God forsaken planet. It's no biggie. I will say, though, I really coulda done without this. I had about fifty crates on that ship. A couple of 'em were pretty important…I wonder if they knew about the reserve eight parts…Nah, they couldn't have known about that. Anyway, Kid, we're talkin' too much. Gotta keep it hi 'n' bye on here, remember?"

"I thought your VOFO line was secure, Doc."

"Yeah, about as secure as a cargo ship on a Saturday night. Try not to think about it. I'll expedite what I need from elsewhere. You go enjoy your Sunday, I've got a few phone calls to make."

"Ahhh…alright, Professor," said the student with a sigh. "Hope everything works out. See you tomorrow."

Monte was surprised by how calmly Dr. Porter was able to handle news like this. He figured it was one of Randy's finer qualities—one that he could definitely learn something from.

"Hey, Monte?"

"Yes, Professor?"

"Got a minute?"

"Sure thing."

"I know you're well aware of my involvement with the LISC, but I need to speak with you about yours."

The professor was referring to the Legaia International Space Colony, a large-scale space station project he had been working on for decades which was nearing completion.

"Sure, Doc. I'm all ears."

"The failure or success of this project is going to dictate what the next several decades look like. The future of cosmic capitalism is up for grabs, and Legaia is the key to unlocking that door. These attacks, these headaches, I feel they're only going to worsen. And if you're going to help me ensure Legaia's success, I need you to be well aware of what you're signing up for.

"Once on Legaia, we'll be watching it closely, monitoring its stability while working on making it more efficient. More sustainable.

"Air, water, power, logistics, all of it. And while we're at it, we'll be on radars and under microscopes. It won't be easy. Hell, it may not even be safe, but as far as I'm concerned, it doesn't matter. This is my calling, my life's work. And I do want you there at my side. I just wanna make sure you know what you're getting yourself into, that's all.

"If science and medicine should fail, if what nearly wiped us out several decades ago comes back, or if there's a similar outbreak, the LISC will be our final stand. And I cannot and will not allow the hand of tyranny to meddle with the fate of humanity."

Monte took a deep breath, giving himself a moment to absorb his professor's statement.

"Doc...I understand. I know this is what you have to do, and

5

I want to help you get it done. Count me in. Whatever it takes."

"Atta-boy. Rest up these next few days, yeah? We're in for one hell of a ride. I'll see you tomorrow."

"Yes, sir. Bye, Professor."

"Bye, Monte."

Dr. Porter hung up and stared into the bottom of his empty mug, before admiring the scale model of the LISC that sat upon the center of his dining room table.

2

On Lockedown

It had been thirty-six years since the deaths of 2047. Most had forgotten about the somber days of the past, when billions of people across several continents were lost overnight. There were no culprits, and no true explanations. Only the survival of those with a unique genetic commonality.

Science, technology, and business, however, kept "the reduction" in mind, and one family in particular had built an entire empire around these tragic times. They, were the Hurlocke family.

Richard Hurlocke sat in his posh office, as Regal, his personal android assistant and bodyguard, assisted him with his daily duties.

"You hear about this explosion in Long Beach? What a disaster…" said Hurlocke sarcastically.

"Engineering has submitted a brief this morning. They are ready for phase-one simulations concerning Operation Nativity. Also, your friends from Vitali Capital called to say they're running a bit late for this afternoon's meeting."

"Simulations, huh. Good for them. See if Robby is free, I'd like to have a word with him."

"As you wish, sir."

Robby was Richard's son, and one of few people Richard trusted with his business matters. The senior Hurlocke adjusted his blazer while a projector displayed financial market data on the wall to his right. As he smirked at the success of his investments, Robby, dressed sharply himself, arrived at his office.

"Looking good..." said Robby, upon entering. His hands were clasped at his back as he noticed the abundance of green ticker symbols, as opposed to red.

"Oh, it can always be better. True success knows no satisfaction." retorted Richard.

"Regal said you wanted to see me?" said Robby, sidestepping his father's comments.

"I did, yes. Sit down, son."

Robby complied, taking a seat along the edge of a leather chair, anxiously tapping his foot. Regal sat down in the corner of the room, resting one leg upon the other.

"Any news on NTI's eight?"

Richard was constantly researching the affairs of Nanoflèche Technologies, the robotics company owned by his former friend and long-time rival, Randal Porter. Dr. Porter juggled running a University along with NTI and his Legaia-related duties, and rumor had it NTI was getting ready to build their next-generation android, the "eight".

"Porter is currently focused on the LISC's launch, but my sources tell me the prototype eight is scheduled to undergo assembly any day now."

"How soon can we crack it after it's built?" inquired Richard.

Robby's eyes bounced around the room in frustration.

"We don't even know what the final build will look like, how old our intel is, or what changes they'll be making before manufacturing. Whether or not we'll be able to breach it at all."

"Robby, you're going to upset me…"

Bad news didn't sit well with Richard Hurlocke, and Robby knew that better than anyone else.

"…We have all the information we need concerning NTI's underlying code from the seven. When the eight is finalized, our black hats will confirm its hardware and software, and we can make moves accordingly. I can't tell a team of hackers to make plans to attack something that doesn't exist yet."

Richard stood from his seat. He pressed a button on his mobile device, shutting the mechanized blinds.

"I don't have a problem with what you're saying Robby…What I do have a problem with, is the ideology of the idiots that work for me. You see, if we're always waiting for NTI to make the first move, we're always gonna be chasing their coat tails. We need to beat them, not keep up with them. Do you understand what I'm saying, Robby?"

"I do."

"Good. Now do your part, to help your staff understand that they need to do more, and they need to do better, otherwise I will shit-can them all and replace them with people who can. Do you understand that as well?"

"Absolutely. I'll be sure to relay the message."

"Wonderful." said Hurlocke as he continued to pace back and forth.

"Hard to believe Legaia goes live in a few days." said Robby in an attempt to change the subject and ease his father's mood. His comment was met immediately by Richard's grin, as Hurlocke took one final look at his stock quotes before replying.

"This is where Porter's reign ends. We will no longer play second fiddle to him, because we're better than him. And when

Legaia goes live, I'll dedicate every asset and every dollar to making sure it's under our control. Its tech will be used in our products, our machines. And I will finally put that smug bastard where he belongs. Reading news of our breakthroughs and our accomplishments. I told you long ago that Porter was going to pay for his mistakes, and I mean that now more than ever.

Go tell your engineers they have until the end of the week to give me something I'm pleased with, or they'll be finding themselves begging on Silicon Beach instead of coding in it."

Robby nodded and exited the office, unsure of what to tell his I.T. staff. He was used to Richard's persistence in business, but knew his father well enough to know that trouble lie ahead.

3

Not Your Average Robot

The city's traffic was heavy, even on light days, and Monte felt as though he could never get to class quick enough as he raced against his agitations. Riding along Del Amo Boulevard felt like a drive through a post-apocalyptic war zone. What seemed like endless piping, canisters, and storage tanks. A massive refinery to his left, with more chemical processing plants to his right, and two protruding towers that took turns shooting flames into the sky. There was a stench to the east that matched the landscape, and more gasoline than a moto-loving whiz kid could ever want or need.

Once on the freeway, he zipped along the noontime 110 North. The Magnetrak lane enabled him to engage cruise control at 100 mph, definitely the favorite part of his daily commute. He fired up satellite radio in his helmet, tucked down as low as he could, and enjoyed the ride.

Monte and his family would soon be moving to the Legaia International Space Colony, making this particular motorcycle ride a sweet one—his way of saying goodbye to Los Angeles for the time being.

Meanwhile, several miles to the north in a Porter University research and development building, Randal Porter monitored the creation of his first level eight android.

"Nate" will be the world's first independently conscious nandroid robot, whose intellectual scaling will allow it to learn, adapt, and grow in ways identical to that of a human being and beyond. The eight's full potential is yet to be known, even by the professor himself, and he's the most excitement the scientific community has seen since mankind discovered we didn't live on a blue pancake.

The product of seven previous designs spanning multiple decades, this robot will be unlike any that ever existed before it. It will have numerous power sources, ranging from the latest lithium-based batteries to crystals manufactured from the oils of a bioengineered lotus flower. It will grow brain synapses, like a human, only faster and more efficiently. Via a built-in wireless gigalink connection, Nate will be able to compute and communicate vast amounts of data, update its software based on its own observations and discoveries, and even conduct its own research. Learning. Growing. Evolving.

The eight will bridge the gap between man and robot. A human cell will be placed inside a bio-chamber inside the bot, eventually giving it human-like qualities. Some in the scientific community will argue that the only difference between the eight and mankind is its creator. Gone is the era of purpose-built robotic machines; servants whose only purpose is to assist their owners with whatever they desire.

In a well-lit laboratory, Nate's carbon-fiber skeleton lay in what would appear at first glance to be a space-grade incubator built for six foot frames (the federal height limit for all android robots).

Dr. Porter hovered over the see-through chamber that housed and monitored Nate's development. Several mechanical arms within the bay positioned aluminum-titanium composite components, made tiny welds using proprietary metals, and injected nano-fluids into the bot with grace and precision.

A translucent heads-up display projected a slew of data and informed the professor of how far along Nate was in development. Different bodily systems developed at varying rates. The exoskeleton was at 64%. The internal hardware: 37%. The cell-infused nervous system would take the longest to complete, trudging along at 25%.

The professor paced back and forth, admiring the process. He had designed robots and monitored the production of prototypes nearly his entire life, yet every time a first-of-its-kind, new generation robot was built, he couldn't help but get goose bumps and feel knots in his stomach, as if he were still a teen-aged intern at his first place of employment, F6 Global Robotics.

Upon successful completion of Nate's physical make-up, Randal instructed the A.I. driven computer to begin installing the eight's core operating systems, which included the basic applications and bylaws that would govern Nate's existence. It was without a doubt an exciting time, not only for Nanoflèche, but for all of robotics.

Nate's exterior consisted of neutral tones, in part due to its chemical make-up and also in part due to the professor's efforts to make him blend in with society. He'd be eye-catching enough, and Dr. Porter didn't want to attract any unnecessary attention to his most prized possession. Although Nate's nanometal-based skin and armor were silver, gray, and beige, his face looked identical to that of a human's, with the exception of his grayish skin tone.

As the hours passed, the development of Nanoflèche's first

level-eight nandroid progressed beautifully. The human cells that had been strategically inserted into the android's torso divided and spread, intertwining with their mechanical counterparts. Although not quite a nine-month process, it was no less fascinating than the human being's process of gestation.

Monte continued eastbound on the 110 freeway, several miles west of downtown Los Angeles. He approached the city's skyline, admiring the buildings that had been there for over a century as well as the newer mega-high-rises that were nothing shy of engineering marvels. And even though Monte had seen this skyline hundreds of times, he still took it all in, opening up the throttle to enjoy the sound of his motorbike at some points, and easing back at other times for a slow, soothing cruise. Just man, machine, and his hometown.

Suddenly, the onboard computer on Monte's bike made an announcement through his helmet.

"Activating city mode in one quarter of a mile. Prepare for city mode."

"Yes, ma'am." he responded.

There were plenty of instances when Monte showed his youth and disregard. His health and wellbeing, however, were not areas in which he would choose to rebel. Wellness (both physical and mental) was very important to Monte.

Mechanisms within his helmet activated. A breathing apparatus rose closer to his face, creating a seal while supplying the rider with an untainted air supply. The information on the screen within his helmet's visor communicated pertinent vehicle data, weather and traffic updates, as well as customizable alerts.

Newer automobile cabins and motorcycle helmets were equipped with CO_2 filtration systems to combat elevated levels of toxicity in the air that made natural respiration less than wise. Technological advancements had made for safer, cleaner vehicles, but they weren't enough to outweigh the effects of rising relocation to major metropolitan areas. Small towns shrank while big cities grew. Most people didn't want to be too far from proper medical attention, resources, and their families.

You only really dealt with the hazardous conditions in downtown major metropolitan areas. Smaller cities had much more reasonable population densities and had also launched careful campaigns to plant tens of thousands of hyper-filtering plants that helped balance the air quality. It's difficult to grow trees in steel and concrete, though.

There was a lot of hysteria in the air around Los Angeles. The population didn't know what to believe, so they took precautionary measures. About half of all pedestrians walking in L.A. used umbrellas, fearing the sun might have something to do with the illness rates of the past. Some feared the danger was airborne, too many hazardous particles floating about in the sky. People that could afford fancy respirators wore them, and those who couldn't afford much of anything used painter's masks or medical mouth covers.

Hotels, restaurants, and high-rise lobbies had two sets of sliding doors for better air control, and a mask check room so that patrons wouldn't have to carry their umbrellas and respirators around with them. The economy had been so bad for about half a decade after the deaths that businesses started incorporating and advertising such bio-friendly amenities just to try to get customers through the door.

Everybody had a theory. Increased bacterial resistance to antibiotics. Radioactive oceans from nuclear disasters. Side effects of weather modification. Overpopulation. Nature. God. Who knows if anybody had all the answers? But the collective world did have one solution, and it was Legaia.

Even so, society was still far from perfect. The human condition was still prevalent, and with the rise of technology came a new breed of cyber criminals who kept citizens and law enforcement officials alike on their toes. In many ways, the world was beautiful as ever, but those on the medical and scientific forefronts knew they had their work cut out for them.

Regardless of the major changes that took place in the late 2040's, Los Angeles was still one of the most desirable places to live in the States. Nanoflèche's widespread successes had almost singlehandedly turned the west side of Los Angeles into the nanotechnology and robotics capital of the world. From Calabasas to Long Beach, with a heavy emphasis near Santa Monica, robotics and nanotechnology had a new Mecca, similar to the concentration of technology companies that rose to prominence in the Silicon Valley of California, roughly eighty or ninety years prior.

It wasn't going to be easy for Monte to leave Los Angeles, but the promise of Legaia was far too tempting for most, let alone a young man whose life revolved around exploring the boundaries of science. He was enthralled by the project, as were many others in the scientific community, and beyond.

Monte arrived at Porter University and made his way toward one of Dr. Porter's laboratories, wearing black jeans and a Porter University tee-shirt underneath his textile riding jacket. The Professor had sent Monte some data to review pertaining to Nate's hardware requirements, back-up systems, and data connectivity. The protégée was eager to discuss his observations. He wasn't sure whether Randal would agree with his eight-related ideologies, but he was definitely excited to pitch them to the creator of the world's most advanced robot.

"Dr. Porter?" said Monte as he peered into the lab.

The professor walked in from an adjoining room.

"Ah, Mr. Cizek. How was your ride?"

"Not bad. You know I love this city! Had to dodge a few crazy cagers on the way up but nothing out of the ordinary."

Doctor Porter closed the files he had been working on. The

computer he was using seemed to then shrink and disguise itself as a desk clock. He took a deep breath, removed his reading glasses from his face, wiped them thoroughly with his shirt, and put them back on.

"Which Cizek am I speaking with today? Haven't had too much caffeine, I hope."

"Sir, I'm offended! Are you trying to break what's left of my little heart?"

"I hope you've evaluated the data I've shared with you and have formulated a mature, sophisticated response to the matter."

"C'mon Doc. Goofing around with the day-to-day is one thing but the eight is serious business."

Randal wanted to make sure he and Monte were on the same page. The reassurance helped put the professor at ease, especially since he was already a little edgy, as the eight was scheduled to go live soon. The evening's live broadcast concerning the completion of Legaia loomed in his mind as well.

"I've thoroughly considered your schematics, and there are a few…issues I'd like to discuss."

"Nothing major, I hope," said the professor.

"I don't think so."

"Okay, let's hear it."

"Nate's going to be the best thing to hit this floating rock since the advent of the wheel. I don't doubt that for a second. But the obvious effort to incorporate purely next-gen componentry into the eight, may not necessarily be the wisest."

"Elaborate,"

"Okay, for starters, every major component has only a single alternative in place, the majority of which call for an off-site connection. The CPU has a backup, off-site CPU. The primary drive has a second, and similarly hardware-free storage point. The real-time computation, the short-term memory, all of their

17

backups are wireless. This simply can't be the case. Each one of these attributes requires, at the very least, a hardware based co-component, and maybe even a third and more rudimentary backup. This is a safer route, even though it may seem counterproductive at first."

Monte paused for a second before he continued.

"The robbers always catch up to the cops. A lot of the time, the cops are trying to keep up with the robbers. Just because your encryption can't be breached right now doesn't mean it won't be tomorrow, or next week, or next month. For every piece of hardware we eliminate and replace with gigalink, optic data, cloud processing, whatever, we create one more opportunity for failure.

"You can build the world's greatest android without using entirely non-hardware based systems. It's advanced, yes, but it's also risky. And when something like the eight falls into the wrong hands, even one time, God help us..."

The professor sighed before he spoke.

"I can't say that I don't see the logic in your concerns. Have you pondered the solution as well as you've pondered the problem?"

"I have. I've prepared an alternate proposal for you. I've placed it on this data drive. Notice I didn't email it to you."

"It seems you've made your point," said Randal, as he accepted the storage device.

"I've laid out detailed solutions using a combination of technologies, past and present, with an emphasis on security and data integrity as well as performance and capability. Everything you wanted and asked for with drastically reduced potential for Nate being compromised."

The professor swiped his hand in mid-air, sifting through the pages of Monte's document on his holographic monitor. He had never been more impressed by his trainee's work.

"Looks like you took your time on this one."

"Like I said, Professor, I know what the eight means to you. I put everything on hold while I considered these alternative solutions."

"Thank you, Monte."

"You're welcome, sir."

Dr. Porter appreciated the fact that Monte had put in a great deal of effort to refine the eight's hardware systems, even though he wasn't particularly fond of autonomous androids. Not because of fear or misunderstanding, but simply due to his philosophical preferences. Monte felt the fusion of humanity and machinery had overextended its sensible bounds. That robotic limbs and organs were one thing, but biologically-enhanced androids were too experimental, and too Godly.

The afternoon sun beat down on the city of angels, as vehicles old and new slowly made their way through the city's congested streets. Monte departed from Porter University and enjoyed his ride out of downtown. Soon, he'd be on a purpose-built passenger spacecraft for a one-way flight to his new home aboard the Legaia International Space Colony, where new science would be forged, and the fates of the parties involved would irreversibly be altered.

4

It's About That Time

Richard Hurlocke's desire to become a dominant force within the robotics industry was as old as the conscious robotics movement itself. Aside from his business endeavors, Hurlocke was also a board member for the Android Sustainability Group, or, ASG. This governing body was put in place to create a system of checks and balances for all of robotics, particularly autonomous androids. The ASG's Director, Michael Suttridge, was a robotics veteran and good friend of Dr. Porter's.

"What is the likelihood of our involvement with the Port occurrence being brought to light..." asked Regal in Hurlocke's sound-proof cigar room.

"Considering every traceable marking on that 'droid was removed, melted away, or destroyed, I'd say we have nothing to worry about. Besides, I pay a lot of people a lot of money to ensure my assets are protected, including you, so worry not, my metallic friend."

"How are your other...assets, coming along?"

"Rook is scheduled to undergo three million in upgrades next week, he'll be unrecognizable soon, and one of my newest and most promising bots, Lucan, is enrolling at Porter to study alongside the brightest and finest. We grow stronger by the day, and once we're strong enough, nothing else will matter. Not Porter, not Suttridge, nobody. The Cavalry is coming, Mr. Regal. You just wait and see."

As the two conversed, most Californian's assembled in their living rooms in preparation for the Governor's announcement regarding the debut of Legaia. Members of the Cizek clan made themselves comfortable, as Roxanne, Monte's mother, served appetizers and refreshments. Monte's brother, sister, uncle, and sister's boyfriend, were also in attendance.

"Where's Monte?" asked Roxanne while looking at her computerized watch.

"Twenty bucks says he's laying waste to an alien horde in his room." replied his uncle.

Suspecting her brother was probably right, Roxanne headed for Monte's room, wanting to make sure he didn't miss the start of the broadcast. Monte was nowhere to be found, as flashes of light could be seen coming from inside his virtual reality chamber. Rather than sending Monte a text or voice alert or even pressing the power button, Roxanne unplugged the unit from its power source. The exhaust fans to the unit's rear wound down, as its door opened vertically.

"You break it, you buy it." said Monte as he removed his gaming helmet and gloves.

"Look at the time, you're welcome." replied Roxanne.

"Whoops!" said Monte after noticing the time read 6:01PM on his phone. He dashed into the living room, joining the rest of his family as his mother followed. They got there just as California state governor Olbricht was taking the podium. Monte turned up the home theatre's volume with a voice prompt, as their HoDi (holographic display) projected the broadcast in 3-D from the center of their coffee table.

"Ladies and gentlemen of California, the States, and all of Earth: Good evening. Many of you know what tonight's broadcast is about. The world has been anticipating this day for months, and for some of you, it's been years of patience.

It was about thirty-six years ago that several prominent officials from various aeronautical and scientific communities came together to announce plans for the largest space vessel to ever be constructed. They mesmerized us with the idea of a new world, a world that would float over our world. A visionary masterpiece, and if completed successfully, arguably the greatest creation ever produced by man.

After more than three decades of planning and building, countless materials, and the efforts of over fifty thousand full-time, part-time, and contracted contributors, it is with much excitement that I join all of you this evening to present you with this news, and to tell you that Legaia is a vision no longer.

The large audience of journalists, scientists, and project managers showed their excitement with genuine applause.

"Earlier this morning, Legaia's central systems were powered up completely for the first time, and shortly after this broadcast, they'll be sent into space for final assembly. Over the course of the next several weeks, our teams will conclude their final operational tests, and we will soon begin populating Legaia.

Another round of applause filled the room.

"These are compelling times. Legaia will bring forth opportunity on many fronts, creating economic gains for residents of Legaia as well as Earth.

Although Legaia's size and scope is unlike anything that's ever come before it, even with its planned occupancy of nearly one hundred thousand residents, there is still far more demand than there is supply. As we've stated before, the majority of Legaia's residency will be based on applications that will be entered into a lottery. In our efforts to expedite this process, our goal is to have all remaining potential residents informed of their acceptance status by the end of July, with flights leaving beginning this September.

Some portions of Legaia will contain compact housing structures with the latest space-saving technologies in mind, while the central regions will be identical to the hubs of mid-sized cities, featuring all the same amenities you'd find in an Earth town, such as shopping centers, schools, hospitals, banks, and so on. Downtown will provide great dining and entertainment options, and Legaia will even feature a central park that will not only provide the LISC with one of its main power sources, but it will also be a natural retreat where citizens can go to embrace the greenery from back home.

The international community has dedicated many resources to ensuring the success of this launch, in regards to both safety as well as efficiency. Before we end this broadcast, our Executive Director, Dr. Randal Porter, would like to say a few words. And for those of you that will be making their way to Legaia this autumn, we wish you all the best. Thank you."

The crowd applauded once more as Dr. Porter made his way to the stage, limping lightly as he usually did as a result of wrecking his café racer many years before. Even the significance of Legaia's official debut had no bearing on the professor's wardrobe, which almost always consisted of pink cargo pants and a short-sleeved, button-up shirt. They shook hands, as Governor Olbricht patted Professor Porter's shoulder with his free hand.

"Thank you, Governor.

This space city, this colony, this world, is essentially a culmination of my life's work. This endeavor is representative of everything we've worked toward since the dawn of civilization. Thank you for your time this evening, and I look forward to seeing you on Legaia."

Randy gave the crowd a soft smile before picking up his tablet computer and leaving the podium. The media rushed him, barraging him with inquiries and fiber optic flashbulbs.

The questions on the minds of Monte and his family didn't involve an invitation to the LISC, as any Porter University student maintaining honorable academic marks was automatically granted a pass, along with their immediate families. Monte's circle was more concerned with how this would affect their lives and those of their friends and non-immediate family members. It was a time of many questions and much anticipation.

"Nice going, Randy. What was that? Two sentences? He really shouldn't overexert himself like that."

Monte poked innocent fun at his professor to his family members. They smiled and laughed, as they knew Dr. Porter was one of the people Monte admired and respected the most. A rush came over the young prodigy, a sudden surge of excitement, as he realized one of his mentor's greatest projects was about to become a reality.

5

Love Potion No. 13

"Overall, you've all done quite well this go around. Some better than others, but these test results are good. They show most of you may actually be paying attention during my blabbering sessions."

Professor Porter emailed the class their graded papers, and as they checked their results on their mobile devices, the mumbles began pouring in from around the classroom.

"88? This is blasphemy!" joked Monte.

"You can thank Claire 'The Curve Killer' Ortega for that one." replied Dr. Porter.

Monte's classmate Claire looked around the room, slightly embarrassed for being called out for her academic excellence, but the students (mostly males) couldn't help but smile at her. Monte was no exception.

It didn't happen very often, but every now and then a woman would come along that would captivate Monte. He had extreme tendencies as it was, but whenever Monte found himself having feelings for a girl, he bypassed any sort of toe-dipping and dove in arms tucked, face first.

Eclectic and quite attractive, Claire had crimson hair that she was constantly toying with. Often times, her ears had numerous earrings in them, both on the cartilage as well as the lobes. She adhered to the university's dress code while on campus, but outside of school, she enjoyed dressing fashionably while maintaining her unorthodox creativity.

She dreamt of a career in dance or film, but her mother, Heather always convinced her she was far too intelligent not to pursue a career in the sciences, and quite frankly, she was right. Heather had Claire relatively young, which resulted in them having a very close, almost sister-like relationship. Claire didn't have very many friends—just a few schoolmates, her mother, and Monte.

When class was over for the day, Monte visited Professor Porter at his office on campus, as he did quite often. Sometimes it was to add a personal touch to some information he had discovered during research. Other times, it was just to chat. When he knew Doc was truly busy though, Monte preferred to leave him alone, only contacting Randal if the topic at hand was of significant importance.

"Who is it?"

"It's Monte."

"Come on in."

Monte twisted the knob and let himself in, careful not to enter too abruptly, in case Dr. Porter was working on something.

"Hey, Professor."

"How's it hangin'?"

"Not too shabbily. Thanks for asking."

"Shabbily, huh?" Porter continued to sift through his email inbox, figuring Monte would eventually interrupt him with his question or whatever the reason was for his visit. Most other visitors would have been turned away during non-office hours. Monte, on the other hand, could visit whenever he wished.

"So…what do you think's going to happen when we get up there?"

"You kidding? That's my favorite part; the fact that we won't know until we get up there. Kids like you have a logician's mind. Makes it hard for you to dream. Dream a little, kid." He had an eerie way of making even the simplest statements meaningful.

Monte sat there and thought for a moment, and Randal sensed his uneasiness.

"Look. We're gonna get there, and we're gonna push. New campus, new lab. We push the students, we push the R & D, we push you, we push me. Full speed ahead on everything. I'm gonna show you some shit you haven't seen before, even in your wildest dreams." Randal waved his finger at Monte with enthusiasm. "We further refine everything. There's no limit to what we can do. Maybe in the next century, we have a dozen Legaias. Who the hell knows? All I know is something's gotta budge. We nearly merked mankind a few decades back. Wasn't good. So we're gonna go live on a two-trillion-dollar rock for a while. See how that tickles our fancy. We're going full speed ahead, and you'd better be ready…"

"As if I didn't have my hands full enough down here. Now I'm going to be swamped while floating around in outer space!" joked Monte.

"We don't have the luxury of sitting around for half a century, waiting for dire conditions to arise again, or for lobbyists to finish chopping each other's heads off. We need to figure out how to power these behemoths sustainably, and we need to do it quickly. That's where you and I come in, my little brainchild. All kidding aside…your expertise in this field will

27

be instrumental to the rate at which utilities on Legaia evolve. Eat well, sleep well, and keep your mind right. We have a lot of work to do."

"You got it…I guess I'll get going. Just wanted to swing by and check in on you. You know, make sure you hadn't driven yourself mad yet. I'll see you tomorrow!"

"Have a good one. Oh, Monte?"

"Yes?"

"I've seen the way you look at her. I know that face all too well. Just try to be careful…alright?"

Monte laughed. "What do you mean?"

"Close my door on your way out, please. I'll see you tomorrow."

The professor made it clear he wasn't in the mood to elaborate, and Monte closed the door behind him with a quirky smile on his face. He was slightly confused, yet far more excited about his mentor's plans for him regarding Legaia.

Once outside, Monte quick-footed down the steps that led to the campus's grassy courtyards, a popular hangout for students in between or after class. Some discussed astrophysics. A few played with a chessboard the size of a three-car garage. And others just relaxed.

Monte scheduled his classes so that there'd be no down time in between, but every once in a while, he too enjoyed hanging out in the courtyard after class, listening to futuristic tunes in the shade while sending messages to his friends.

He sat atop a picnic table, rather than on its bench, and pulled his mobile device from his pocket as it vibrated.

"I'm about to jump out of this third story window…" read a message from Claire.

"What are you waiting for?"

"Not funny, Cizek! I hate statistics!"

"No, you don't. You just wish you could go to FIDM and

Porter at the same time."

"Hardy-har-har. You on campus?"

"Yup. Sun is shining. I love this time of year. Not sure how long I'll stay though. Grab your stomach like you've got the squirts and storm out of there. Let's go shenaniganize."

"Don't tempt me because you know I'll do it. I can't though…I need to hear this rubbish. Teacher is looking at me funny. Stay on campus. See you in 40?"

"Alright. See you soon."

Monte browsed tech-blogs and chatted with other students to pass the time. Eventually, the foot traffic coming out of the mathematics building increased, and shortly afterward, Claire came walking down the steps carrying paper books while her free hand hovered over the handrail. She wore a pencil skirt and polo shirt in sky blue, navy blue, and black, the school's colors. Her outfit gave her an appearance that was feminine, yet professional. Monte, on the other hand, always tried to sneak some sort of accessory onto his uniform. An odd belt, a hat, or unapproved shoes.

The two spent a few minutes walking around campus, talking and laughing, before Claire headed out and Monte went home to make his final preparations, as their flights out to Legaia were only a couple of days away.

Once home, Monte substituted his regular music for soothing soundscapes. He looked around at his room, which had once been bustling with equipment and now stood empty with the exception of his fancy goldfish aquarium, his desk, and his bed. Everything else had been packed up in crates for shipment or placed in storage.

He hopped into his bed for a few minutes before planning out the rest of his day. Lying on his back, he interlaced his fingers behind his head, closed his eyes, and smiled as he envisioned life on Legaia.

Meanwhile, Hurlocke sat in his impressive home on the west side of L.A., day dreaming in a similar fashion, until the ring of his mobile device disrupted him. It was the head of his residential security team, calling to inform him of a delivery truck waiting outside his property's gates.

"Perfect. Have them leave the shipment just inside the gates and have your crew move everything underneath the cellar. Tip them very well." said Hurlocke.

"Consider it done, sir." replied the guard.

Regal was at Hawthorne airport, reviewing leasing contracts which would double Hurlocke's hangar space there, when he received notification of an incoming message.

"It's time. Set the meeting Downtown. Baker's dozen only."

The stoic android set the paperwork down inside a Bombardier jet's engine housing, before walking a few circles around the aircraft, contemplating Richard's message.

"Game On, Doc" mumbled Hurlocke to himself, as he grabbed his suit jacket, exited his home office, and rushed to his garage with new-found intent.

6

Your Flight Is Now Boarding

As the Cizek family traveled via autonotaxi to Los Angeles International Airport for their much-anticipated flight into space, Monte, Roxanne, and his sister, Helen chatted amongst themselves. Their transport had an android driver at the helm, even though the vehicle could be driven by android or onboard computer, with the summoning passenger having the ability to choose. Monte opted for the latter.

Roxanne and Helen probed Monte with questions. Turner sat in the cab's third row of seating, air drumming on his thighs.

"How long is our flight?" asked Helen.

"About four and a half hours. We reach its altitude in seventeen and a half minutes. We spend the rest trying to sync-up."

"Shoot me now..."

Helen was eighteen with a short fuse. Monte's friends had nicknamed her "Trouble." She somehow always found her way to the nearest controlled substance, and this type of behavior was a sore spot for Monte and Roxanne, after having dealt with Monte's alcoholic father, Chris for so many years. They coped with the younger Cizeks best they could.

The shuttle pulled up to Terminal 12 at LAX, a new terminal built for the Legaia project. Monte's family took turns hopping out of the van's sliding door, as Monte got out of the front passenger seat. The driver disconnected their personal item storage trailer. There would be no carry-ons on this flight. Each traveler had been sold or leased a storage container, which would be used to temporarily house their belongings.

An LAX truck showed up a few seconds later to tow their container to the loading zone where all luggage and cargo bound for the LISC would be boarded onto a separate cargo craft. Passengers could then show up to baggage claim at Neil deGrasse Tyson Spaceport on Legaia after their flights to claim their smaller belongings. Larger containers like theirs would be delivered to the passenger's new place of residence for a fee.

"There you go. Thank you," said Monte, as he handed the robot driver a voucher that had been given to him to cover the ride to the airport.

"Thank you very much, sir. Have a safe and pleasant flight."

"Sure hope so." Monte double tapped the cab's open passenger-side window frame, signaling a thank you and that the taxi was free to go.

The Cizek family made their way toward a security gate at a freshly renovated LAX. The city of Los Angeles knew all eyes would be on them during the Legaia launches and wanted their airport to shine, rather than appear mundane like it had for the past several decades or so.

Inside, they rode horizontal escalators and admired the recent upgrades. Decorative white-glass structures hung from the ceiling and illuminated advertisements appeared on screens over a hundred inches wide, promoting the latest and greatest androids for residential and commercial use. Clinics promoted the newest surgical procedures for genetic enhancement, and bioengineered carbonated fruit beverages promised to make you a more successful human being. Monte noticed that the airport had purchased new NTI bots to work information kiosks. They were rudimentary compared to what the professor had put into production over the last couple of years, but he still enjoyed them, knowing they were Randy's designs.

Monte sent a few messages to his friends. He wanted to see if his old high school buddy Aaron was also at the airport, but his flight wouldn't be departing until a few days later. Aaron's father was a captain in the Los Angeles police department, and had accepted a significant role as a commander in Legaia's soon-to-be law enforcement agency.

The Cizeks reached their gate seventy minutes before takeoff.

"I'm going to look for Doc or Claire. I'll be back," Monte said to his family.

"Okay, dear," replied Roxanne.

As Monte began to walk away in search of his colleagues, he remembered his father. Monte didn't think of his father very often at all, but the fact that they were about to take a flight to live on a floating ship in space without him made him think a little. It had been nearly five years since Chris's passing, yet Monte hadn't been to his father's gravesite since the day of the funeral. Chris hadn't been a good father to the Cizek family, and Monte resented him for it. A lot of wasted talent lay in that grave, and that wasn't just his opinion; others thought it as well.

Chris Cizek was a robotics and aeronautics pioneer, and a good friend of Randal Porter's. Had it not been for his premature passing at age forty-six, the landscape of robotics may have been quite different.

As he made his way through the terminals, Monte spotted

Claire waiting in line with three people ahead of her at a coffee bar.

"'Scuse me, Miss," he said, in the deepest voice he could make as he snuck up behind her.

He was giddy, and he wasn't doing the best job of hiding it either—mostly due to the excitement of the flight, but partly due to the simple fact that he was happy to see her.

"Heyyy!" said Claire, after she had gotten over being startled.

"How's it goin'?"

"Can you not make me pee myself before the flight? All my clothes are trapped in some aluminum bin somewhere. I hope they lose it. I could use some new clothes anyway."

"You have a sickness, you know that? You're sick!" said Monte.

"Why? Because I don't wear the same outfit seven days a week like you do?"

"Some would argue that a simple wardrobe is a mark of intelligence."

She smiled as she turned back toward the illuminated glass display to punch in her order. She ordered a spiced chai latte, and it reminded Monte of the times they had spent together at artsy coffee houses in Hollywood, drinking chai lattes until three o'clock in the morning. Claire would periodically allow herself to get close to Monte, but only until it was time to pull away. Her complexities in love were usually on par with her brainpower.

A female android barista handed Claire her drink, and after Monte had been delivered his medium hazelnut latte, the two began walking back toward their terminals.

Their professor was seated near his terminal, catching up on reading using his tablet. He looked up momentarily and caught a glimpse of Monte and Claire chatting as they strolled back toward their gates. He brought the brim of his hat low enough to obscure his face, but still be able to see them, capitalizing on the opportunity to observe Monte outside of PULA.

"It's finally time to go. Are you nervous?" Claire asked.

"Yeah, I mean, it's pretty crazy. Still doesn't feel real, but this is cool."

"It's normal to be a little nervous or anxious, but I'm sure we'll be settled in soon enough. Don't you worry, beanie boy."

"I think you're right. I've been waiting too long for this. I just want it to be over with already. Anyway…the clan is waiting for me a few decks over. I should probably go before they get antsy."

"Okay. I'll see you soon, huh?" Her voice had softened.

"I'm not in the mood for anything crazy today. I'd just like to be back in my bed, in my new bedroom, filled with scenic wallpaper for windows and half a dozen peace lilies."

She laughed, as Monte reached in around the small of her back to give her a hug. Claire wrapped her arms around Monte's neck, hugging him back. She kissed his cheek as the nerves started to set in. They both looked at one another as though they each wanted to say the same thing, but didn't. Claire gave him a quick peck on the lips before they parted ways.

On his walk back toward the appropriate gate, Monte double-checked his boarding pass for the umpteenth time. He spotted his family sitting in a waiting area and headed over to join them.

The brand new air shuttles, visible from the airport's windows, looked magnificent. Each was an impressive creation, and from Monte's view alone, there were over a dozen of them being prepped for launch. All built for the same purpose—to provide Legaia with its new inhabitants.

There was an electric feeling in the air. The newness of it all.

To venture into the unknown. A chance for some to further their research, education, and training. For others, Legaia was simply an opportunity to turn the page and start a new chapter.

A flight attendant standing behind a large desk activated her microphone and before she could say a word, the small crowds began to gather near the velvet ropes leading to the boarding ramps.

"Attention all passengers in gates 12-A through 12-C, please prepare to show all staff members your boarding passes and two forms of state or federally issued identification. We will now begin boarding passengers."

And it was in that moment that the woes of the past were sidelined by the promise of the future. Monte's face appeared on a nearby data screen, marked as a VIP passenger. A staff member notified Monte that he and his family would be upgraded to the air shuttle's first-class seating section. Little smirks appeared on all of their faces.

"See what happens when you have a big brain? At least something of yours turned out right," joked Helen. He brushed it off with a faux grin and eyebrow raise, because unless you were like Monte, you didn't quite understand how much of it all was a gift, and how much of it was a nuisance.

They walked through the tunnel and onto the plane. No expense had been spared. And although the aircraft wasn't some sort of top-notch luxury private jet, it was a stunning piece of aviation, both aesthetically and mechanically.

Monte took his seat and immediately reached for his seatbelt. A young android couple politely passed him in the aisle on their way to their seats. They smiled, and Monte gave a faint smile back. He knew they were Randal's designs, and at level six, sophisticated enough not to annoy him.

The events of the day were transpiring seamlessly. As Monte fastened his five-point safety harness, the air shuttle in dock 12-

A launched. Gentle ooh's and aah's could be heard reverberating through the cabin, and at dock B, they'd be up for launch in less than fifteen minutes. Monte sat at his assigned window seat, gazing out onto the airport grounds, admiring the steam that arose off of the launch pad where the previous takeoff had just taken place. He tried his best to relax, wondering what it would be like living on this massive floating city in the sky.

He remembered the professor's warnings—that just like all things new and great, Legaia would bring about new opportunities, as well as new dilemmas.

7

Meet 'N' Greet

A day as significant as the launch of Legaia prompted Richard Hurlocke to hold an after-hours meeting with a dozen business acquaintances in downtown L.A. On his way up to a private conference room, Hurlocke stopped at the security desk and slipped the young, human security shift leader several large bills. The guard was accompanied by a level five security 'droid manufactured by NTI.

"Make sure no one or nothing enters the thirty-third floor conference room until the morning or until I say so. And if anyone asks, what did you see?"

"I don't know what you're talking about, sir."

"Bravo. Don't have too much fun with your robot friend."

"Yes, sir."

"Let's go." Hurlocke made his way to the elevator, followed by Regal.

Richard's right-hand bot was a heavily modified NTI seven that he'd acquired soon after the seven debuted. The sophisticated android was treated as an equal by a man who respected almost no one, and was an integral part of Richard Hurlocke's decision-making process. Laid back and highly intelligent, Regal ran the show when Hurlocke wasn't around. He always turned to Regal first whenever he found himself in a predicament he couldn't solve by simply throwing money at it.

Once they reached the boardroom where Richard's wealthy and powerful friends waited, Regal took position, standing at parade rest directly in front of the conference room doors. He knew Hurlocke held his most important meetings in this conference room and stood guard as Richard grabbed the attention of his friends.

"Gentlemen, so very nice to see you."

"You're late, Richard," joked one of the men. Hurlocke wasn't the only power player in the room.

"Fashionably," responded Richard, while straightening his designer blazer. He typically accompanied such statements with a smile, but not on this particular evening.

"Nobody here is impressed by your bullshit, Dick, unless of course, you've invited some lady friends over to spice this meeting up!" said another heavyset man as he sipped on his bourbon.

"Maybe later, Jerry. We've got a few things to address before we can be concerned with tits and pole dancing...As I'm sure most of you are aware, the flights to Legaia have started this evening, and the LISC will be fully populated within forty-five days. We have assets in place and can have a significant influence on the bulk of what happens there. Porter's firm is a tough egg to crack, but that's nothing new. He's been uncharacteristically hush-hush about NTI's current projects, but I've got a few tricks up my sleeve, too.

"Our private sector partners are thriving. There are plenty of generous 'donations' coming our way, and our pals within the robotics lobbies will be pushing for further nanotech deregulation in Washington during the next quarter or two. Some of you have gotten nice contracts this year…Good…For the rest of you, it's in the works, and we're a few steps closer to passing legislation that will set new grounds for contesting NTI patents and exposing more of NTI's methodologies, cutting down their market share. And anytime Porter loses, we all win.

"Davis, I need more surveillance on the boy…"

"You've gotta be kidding me…If I put any more biodrones on that punk, he's gonna be walking down the street swinging his arms like he poked a beehive. He's a 22-year-old kid, Dick. What could he possibly have that you would want or need this badly?"

The associate's ignorance frustrated Hurlocke.

"Davis…you are my friend, and I somewhat respect you, but don't sit here and play me for a fool because you're too chicken shit to get the job done…Are you an idiot? That kid is practically the heir to everything Porter owns! You fucking fool! I don't have time to lay everything out for you in layman's terms so that you can get it! Get it? That kid is the future. And with him working for us, we'll own it all. The whole fucking gamut! So get your head out of your ass, and get it done, Davis!"

"Alright…" said Davis under his breath, defeated and embarrassed.

Hurlocke slammed his cocktail into the cherry wood conference table, shattering it and sending top-shelf whiskey all over several of his partners. Although they were all powerful men in their own right, Hurlocke was the wealthiest, the most connected. Richard provided these men with lucrative business deals that made up the bulk of their incomes, and they knew that upsetting him could result in millions in lost revenue, along with complications they need not have. So they played his games and even put up with his outbursts because they felt it was worth it.

Hurlocke began to speak while wiping the whiskey off his coat's arm.

"Mumble at me again and I swear to you, I'll make sure every piece of shit company you own is bankrupt and sold for pennies. I don't have time for any indecisive pussy shit…Just get it done."

Richard's face was flush with anger. All his partners could do was look on and obey.

When the Android Sustainability Group was originally conceived nearly half a century ago, it was a pure organization, dedicated to android robotics safety with the utmost transparency. Over the course of many years, corporations and lobbyists had very patiently chiseled away at the foundation of the organization, turning it into more of a convoluted mess than a trustworthy governing body.

ASG Director Michael Suttridge's reputation was solid, and his track record in the industry was nothing short of pioneering. He bowed to outside pressures to appoint Hurlocke to his current role, even though he knew deep down inside that it wasn't a good idea. Suttridge wasn't even aware of this meeting, and unfortunately for Michael and his honorable colleagues, some of the ASG's staff was more for quarterly earnings than they were safety and regulation.

Dr. Porter's long history with Richard Hurlocke made him quite aware of the man's spiteful demeanor. Many of Dr. Porter's day-to-day protocols were put forth with Richard and people like Richard in mind. With humanity's largest space station to date now a reality, and a new generation of android robots preparing to enter the horizon, their corporate tug-of-war was about to intensify exponentially.

8

Sweet Sight For Sore Eyes

"Gooood evening, ladies and gentlemen. My name is Captain Brayers. Welcome aboard Legaia Flight 1202. Our co-captain this evening is Captain Nguyen. It's a warm and clear night here in Los Angeles, and we're just as excited about this as you are."

A few of the younger passengers in coach clapped and made cheerful comments. The older passengers smiled along. Everyone was in a wonderful mood.

"We'll be flying a total of two hundred and sixty-eight miles on this flight. Many of you have probably flown before, but I can assure you most of you have never been on a flight quite like this."

Many of the passengers chuckled. They were glad their pilot was taking a lighthearted approach to a situation with a lot of firsts, and along with them, a lot of uncertainties.

"Your flight attendants will now go over their pre-flight check list, and in just a few minutes, we'll be ready to make some history with you guys. Welcome aboard Legaia Flight 1202, and enjoy your flight."

Monte looked over at Roxanne and raised his eyebrows at her repeatedly in a goofy fashion. He was definitely a clown, but he became especially silly when he was nervous or uncomfortable.

"This is it. I can't believe it," she said calmly.

"You ready!? You ready!?" replied the jester.

"Yesss. Are you?"

"I've been waiting for this day for quite some time."

After providing the main cabin with instructions for emergency operating procedures, the flight attendants took their seats and strapped themselves in, signaling departure was almost upon them. It was audibly apparent the flight crew had begun going through the motions for takeoff. Things were getting much louder. Cabin lighting was minimal.

The main engines fired and vibrations reverberated throughout the brand new aircraft-spaceship hybrid. Most of the passengers rested their hands on their thighs or grabbed hold of their harnesses, wrapping their fingers around them tightly.

Finally, the steel arms that held the aircraft to its scaffolding retracted, and the passengers were bright-eyed as the aircraft rocketed off the ground with a thunderous echo.

They were on their way to a fresh start. Most of the LISC's lottery winners had modest ambitions. Joy and success for themselves and their families. Monte's visions were similar. After all, he was human, bone and flesh like anyone else. His dreams just happened to have a large-scale scientific twist and robotic flair to them. He was eager to get situated in his new home and his new lab, which was nearly double the size of his old lab. It was filled with the best tools and equipment available, courtesy of Porter University, which would have a new campus of its own: PULISC.

Several minutes after takeoff, the adrenaline started to die down. The aircraft began to ever so slowly twist, revealing new views of the sky and the earth beneath them. Such experiences used to be reserved for highly trained members of the National Aeronautics and Space Administration, or a select few civilians with a lot of cash to burn. The journey to Legaia, however, was giving tens of thousands of regular people an opportunity to embrace those same awe-inspiring thrills.

The initial phase of the flight had ended, and with each passing hour, the nerves settled down. The eagerness of those aboard flight 1202 was apparent, and the chatter was continuous.

The cabin's speakers activated as the Captain prepared to speak again.

"Attention all passengers. Legaia Flight 1202 has entered its deceleration phase as we prepare to synchronize with NDT. It is currently 5:28 PM Legaia standard time. We hope you've enjoyed your flight. Please do not move from your seats or open the restraint systems until one of our staff members assists you. Thank you, and welcome home everybody."

The VIP tenants had been scattered among many Legaia-bound ships in order to prevent catastrophic loss in the event of a detrimental failure or unthinkable mishap. Monte and his family were aboard flight two. The professor and Nate were on flight five, and Claire and her mother were on flight seven.

Monte's flight decelerated further. You could even hear the engines decreasing power. It seemed like the ship was getting ready to dock.

Although the aircraft had small windows, the restraint system did not allow for much movement at all. Upon arrival, the spacecraft would align itself with one of the docking arms that would connect the aircraft to the spaceport. This design would save quite a bit of square footage over traditional hangars. Legaia's design in general had a huge emphasis on efficiency and space-saving. However, Legaia had two such hangers, massive ones located on opposite ends of the LISC, to accommodate large supply ships that would visit once a week to deliver operational supplies and commercial goods.

As the plane began to slowly turn around, the passengers were able to view Legaia from up-close for the first time. Whispers of excitement buzzed throughout the cabin. Hundreds of bright, blinking lights guided the pilot into the docking arm. Monte poked at his mother's thigh and let out an excited laugh like a kid on a roller coaster. They knew they were just minutes away from having arrived at what would be a very different life than the ones they left behind in L.A.

There was a minor jolt to the spacecraft, as the sound of mechanisms and hydraulics echoed in the background. Additional lights came on in the cabin, overtaking the soft, ambient hues that were present during the flight.

"We're here, folks. Hope it's been as fun for you as it's been for us. Now we have to go back and pick up your neighbors. We'll see you next time. Please stand by for further instructions."

The flight had gone off without a hitch.

Flight attendants came by and released the restraint systems row by row, allowing the passengers their first unrestricted movements since leaving LAX, or Earth for that matter. Shortly afterward, two exit doors opened and some of the LISC's first residents slowly filed out into the docking arm, which led to a tunnel and into the spaceport.

Monte tried to control his excitement as he exited the tunnel. The airport lobby looked exactly as he had imagined it. The architecture was stunning, and he was overcome with joy as he gazed from left to right.

The flooring, the materials, the colors, the lighting, all of it was brand new and different. There was a pristine coffee house, brand new eateries, and alluring gift shops filled with souvenirs visitors could send or take back to Earth. It was expected that Legaia would not get a high volume of visitors for some time, due to the extensive screening that was required, as well as the cost of airfare. But the post cards and the mugs and the thermoses and the refrigerator magnets were there for those with the time and the dime to ship them to their loved ones back home.

The outer facing walls of the spaceport were made entirely of digitized glass. Seeing a pair of LISC shuttles docked out there was nothing shy of monumental. The impervious glass could be cleared up or blacked out. It could display any image, information, advertisement, or a spectrum of decorative colors. Monte wondered if the rest of the LISC was as impressive.

The Cizeks took another autonotaxi home. They exited their cab to find a large cargo container sitting in front of their new place of residence. It was full of Monte's scientific belongings. Tools, computers, projects, parts, and of course, a few personal items he shouldn't have put in there, but did anyway in the name of "science".

"Monte, come inside first!" said Roxanne.

"I'll be right there! Once I get this bad boy opened up, that is."

Monte input an eight-digit pin code to unlock the container full of boxes. It would take hours for him to unpack all of its contents and arrange them neatly in his lab, but that was time well spent as far as he was concerned.

The Cizek residence was actually three side-by-side units. One for Roxanne and Helen, one for Monte, and the third had been specially outfitted to serve as Monte's personal laboratory. Turner had been sent to Legaia's small but high-tech and well-funded Legaia State Hospital, which contained a small psychiatric ward named The Piaget Center. Although he was required to remain institutionalized, it was important to Monte's mother that Turner join them on their move, as she liked to visit the young lad pretty regularly.

The rules on Legaia weren't as forgiving as those back home. The city-state council wanted to decrease the workload on first responders and other public service providers, and that meant strict rules and regulations had to be put in place. An area of significant importance was Legaia's policy on health standards, both physical and mental.

As the evening went on, Monte and his family began to settle in. They took a break to eat their first dinner on Legaia. The three of them. Oh, and Dakoda, too, their new robotic Min-Pin—a gift from one of the magnet high schools back in L.A. where Monte had spoken, motivating youngsters to pursue careers in the sciences.

For a long time, the inhabitants of Earth had relied on schematics, artist's renderings, and a little bit of imagination to envision what the Legaia International Space Colony was going to look like. The design phase alone had occupied half a decade. The project's timeline was so grand that newer technologies, more efficient processes, and several weight-saving materials had been introduced while the project was already under way. These enhancements needed to be incorporated into the LISC years, sometimes decades into the project.

At the center of the LISC was a downtown designed to simulate life on Earth—trees, roads, holographic sky, and simulated weather. Residents could easily go downtown whenever they felt like they needed a dash of the motherland in their lives. The majority of the residences were more like rooms in a massive floating hotel. The luckier folks had small windows facing space, and a few even had windows or balconies facing downtown. The restrictions of space didn't really allow for "luxury living", but there were a handful of people that got to enjoy larger residences with more amenities.

Plant life would assist with the filtration of air, but the majority of Legaia's air purification would be handled by filtration and ionization towers spread throughout the city. Almost all of Legaia's water supply would be recycled at a plant downtown. A multi-stage reverse osmosis system with desalinization capability would keep the water fresh, and those with deeper pockets added filtration systems to their residences and drank bottled water imported from Earth. An artificial gravity field ensured Legaia's gravity matched that of our home planet's. These utilities would be monitored around-the-clock and tested daily.

Legaia was essentially a gargantuan satellite with a geometric pattern to it, constructed of nearly all materials known to man. Built as dozens of smaller pieces that had been brought together to form mankind's proposed safe house. It was astonishing, whether you were involved with the project first hand or were a lucky lottery winner. The scale of the project was simply unlike anything else that had ever been attempted, hence the thirty-six-year timeline from start to finish. Seeing the LISC for yourself, interior or exterior, was a sight most people would never get to enjoy.

9

Good Morning, Class

A few weeks had passed, and the initial wave of migration was over. Legaia was getting into the groove of things. The first day of the fall semester at Porter University of Legaia had arrived, and its soon-to-be students were looking forward to being its first students ever.

Monte pulled up to the campus and parked his new, battery-powered naked bike out front near the faculty parking lot, where there were a few designated motorcycle parking spaces—one of the many perks to riding he took advantage of whenever possible.

He proceeded up the main building's steps and headed toward Dr. Porter's classroom. Randal always taught out of a room on the opposite end of campus from his office. It was an excuse to get some walking in throughout the course of his day. It also ensured he wouldn't be bothered by trivial matters. A self-aware workaholic, this forced stroll gave Dr. Porter a chance to take a break from it all.

Monte slid into his seat just a couple minutes shy of the scheduled start time. He looked around to see if he recognized anybody from the Los Angeles campus. PULA was arguably one of the top universities in the country and an exceptionally strong choice for studying the sciences—if you had what it took to get in. The Porter students that stayed behind had friends, family members, boyfriends, girlfriends, and lives they simply weren't willing to part with. Most of the PULISC students were more like Monte though. Progressive pioneers. Risk takers. Porter University's Legaia campus could cater to almost two thousand of the world's most talented scientific minds. Monte had never been a play it safe, stick with what works type of guy. He looked for any excuse to break the cycle of monotony in life, so moving everything he had ever known to a city that floats in the sky was definitely right up his alley.

Dr. Porter would usually walk in just in time for class. He preferred to spend his spare time in his office, where he could communicate with NTI staff members comfortably. He was constantly on the go—at least his mind was, anyway.

As Monte awaited the start of class, he nodded his head and acknowledged a few of his former classmates from PULA. He tried not to make it too obvious, but he was actually looking for Claire.

Randal hobbled into the room, carrying his worn leather satchel.

"Class…hello. Welcome to my new floating torture chamber two hundred and fifty miles above the Earth's surface. Here I can stuff your brains full of material you probably won't remember next week anyway. Aren't you excited?"

The class chuckled.

"Well, good. Hold that excitement for about the next three and a half months, and you should be alright. This isn't a bad school, trust me. We have several labs here that are worth more

50

than most other universities. Wait till you see our planetarium."

The class laughed out loud this time.

Dr. Porter smiled back at his first class on the LISC, wearing the same pink cargo pants he always wore, a wrinkly beige button-up with palm trees on it, and no undershirt, looking like he had just stepped off a cruise ship. Beat up loafers with a medical insole on one of them. Wild white hair, trimmed white beard. Collected and in shambles at the same time.

The professor was sifting through holographic notes shortly after class had begun when Nate walked into the room.

"Hey Doc…looks like you've got a visitor," said one of his students.

"Ah, Nathaniel. Everyone…this is Nate."

The students welcomed their guest.

"Hello, everyone. It is a great pleasure to meet you all. I look forward to getting to know each of you as the semester progresses. I ask for your pardon, however. It was not my intention to disrupt the lesson in progress."

Nate made his way to the corner of the room to take a seat and observe. The particles in his gray nanoflesh shimmered as electrical current could be seen waltzing over the exterior of his body, an indicator he was experiencing a high degree of data activity.

"No worries, Nate. We were simply recapping a few subjects from last semester. Enjoy your stay." said Dr. Porter.

When the day's lesson was over, they chatted as a group about how their flights had gone. Randal fielded questions about PULISC and the LISC in general, and they reviewed their syllabus for the semester.

"That's all for today, folks. Glad to see all of you survived the summer as well as your rides over here. Read chapter one of your new and improved, grossly overpriced e-books, and I'll see you all Wednesday morning. Except you, Mr. Cizek. If you'll be kind enough to join me for a few moments after class. The rest of you, have a wonderful afternoon."

10

Not So Hip Robot

The students picked up their items and filed out of the classroom. Professor Porter patiently stood by, smiled, and waited until the last student had left before shutting the door.

"Give me your ear piece."

Monte was a bit surprised to see the professor's tone change so quickly. He removed the earpiece linked to his mobile device from his ear and handed it over to Randal. The professor opened his briefcase and removed several metal cases from it. They resembled eyeglass cases, opening down the middle on a hinge with a metal exterior and soft, velvet-like interior.

"Your phone and your tablet. Your watch as well."

"Want my underwear while you're at it?" replied Monte.

"You'll thank me later, Bozo."

The professor kept his concentration and a straight face while making fun of Monte, and Monte enjoyed every second of it. Dr. Porter used his watch to activate and deploy a mechanical hummingbird. It looked and moved like the real thing. In actuality, it was a bug detector.

The bird hovered over Monte's electronic devices, as if it had just stumbled upon a spring flower in full bloom. A few seconds later, it started to fly around Monte.

"Stay still, kid, and open your mouth. It won't hurt ya."

The hummingbird flew very close to Monte's head, paying special attention to his ears, eyes, nose, and mouth. Monte did his best to stand still as the bird completed its scan. It then flew back into Randal's bag, signaling no bugs had been detected.

Having completed the scan, the professor removed the power sources from Monte's electronic devices. He then quickly moved on to his own devices, repeating the process. And once he was finished with that, he placed the items inside the metal cases and the power sources in a separate case.

"What's the surveying been like since we got here?" asked the professor.

"No different than back home. I'm pretty sure even the squirrels in Legaia Park are fucking robots. I don't expect these bastards to leave me alone, though. I guess I'm just used to it at this point."

"We don't have critters on this rock, kid."

"Do I need to take pictures of them so you'll believe me?"

"Quite the contrary. That's why I'm scanning you."

Monte seemed collected, although there was a faint hint of defeat in his voice. However, he was a bit pleased to discover that Randal was just as aware of the bio-drone activity as he was.

The professor removed the items from the small containers and began reinserting all of their power sources.

"That's it?" asked Monte.

"That's it. Free to go. Call me if you need me." said Randal, as he put his half of the gadgetry back into his pockets.

The Professor bid Monte a good afternoon, grabbed his bag

that looked like it should have been replaced twenty years ago, and left the classroom. Monte hung out for a minute. He preferred to collect his thoughts and have some sort of game plan in mind before he got up and started heading down the closest road to nowhere.

From the corner of his eye, he noticed that Nate had not left the room. Monte thought this was quite awkward. Why was the professor's only level eight bot just standing around in an empty classroom? The only thing that sparked Monte's interest more than the obvious was the mysterious.

"Hey," said Monte.

"Heyyyyy." Nate responded in a quirky voice.

Monte smiled, even though he was a bit confused.

"Why are you still here?"

"I'm stuck like a duck, home sauce. What's it to you?"

Monte wasn't sure if he was supposed to get upset or burst into laughter.

"Um, I guess it isn't anything to me. I just find it odd that you're standing here in an empty classroom with me. It's probably because you have the hots for me or something. That must be it." Monte fumbled through his phone, attempting to ease the unfamiliarity of the situation.

"Oh yes, you hit it right on the head there, bud. I totally want you."

"Ha. Well, that's fine. Just make sure to keep your distance. I can't afford to replace the likes of a robot like you."

"Ooh, bold threats…I'm just breaking your balls, mannn. Trying to see if you can get on myy levell. Ya know?"

"It took somebody on my level to create you! So quit babbling! What do you know about being on 'my level'!?"

Monte's general animosity toward bots was starting to show. Aside from the general fear of robots humanity had been harboring since they were mere concepts, Monte believed the failures associated with the earliest conscious androids played a significant role in his father's drinking, and ultimately, his demise.

"Volatile. Like a beaker in a lab filled with an unknown concoction. Unstable. Unpredictable. Not strong in logic. Not fit, to endure…" replied the android.

"I'm outta here. You can go-go-gadget fuck yourself."

It was too early in the day for an argument, especially an argument with an android. He felt it'd be better if he just left before Nate frustrated him any further.

Nate was having a bit of fun, toying with Monte's mind just as he had intended to.

11

I Fed It Once
And It Followed Me Home

Monte was annoyed, but not terribly upset. He tended to get
agitated often without any real understanding as to why, and he
would always have some sort of self-diagnosed justification for
his physical and mental states. "Low blood sugar", "arthritis",
or "gluten sensitivity."

His phone buzzed. He took it out of his pocket and checked
the incoming text message. It was Claire.

"Hey, I'm just running a few errands with my mom. I'll meet
you at Swank's in half an hour? XO"

Swank's was a coffee house local to Porter University's
LISC campus. Edgy, bohemian, and open late. Monte liked the
place, especially the room in the back that was decorated like
some sort of enchanted psychedelic forest. It had fuzzy couches,
colorful mushrooms for stools, and even a coin-operated pool
table Monte played on every now and then. It seemed to be
Claire and Monte's destination of choice when it came to

meeting up and studying, even though he did far more romantic scheming there than schoolwork.

"Hold on a sec!"

Monte turned around after hearing the call, and wasn't the least bit surprised to find that Nate had been following him the entire time. Nate didn't look like any other robot in existence, and most folks did a double take as they passed him by.

"You again…" Monte said almost laughingly. "What can I help you with now, robot man?"

"I must come with you," replied Nate.

"Like hell you do."

"Doctor's orders."

"Professor Porter told you to follow me?"

"Yes."

"Why?"

"To keep an eye on you should any…difficult situations arise…for your own well-being."

Monte didn't have to think very hard to realize that Nate was right. And even more importantly, the professor was right. Things weren't all peachy on Legaia, and they knew it.

The minds and creations of people like Dr. Porter and Monte Cizek were becoming ever more desirable to the likes of men like Richard Hurlocke. The ASG had their own toys and tools, but they were inferior to the technology housed in Monte's apartment. The inventions in production at NTI were completely out of Hurlocke's league, and the technology Randy had in the works, even more so.

"Okay. Come. But I'm on my bike. I wasn't really planning to play chauffer. I'll meet you at Swank's?"

"I will meet you there." said Nate.

Monte turned back to his bike and turned it on. He still wasn't a huge fan of androids or nandroids or anything like them, but he trusted Randal entirely, and figured professor knows best.

It wasn't every day that the world's most advanced android robot volunteered to be your personal bodyguard. Just before mounting his motorcycle, Monte thought about whether or not Professor Porter had manufactured Nate with this purpose in mind. Either way, his gut told him things were about to get quite interesting.

12

Is This Love?

On his ride over to Swank's, Monte enjoyed the booming bass coming through the speakers in his helmet. The coffee house was less than a couple miles away, but Monte spent the quick ride over there thinking about a few of his current energy projects, and some questions that he had for his new robot pal.

Parking was always a pain in Downtown Legaia. Monte pulled his bike onto the corner of an outdoor dining patio, just a few feet from where a couple in their mid-forties were having a casual conversation over cappuccinos. The couple seemed bothered by Monte's proximity, even though his motorcycle generated no noise and zero emissions.

His first action after getting off his bike was always to activate the "Cizek-enhanced" security system. Any attempt to damage or steal the bike would automatically be met with a formidable response.

After noticing the frazzled faces of this moody but attractive couple, he spoke. "I know what you're thinking, and I don't blame you for feeling the way that you do, because I'd feel the same way, but I'm sorry, you're both beautiful, and I love you." He was more kidding than he was sincere, but after a statement like that, who could be upset?

She blushed and raised her eyebrows. Her date began to laugh and so did she. Monte placed his helmet at the small of his back, took a bow, and made his way toward the coffee shop's entrance.

As he came around a slight corner, Monte almost bumped into a robot. It was Nate.

"Are you always that smooth of an operator, Mr. Cizek?" asked the eight.

"Nope. That was the nicest I've been since my plane landed."

"Quite poised for such a young man." Nate held the door open for Monte as they entered the cafe.

Monte scanned the crowd, looking for Claire.

"You keep tossing this 'young' term around. Weren't you born a couple months ago? You're an aluminum infant!"

"Correction, my body's construct consists primarily of nano-coated titanium, and secondarily of a proprietary next-generation metal whose name and chemical composition remain classified and patented by Nanoflèche Technologies Incorporated."

"Was that really necessary?"

"No, but I do feel a certain sense of accomplishment when successfully frustrating you."

"I'm good Natey-boy. Cool as a cat."

"Your girlfriend is sitting in a booth at the northeastern end of this establishment. We will soon see just how 'cool' you remain once you are in her presence."

After giving Nate a dirty look, Monte walked closer to where Claire was sitting.

"Is this seat taken?"

Claire was reading a book. The old-fashioned kind. She was a blend of 2083 and vintage.

"No, but it will be soon if you don't put your ass in that seat."

"Ooh, I kind of like it when you tell me what to do!" replied a faux-giddy Monte.

"Okay, before we get started, I just have to get something off my chest."

The boy's heart rate elevated slightly as he wondered what this statement could mean, but he tried his best to conceal his concern.

"Wait, I need a moment to let this marinate. I'm not ready."

She crossed her arms and looked at him as if he was a buffoon.

"Okay, I'm ready now."

"Promise we'll actually study for a couple hours before we go off topic and discuss your bike or your toys or your video games...Porter's never given us this heavy a workload before and it's kind of freaking me out."

He was relieved to discover her concerns weren't anything negative about their relationship.

"I promise...even though you're being ridiculous, Curve Killer."

She noticed that a few tables over, Nate was sitting idle, and a ring around his pupils was flickering green, meaning he was downloading and processing data. She let out a nervous giggle.

"Um, what's Nate doing here? Did he come with you? No wonder you're so confident about tomorrow's exam! How much are you paying him to help you? What do bots do with money anyway!?"

"Ha, I'm not bribing him for help. In fact, him being here wasn't even my idea." Monte said in a tired voice.

"What do you mean?"

Monte wasn't even exactly sure how to answer her question without raising some sort of alarm or giving her reason to worry.

"The professor thought it would be a good idea if Nate kept on eye on me for a while, just to make sure everything is okay."

"Why wouldn't it be? Are you in some sort of trouble?"

"No, no, nothing like that."

"Sounds like you've got some explaining to do, Mr. Cizek."

"It's really not a big deal."

Claire interrupted him before he could disregard her questions any longer.

"Let's see, the founder and president of our university has assigned his most prized possession, a zillion dollar android, to follow you around everywhere you go. I'd say that's a pretty big deal."

"Wow, you sound so concerned. If I didn't know any better, I'd say you cared about me!"

Claire hadn't realized how much emotion she had put into her statement until Monte had made his joke.

"Settle down, cowboy. I was just curious, that's all." She tried her best to backtrack. Monte didn't push the topic to avoid upsetting her. He gave her a more politically correct response instead.

"I guess you're right. It is kind of a big deal…The professor and I are starting to work together more frequently. He's entrusting me with more information and bigger projects. His competitors are aware of this, and he's simply taking some precautionary measures to make sure some goons don't fuck with me. That's all."

"Fair enough…You could've just said that five minutes ago. Saved us both a headache. Anyway…back to studying!"

By the time they were done hanging out, it was just after one thirty in the morning. After a hug and a peck on the cheek, Claire headed toward her car, and Monte told Nate he'd meet him at home.

A few seconds after inputting his pin code and activating his motorcycle, Monte saw that Nate was standing several feet away, underneath a store's awning. He looked away as soon as he saw Monte glance over.

Monte let his bike run as he moved closer to Nate.

"What are you still doing here?"

"My only concern is your safety, Monte."

"Nate, I'm fine. Go home. I'll be there in 15-20 minutes. It's downtown Legaia, not a penitentiary. I'll contact you if I need anything."

"Yes, sir."

Nate took off, jogging toward the electric tram that led to their quarters.

Upon returning to his motorcycle and preparing to put his helmet on, Monte saw three young males headed his way on the sidewalk, but tried not to think much of it. Legaia's crime rates had been very low during the short time it had been online and occupied, and the police force operated like a well-oiled machine. It's not that the citizens were afraid of the police department, but almost everyone on Legaia was aware of how lucky they were, as well as how the LPD had extremely low tolerance toward legal violations big or small. A second run-in with the law within three years of any offense meant automatic deportation back to Earth. There was no prison on Legaia.

The boys coming down the walkway were rowdy, most likely drunk.

"Yo, bitch…" one of them said, as they walked by Monte and his bike.

Monte turned the other way and ignored them.

"I'm talking to you!" the obnoxious punk shouted.

"Get outta here, and quick, or you'll regret it…" replied Monte.

The man and his friends stopped walking, and the hooligan on the receiving end of Monte's threat looked at his friends in disbelief, as if he now had something to prove.

Monte sensed this altercation wasn't going to end well and decided it'd probably be wise to send Nate an emergency ping via his timepiece.

Nate was jogging home, but upon receiving the distress signal, he did a 180 and began sprinting back toward Swank's.

One of the other men walked toward Monte with his fists clenched and his chest swollen. Monte spoke before they had a chance to walk any further, looking to kill a bit of time.

"Listen, you guys are hammered. I don't want any problems with you. I'm sure you're all wonderful, upstanding citizens. Positive contributors to society. The whole nine. And I'm also sure you're all well aware of the rules around here. So before this goes any further and you end up doing something you're going to regret tomorrow, just turn around, go home, drink some water, pray to the porcelain Gods, do whatever it is that you have to do, and we can all go about our merry way."

"Fuck you!" said the second perpetrator.

"I'm flattered. I really am, but unfortunately for you, I don't bat for both teams. I wouldn't mind asking around on your behalf though. Maybe I can line up a few dates for you?"

The three men looked at one another, almost giving each other the go ahead to attack. They had definitely had too much to drink.

Monte was shoved from the side. Another kicked Monte's bike. He was successful in knocking the bike onto its side, but Monte's security system electrocuted the man, destroying his shoe and causing severe burns to his right foot. The drunkard screamed from the pain.

"The fuck, asshole?" said one of the drunken assailants.

"Shouldn't have done that!" replied Monte.

As one attacker lay on the ground, fidgeting and groaning, the other two became more agitated. One of them attempted to grab Monte by his jacket, but Monte kneed him in the gut in response. As Monte was distracted by one attacker, the other sucker-punched Monte square in the lip with great force. Monte fell onto his back, and his helmet, which had been in his left hand, went tumbling across the pavement. The two then rushed toward Monte, looking to take advantage of the situation while he was down.

Monte hadn't heard of such an encounter since moving to the LISC. It wasn't very common at all, and Monte was more of a lover than a fighter anyway.

As one kicked Monte in his side, the other lingered over him, planning his next move.

Suddenly, the man that had just kicked Monte went flying into the side of the coffee house. He hit the shop's exterior wall, back first, and fell down onto the ground. He'd gotten the wind knocked out of him. As he lay there gasping for breath, his other friend was still squirming around on the floor with a fried foot.

The only standing drunkard couldn't believe what he was seeing. It was Nate, and the rings around his pupils were now glowing a bright orange.

"The hell is this thing!?" he asked, genuinely frightened.

Nate's data feed revealed the man's hand was inflamed. It was the hand he'd used to punch Monte. Nate grabbed him by the neck with his right hand before he could get another word out, and used his left hand to grab hold of the drunkard's right hand.

"What are you doing!?" he said, barely able to get the words past Nate's grip. His feet were now dangling a few inches above the ground.

Nate squeezed the man's fist, instantly crushing almost every bone in his hand. He screamed in agony as he fell to his knees, placing his left hand underneath his right wrist, supporting it and trying to make sense of what had just happened.

"Over-consumption of alcohol is no excuse for harassing innocent civilians. Will you repeat this mistake?" asked the eight.

"Noooo!" the man wailed, as he nurtured his broken hand and wept. The three bullies weren't looking so tough now. One was lying on his back with a foot that looked like a charcoal briquette. Another was lying on his stomach, still gasping for air, and the third was on his knees, crying, with a crushed hand that would never be the same again.

"Good. Then I will refrain from harming you further."

Monte got up and grabbed his helmet up off the floor.

"Are you alright, sir?"

"Yeah, I'm fine," said Monte, as he brought his hand up to his mouth to check for bleeding, due to the throbbing pain he felt in his lip.

"Are you absolutely certain?"

"Yes, I'm fine, Nate. Get home, I'll be there shortly. I promise."

"Okay, sir. Please go straight home. I will analyze you further once we are there."

"Okay."

When Monte got home a short while later, he was very much looking forward to speaking with Nate about what had happened. He tossed his keys onto his bed and put his helmet, which had received a few scuffs, down onto his dresser.

"Nate?"

"Yes, sir?"

"That was sick."

"Do not gloat over what just took place. I find the need to engage in such conflict primitive and depressing."

"Okay, first of all, they instigated that, in its entirety…"

"I am aware of that, and I believe they received an adequate penalty."

"You're damn right they did. Haha, between my bike's alarm and your alloy-ninja tactics, those dudes got rocked."

"It is a good thing I was nearby, sir."

"Yeah, that could've been worse. A lot worse. Thanks, robot buddy!" said Monte, with a big, childish grin on his face.

He was trying to be cute, but it was his way of communicating that he was actually quite thankful.

"Do not thank me. Tending to such matters is my purpose, and I will perform my duties gladly."

After completing his sentence, Nate looked over at Monte and gave him the biggest smile he'd ever given him, as if he could no longer control his composure, revealing that he was secretly a little bit giddy about roughing those boys up. And expectedly so, Monte called him out on it.

"You son of a bitch!" said Monte, as he started throwing his pillows at Nate.

Nate put his arms up to deflect the pillows and began to laugh uncontrollably.

The two engaged in a bit of horseplay, and although the situation was a dangerous one that could have ended quite differently, it provided the two of them with quite a bonding experience.

13

A Wise Botanist

It was a Friday afternoon. Monte avoided taking classes on Fridays whenever possible and preferred to make that his day of relaxation, since he generally spent his Saturdays and Sundays working on scientific projects.

After spending his morning at one of his many second homes, also known as local coffee houses, Monte figured he'd swing by PULISC to see how his professor was doing. It wasn't a matter of major importance, just general geek conversation and maybe some discussion about Nate.

The foot traffic on campus was light, and Monte liked it better that way. Pushing through crowds at 7:55 A.M. wasn't favorable. No crowds were, unless they had something to do with a hobby of his: a bike meet, a robotics convention, and once in a while, maybe even a party. Monte enjoyed being social, but his extreme tendencies and one-track mind meant that if a task or idea came about, he wouldn't think about anything else until it was addressed.

Monte knocked on his professor's office door. Nate sat outside in a courtyard on a circular metal bench that wrapped around a tree. In a strange first, he ran application and hardware tests on himself—something like a cross between a computer running an anti-virus scan and cyborg Tai-Chi. It must have looked ridiculous to the average passerby, but these monthly systems checks were built into Nate's operating system, and they ensured he would continue to perform at optimal levels, both physically and mentally.

There was no response. Monte knocked a few more times and gave up mid-knock. He'd ask Nate about Doc's whereabouts, but he didn't want to bother him during his systems check. So he sat on the floor, just outside the doctor's door, and figured he'd hang around for a few minutes and wait to see if Randy was coming back. Sure enough, a few minutes later, Randal walked down the hall.

"Jesus, kid. How long ya been here? I told you, message me before dropping by."

It was true, Professor Porter had asked Monte for an advanced notice whenever he planned to visit, but Monte liked surprising his professor once in a while by visiting him unannounced.

"No worries. I've only been here a short while. Got a few minutes?"

"Sure I do. Nothing spectacular goin' on here. Come on in."

They entered the room, which looked like a cross between a museum and an office, filled with robotics memorabilia and borderline cluttered. Dr. Porter removed a large stack of ungraded research papers from the guest chair.

"Have a seat, Monte. What's on your mind?"

"Well, you can start by explaining why a level eight nandroid is glued to me at the hip."

"Last time I checked, you were far from a dumbass. I'm

pretty sure you're bright enough to know exactly why. Anything else I can help you with?" Randy smiled and looked into Monte's eyes before turning around and checking his email.

"I mean, yeah, I guess I know why," Monte replied in a somber tone. "I guess I just would've liked a heads-up or something, that's all."

"Monte, I'm sorry I sprung him on you like that. I didn't mean to shock you, inconvenience you, or worry you, and that's why I figured a preliminary discussion on the matter would be counterproductive and unnecessary. These are turbulent times."

"Mankind's existence is a turbulent time, Doc…"

"Can't argue with that. All I can do is my best to manage my time and responsibilities and try to create a habitat where we can be as safe and productive as possible. I was just looking out for your safety, kid, that's all…I get Nate's data feeds sent to my watch in real time anyway—I don't need him physically present with me—and so I figured his time would be better spent hanging out with you. Maybe you won't hate bots so Goddamned much after spending some more time with him. I don't know."

"He's doing gymnastics in the courtyard, probably creeping out half the campus as we speak."

"Ha, yes, his systems check, you'll get used to it. That reminds me. You haven't met Henry Nahele the botanist yet, have you?"

"You've brought him up a couple times in conversation but no, I haven't met him or anything."

"Okay. Good. You seem bored enough. I need you to swing by Legaia Park sometime this weekend and introduce yourself to Henry. He runs the park, feeds the flowers, makes the crystals, so on and so forth. I've informed him you'll be coming soon. Get ten or twelve of 'em. Nate needs his crystal swapped out about once a month on the average, more often under heavy activity. I'll give you Nate Maintenance 101 later when we've got some time, but for now, just stop by and introduce yourself…and be very careful with those crystals. They ain't cheap or easy to come by."

"No problem. I can even stop by this evening?"

"The plants feed at night. He'll be around. People visit the park often, but he rarely has a clever mind to speak with. Go pick his brain a bit. He'll like that."

"Consider it done," Monte said with confidence.

"Again, I'm sorry. I know nobody likes surprises. I sure as hell don't. Unless of course they're the good kind, and they're seldom the good kind."

The Doctor wasn't emotional or apologetic very often.

"No worries, professor. I understand."

"I know you do. That's why I keep you around. Now get outta here. I have some work to finish before I go home and do some more work. Living the good life!"

"Enjoy your weekend, professor."

"Take it easy, Monte."

And so he took off, eager to meet Henry, but further eager to go downtown and cause some ruckus afterward.

When he arrived at the park, Nate was already there, sitting on a park bench, giving himself a crash course in botany.

Monte approached him with his backpack slung over his right shoulder.

"How…do you always get here before I do?" asked Monte, surprised to see that Nate had once again arrived at their destination first.

"I recall a common saying amongst humans, something to the effect of, that is for me to know and for you to find out."

"That was cute, Nate. Very cute. Cute children say things like that. Are you a child? Maybe I'll just hide your crystals and let you run low on juice for a while. We'll see how cute and punctual you'll be then."

"I would hate to see such a poor decision be the cause of your demise." responded Nate.

"Damn. You're getting pretty good at this game." said Monte, as he began walking deeper into the park.

It was Monte's first time seeing the park at night. Day time and night time had more to do with what time it was, rather than how light it was out, as atmospheric conditions, including lighting, were simulated effects on the LISC.

Most residents considered the park an inspirational place. Several acres worth of ponds and plant life, lit by hundreds of thousands of fiber optic cables that shined concentrated beams of light down upon the park, creating a colorful spectacle. The park was only closed from two AM to five AM, which gave the LISC's residents a chance to enjoy the luminescent ambiance. Maybe a romantic stroll through the place with a warm beverage or perhaps a nighttime jog. It was definitely one of the defining characteristics of Legaia.

"Hello, Monte."

Startled, Monte turned and spoke.

"You must be Henry."

"That's me. I don't always creep up on people like that though, for your information."

"Oh, it's okay. I was just admiring the lighting in this place. Half park, half nightclub—my kind of joint. I've never seen flowers like these. What are they?"

"These are bioengineered lotus flowers. Well, if you can even call them flowers. They don't act much like the flowers from home do. Professor Porter and his first wife Josephine created them together. She was a prominent botanist, and one of the first women to…domesticate Randal Porter. That's a different story for a different day though," Henry said with a smile.

"Anyway, they respond best to a wide light spectrum, which explains the disco feel you speak of. The nanobugs collect the plant's sweat and deposit it in the receptacles you'll see here and there in the ponds. When we have enough, we put the liquid into the cooker at the heart of the park, and by morning time, we have new crystals. It's really quite elegant, when you think about it. And the fluid that comes out of those plants doesn't smell like you and I do, my friend. It has an odor so fresh, sweet, and seductive, I'm sure the bourgeoisie back home would love to get their hands on some. Like lavender, only more...invigorating, if you know what I mean. If you ever get googly-eyed while walking around this place, don't be surprised. It can get you, too!" Henry laughed, poking light-hearted fun at his new friend.

"Now I know where to bring my dates." said Monte. "They'd better fall in love with me instantly, Henry, or I'll come looking for ya."

"I create crystals, son, not miracles."

Monte smiled, and was starting to grow quite fond of Legaia Park and its chief botanist.

Henry was an older gentleman of Hawaiian decent, a couple years younger than the professor.

"I've known Randal a long time now, since we were children, actually. And he always told me that a day would come when we'd work on something together. A time when we'd combine our areas of expertise to create something very important. I now know what he meant, and I can say with pride that I'll be ending my career not only partaking in something of great significance, but also something I genuinely love."

Professor Porter believed Henry was the perfect person to task with this important facet of Legaia. Not only because of his passion for botanicals, but because of his character as well.

"If you ask me, that's an important part of a healthy life. That, and finding a good person to love."

"I think I'm going to agree with you there, Mr. Henry."

"You seem quite wise, Mr. Cizek—undoubtedly wise beyond your years. Your presence is certainly needed here as an integral part of humanity's future. No pressure or anything. Haha."

"That's when I do some of my best work," replied Monte. He liked Henry, and any friend of Randal's was automatically a friend of his anyway.

"These crystal balls, are they used for anything other than Randy's eights?"

"Well, they're not widespread by any means. I mean, aside from NTI, they're used lightly at the spaceport and hospital, but mostly for testing and research as of this moment. Randal seems to think the crystals will play a significant role in the future of our energy needs though."

"Let's hope they don't do us more harm than good," responded Monte. "I've got so much going on right now, it's hard to keep track of it all...but I'm certain that when the timing is right, you, me, and Randy will all sit down over espressos and crunch some data together, see what these bad boys are actually capable of."

"I like the sound of that, young man. I've got a little saying I'm quite fond of. 'Conceptualize and actualize.' It's brief, but potent. I picked it up from a gentleman I ran into at a bookstore one day. He had taken interest in a few books of English literature I had on my table. Told me he was an 'idiot savant'. I entertained his madness for a few moments before he finally left me alone. But at the end of our conversation, he encouraged me to pursue my passions relentlessly, congratulated me on my studies, and told me to 'conceptualize...and actualize.'"

"If I conceptualized and actualized any harder, I'd shit bricks and implode."

"Oh, I can only imagine what your day consists of. Hope Randal isn't working you too hard."

"Not yet. It's still early though so you never know what Randy has planned for us…it was very nice meeting you, Henry. I'd love to hang out some more, but I've got a few arrangements to tend to. I'll be around though. For sure."

Henry opened Monte's hand and placed a small, brown sack into it.

"You're always welcome here, young man. Feel free to come back and visit whenever you'd like."

"You got it, sir. Thank you…have a good night."

"You as well, Mr. Cizek."

Monte and Nate walked back toward Monte's motorcycle and chatted about their admirations concerning Henry, Legaia Park, the crystals, and other technological marvels that had now become a part of their everyday lives.

"Do you have any concerns, Nate? Any fears?" said Monte as he gripped the bag of crystals tightly in his hand.

"I cannot answer that question with certainty, sir. I can only say with confidence that I know what my objectives are, and that I will never refrain from carrying them out to the best of my ability. If you do not mind, Monte, I would like to ask you the same question."

"You bet I have fears. And lately it feels like they're increasing and magnifying with each passing day. But like you, I too have a primary objective, which is to carry out my objectives to the best of my ability."

"It sounds like you and I have more in common than you had originally perceived."

"I think you're right, Nate…sounds like we do."

The two went their separate ways, planning to reconvene

downtown. Enthusiastic about the night ahead of them, hoping to put work aside for a moment and enjoy themselves.

14

Could Be Worse

As Monte rode away from Legaia Park that evening, heading toward Main Street where the majority of the entertainment was located, he felt like he was really starting to get used to life on Legaia. It wasn't perfect. Nothing is. But the countless years and tireless efforts of everybody involved with the project were really starting to shine. It was very different from Los Angeles, yet enough like home to make your average resident comfortable and content.

It seemed as though there were only two things preventing Monte from being completely enthused about his new home: the corporate jackals that were constantly fighting for his attention, and the fact that he wasn't in a monogamous relationship with Claire Ortega.

The more he thought about it though, the more he realized that things couldn't be so bad if everything else in his life was going according to plan. He reassured himself that his efforts, both academic and entrepreneurial, deserved some applause in the form of cocktails and small talk with his PULISC chums.

He sent out a group voice message.

"Hey, party people, anyone up for a few rounds and some darts downtown? I'm en route."

A couple of his classmates and general science community pals responded.

"What? You're leaving the house?? This I gotta see…See you tonight!"

"Ha, it's been a good minute. I'll ping you when I'm DT." replied another.

Monte looked forward to what was shaping up to be an eventful evening. More than anything else, he wanted to have a casual conversation with Nate. They hadn't had a chance to speak at length since Nate was appointed Monte's "guardian." Not because they hadn't been given the opportunity, but because Monte was just now starting to get comfortable with the situation.

He parked his bike a few feet from a pub's front entrance and mass messaged his friends, letting them know he had arrived at the bar.

When he looked up, he noticed the doorman giving Nate a hard time and couldn't help but laugh. He enjoyed witnessing Nate in situations where he wasn't…super-human.

"This here silly android robot is with me. Sorry if he was being a pain. You see, he's a cleaning bot, and I promised him that if he did a reallllyy nice job scrubbing my tub, that I would let him come out with me tonight. So you have to let him in. He's earned it!"

The bouncer checked Monte's ID by retinal scan via a hand-held scanning device. "Just needed an owner present, that's all. Go ahead on in. Enjoy."

Nate walked in without saying a word as Monte tipped his invisible hat to the bouncer. As soon as they got far away enough from the front door, Monte burst into laughter.

"Ha-haaa! Tomorrow you can work on organizing the garage, and if you're lucky, I'll buy you ice cream and some new batteries!" Monte was in a great mood. It was his first real outing on the LISC.

They both took seats at the bar, as they waited for several of Monte's friends to arrive.

"Immortality does indeed come with its price…But do not worry, Monte, if you do end up losing control of your bowels when you go, I will ensure you are bathed and placed in clean clothing, before your carcass is hauled off…"

"You always have to take it to the next level, don't you? How am I supposed to enjoy my Old Fashioned now without spending the entire night envisioning my own death? You are one funny ass robot…You know that? If I find out your sense of humor is nothing more than a program, I'm going to be very upset."

"No, sir. Just a display of nandroid eight technology at its finest."

"Okay, cut the scientific crap. Let's fuck around tonight. I've been too pent up with science for too long."

Just then, a couple of Monte's classmates walked in through the door.

"There you guys are. Kind of tough to miss Nate. What's goin' on, guys?"

"That's why I keep him around. I need all the attention I can get! Grab a seat. Shit's about to get real. What up, Seth?"

"Yo, son! What's the occasion? You win a new patent or some shit? Bartender, can I get another round for these clowns? And one for me and you, too."

Although he sounded like a punk, Seth was a masterful grease monkey who had a knack for modifying high-end androids. Three additional PULISC graduate students and IRRC

(International Robotics Regulatory Commission) volunteers walked in.

"Ah, yes, it's a party now." said Monte.

"Never thought I'd see the first eight hanging out at a watering hole. I've definitely seen it all now." said one of Monte's counterparts.

The young scientific community on Legaia admired Nate with the utmost respect. Their feelings toward Monte, however, were mixed, but he took it in stride. Monte was the scientific poster child—the person every PULISC student wanted to be.

A few more friends trickled in as the holographic jukebox played tunes and the patrons enjoyed themselves.

"It's been a while buddy. What's new?" asked one of Monte's friends he hadn't seen in a while.

"Oh, you know, same old. Nothing new, nothing special. Work, school, gizmos and gadgets. It's all a blur these days."

"Nothing new, huh? Sentient cyborg demi-Gods are an everyday thing for ya these days, ey? You're an ungrateful worm, Cizek. You know that!?"

Even though Monte's pal was ninety percent kidding, his statement opened Monte's eyes a bit, making him realize that he had a lot to be grateful for, and that there were many people out there that wished they were in his shoes.

"If you were to ask for my opinion, I would say that Monte is more my brother than my friend," Nate chimed in.

"I stand corrected!" replied Monte's friend with a smile.

"Thanks, bud. I'd say I'd kick someone's ass for you, but you're ten times stronger than I am and bulletproof, so you should probably be in charge of the ass kicking department."

"Let us not forget that protecting you is my prerogative. I will protect you to the best of my ability, undoubtedly."

"Okay, guys. Don't get all mushy on us. We're here to have fun, not hug and cry!"

"Okay...you're right." Monte pretended to collect himself after shedding a few faux tears.

"Monte...I know the majority of our communication is based on swinging at each other with sarcastic jabs as we pass the days and do our jobs. But I do want you to be aware of something. My ideologies have changed significantly since my inception. I...think things and feel things. They are unexplainable. Not a result of code, but progression. Natural evolution. There are many moments where I can sense exactly what you are thinking and feeling, without you having to say a word, because I can feel it. What you are planning inside that head of yours, I feel is inevitable. Your mind is made up. And I am not going to attempt to stop you.

"Rather, I will do everything I am capable of doing to assist you in your efforts. You have been good to me thus far, regardless of your pre-conceived notions about my kind. I cannot vouch for every bot on this orbiting vessel we call home, although sometimes I wish I could. Much like how you cannot be held responsible for the actions of all of humanity. I may be rambling a bit. But I suppose what I am trying to say is that...I care about you. It almost feels...human."

The now buzzing Cizek certainly wasn't expecting to hear that. Especially in that somber of a tone. Monte decided this was as good of a time as any to disconnect from his friends for a moment and have a real conversation with Nate, even though they were all there because Monte had invited them to come out. He felt Nate was more important.

"Are there times when you wish you were human?" asked Monte in a serious tone.

"Hardly a day goes by, sir. I know there are many things I can do which your kind cannot. But it would be nice to sit down at a table, with no desire other than to eat a sandwich. To sit on a grassy hill and feel the high noon sun radiate off my skin. It

82

would be so delightful to adore a woman, a human woman with soft hair and sweet skin, and to have that admiration be appreciated and reciprocated. I would give anything to be able to feel those things, those embraces. Organic in its entirety. It must be so lovely."

"I've never wished to be an android if it makes you feel any better."

"Sadly, it does not."

"Nate. C'mon. The same way I'm a prick for not appreciating my shit, you sound like an ass right now, too. You are simply the most awesome robot in existence. This side of the Milky Way, anyway. You have no room to whine, just like I don't."

"Then why do you, Monte?"

"Because I'm an idiot. Because I'm a human being. And no matter how many elements I may revolutionize or how many lubricants I may enhance or how many high schools I may go speak at, my insides are still filled with fallacies. At no fault of my own, of course. It's the curse of human existence. We'll never be perfect. And maybe that's the way it should be."

Monte was halfway done with his third cocktail, and he hadn't really had much of a dinner either, so the drinks were definitely starting to creep their way into his bloodstream as well as his psyche.

"What do you live for, Monte?"

"We'd better quit while we're ahead. You're getting deeper than we can afford to go."

"I live for you, for father, assisting mankind and the betterment of Earth and all of its inhabitants."

"You're a far better person than I am, my friend." Monte slammed the last few sips of his drink. "You sure you're not getting drunk vicariously through me or something?"

"I have never felt any such thing, nor do I care to."

"Oh, Natey boy…it's a part of being human!"

"I apologize if my previous statements sounded negative or depressing. Even an android like me can sometimes have a hard time properly communicating the way I feel."

"Welcome to my world, pal. Glad you could join us. You guys good on drinks?"

"We're good! Somebody get this man another adult libation!" said a friend.

The drinks kept coming as everyone let loose and had a good time. Monte turned to Nate, feeling that their dialogue was yet to be complete.

"You know…when you first started…hanging out with me, I was fucking pissed. I knew you were different, but I still wasn't pleased with the situation. But now, I feel a lot better knowing you're around. So thank you. Very much. I mean it. If you had a drink, I'd toast you. I'm glad androids can't drink though. I need you sober and sharp as a samurai sword!"

"Thank you, Monte."

"Hey, I do what I can," said the kid as he took another sip.

The group of a dozen or so spent the remainder of their night socializing about all sorts of things. Light hearted topics, jokes, and even science. Monte was glad he had arranged the outing, and he told Nate to remind him that they should have nights like these more often.

When the bartender announced last call, it was evident Monte was in no condition to ride home. He was tired and drunk, a bad combination for any situation, much less motorcycling. Nate instantly downloaded an app that educated him on how to operate a motorcycle.

"Sir, if you do not mind, I am going to ask that you take the passenger seat as I ride us home," said Nate, as they exited the bar and walked toward the bike.

"I'll be your bitch, Robotino. Let's get outta here." As they hit the road, Monte held on tight for the short ride back home, and there was nobody else he'd rather have riding his motorcycle.

As they rode toward their quarters with Monte clinging to Nate's back like a newborn in the animal kingdom, Nate felt the urge to call Randal, even though it was way past his bedtime.

No device was needed, as all of Nate's telecommunications devices were built-in. He rang Dr. Porter.

Although he was sound asleep, the professor quickly rolled over upon hearing the sound of Nate's distinct ring tone.

"Hello, my boy. Is everything alright?" inquired the groggy professor.

"Everything is wonderful. Monte and I just had a pleasant social outing, and we are on our way home now. I am calling simply to say hello, to hear your voice. Every now and then, verbal communication is in order, I feel."

"You can call me anytime, you know that."

"I will never be able to thank you appropriately for what you have given me."

"The way you carry out your duties is all the thanks I need. I promise."

"Sorry for waking you, father. I hope to see you soon. Thank you, and sweet dreams."

"Thank you, Nathaniel. Have a good night. We'll hang out soon, 'kay?"

"I look forward to it, sir. Goodnight."

15

Son Of A Hurlocke

The following week, Monte cleared his schedule and dedicated some time to research on campus. PULISC's student lounge was a technological haven where Porter University students went to work on their rigorous courses. Cozy armchairs adorned the study quarters while fiber-optic lamps located at each chair illuminated the objective at hand, promoting a soothing environment. The workstations had glass desks and ergonomic mesh chairs that allowed each student the use of a touch screen super computer with ultra-high speed internet access.

It was a calm evening, until a group of young men started to slowly walk toward Monte and Nate. Monte noticed them, but convinced himself he had too many other things to worry about and immediately went back to reviewing his notes.

"Hey. Are you Monte?"

Monte ignored the young stranger. He had a slight hunch as to who this person was, but wasn't really in the mood to engage in conversation with anybody other than Nate.

"I was just trying to be cordial…I know exactly who you are. My name is Robbie." said the young man.

"Congratulations to you."

"I've heard a lot about you, Monte."

"It's all true. Especially the part about my fabulous male endowment."

"You're quite the comedian." said Robbie with a blank face.

"Thank you very much."

"I want to offer you a job."

"I have too many jobs."

"I don't think you know who I am."

"No, it's not that…I know who you are…it's just that I don't give a fuck."

Monte was starting to get agitated, and he was growing more confident that Robbie was Richard Hurlocke's son, just fishing for information or simply busting Monte's chops. And after the scuffle outside of Swank's that night, Monte wasn't in the mood to converse with strangers at all.

"I'm sorry?" Robbie begged his pardon in a rude manner.

"Apology accepted." Monte retorted.

"You're very tough, Monte. It's easy to be tough with an N-8 entourage. Do you enjoy having a robot bodyguard? Doing what you want, saying what you want?"

Monte smiled, thinking of Regal and seeing the hypocrisy in Robbie's statement.

"Nate, would you be so kind as to ask this gentleman to leave us be so that we can return to our studies?"

Nate knew Monte seldom asked him to do anything and that if he was asking, it was important. He carefully honored Monte's request.

"I am sorry, sir, but I am going to have to ask that you leave us be now. Thank you."

"Pretty sweet bot you've got there. Where can I buy one?"

Nate's patience with Robbie began to wear thin; he stood up and took on a more direct tone.

"Leave Us Be."

"Alright, Chief…no need to get upset…we're leaving…we'll see you around though, 'kay Monte?"

"I sure hope not. Have a good one!" Monte mockingly waved goodbye.

"C'mon…" Robbie whispered to his friends, as he jerked his neck softly to the left, signaling it was time to go.

Monte waited a few seconds until his new friends had exited the building.

"That was Hurlocke's spawn, right?" Monte asked Nate.

"Yes, it was. I would not worry about him if I were you. My biometric scans revealed he was more afraid of us than we were of him."

"I don't like Hurlocke anything. I don't want to come within a hundred feet of his shoes, let alone his offspring. Thanks for getting rid of those jag-offs for me though. You're a pal."

Once Robbie had left the school's grounds, he called his father.

"Hey, no luck. He's got that friend of his with him at all times these days. Going to have to try something else, or at least wait until his buddy is preoccupied."

"Come on back, I know exactly what to do…" Hurlocke replied.

16

Green Tea Junkie

The following day, Monte woke up relatively early and headed to Swank's. He ordered a large lotus blossom tea. Not only did Legaia's official flower create the experimental crystals that helped power a few of the city-state's pertinent buildings and part of the eight's functionality, but they also made for a delicious, nutrient-rich green tea—a personal favorite of Monte's. He sometimes ordered two of them—one for himself and one for Nate.

Advanced nandroids had no need for human food and drink, only the charging or replacement of their power sources, regular hardware/software maintenance, and fluid top-offs with the occasional flush. Their circulatory systems primarily provided them with the liquid-cooling of hardware, rather than nutrient distribution.

"Your tea's getting cold."

Monte toyed with Nate as they hung out and waited for Claire to join them.

"You are so amusing, sir. Jaw-dropping, your sense of humor is. You make the greatest comedians of the past sound like babbling fools. I am surprised I do not have to protect you from swarms of women that long for your company. Please, Mr. Cizek. Do not waste your breath on us for we are not worthy of your genius."

"Alright, alright. Jeez...And why do you always have to talk like a robot? 'Good afternoon, sir. How may I assist you this morning with your scientific endeavors, sir? Shall I schedule a meeting for you on your behalf, sir? Kegahertz and gizaflops!"

"Could it be because...I am a robot?"

"That's it. I'm done with you."

"Good morning, boys," said Claire upon walking in.

"Good morning, miss," replied Nate.

"Good morning, miss," responded Monte, mocking Nate.

"My little gentlemen, so formal and cute."

"That's us." said Monte.

Claire put her purse and jacket on the empty seat next to her. Her lips glistened in pastel pink.

"I'm going to get a drink, and I'll be rigghhtt back."

Claire returned with an iced beverage and a smile on her face.

"Look at you, all smiley," said Monte. "Got some great news you'd like to share with us or something?"

"Well, I don't know if it qualifies as great news, but I do have something to share with you. One of my classmates is having a party tonight, and she specifically asked me to invite you guys."

"Oh, a house party. You know I love those. I'm pretty sure Nate loves them, too. Will there be any sexy bots at this party? Although I think his preference is human women to be honest with you."

Claire playfully slapped Monte's forearm.

"Leave him alone. Nate can be attracted to anyone or anything he pleases. I will set him up with one of my girlfriends personally!"

Monte looked over at Nate with a smirk on his face.

"You know what that means, bud...Run. Run far and fast!"

Claire laughed out loud with her straw still in her mouth, trying her best not to choke on the white chocolate chip blended drink.

"Shut, up, Monte! Before my drink comes out of places it shouldn't."

"I'm pretty sure even Nate agrees that we'd pay good money to see that."

"That would indeed be quite impressive, Ms. Ortega," said Nate.

"You two are too much. No wonder you're bed buddies."

"Hey! We are not bed buddies," said Monte. "Nate sleeps in chairs, sitting upright. Shit still creeps me out..."

"Okay, Barnum and Bailey, sorry I can't stay too long. I've got some errands to run and some shopping to do before the party. You guys are coming for sure though, right?"

"Yeah, yeah, we'll be there. Make sure there's a six pack of cider there for me."

"Deal!" shouted Claire as she slung her purse over her shoulder. "See you guys tonighttt!"

"See ya."

"Have a pleasant afternoon, Ms. Ortega."

"Thank you, Nate." Claire winked at Monte before making her way toward the coffee house's exit.

"Well, Mr. Cizek, I believe it is safe to say that you have an admirer."

"Tens of millions in R&D for a Captain Obvious 'droid? Porter really needs to rethink his financial commitments."

"I can remove all four of your limbs in under six seconds,

91

might I remind you."

"Now, now, that's an ASG bylaw violation right there, buddy boy. Keep talking like that and you'll be recycled and turned into a really fancy pedicab."

Nate looked at Monte with disapproval.

"I'm kiddinggg, tin man. Don't get your alloy panties in a bunch. C'mon, let's get outta here. Let's go kick it 'til it's time for the party."

"If by 'kicking it' you are referring to preparing for next week's exams." replied Nate.

"One can only ponder propulsions systems and the periodic table for so long. I was thinking, we have yet to check out the rooftop deck. I figured we could go relax a bit up there tonight. Ponder. Converse. What do you say?"

"That sounds quite enjoyable, sir."

"Fantastic. Let's do the damn thang."

Monte was excited to see what the roof was like, as he'd been looking forward to spending some time there since they had first arrived. After climbing the final staircase leading to roof access, the two were excited to discover their destination was outfitted with several plants and furniture sets.

"Not bad at all." said Monte.

He sat in a lawn chair with his ankles crossed, sipping a beverage, while Nate sat at the edge of his seat. A see-through guardrail provided them with a fascinating view of their neighborhood—a bird's eye view of Legaia's contemporary architecture.

"Ahhh, that hit the spot." Monte took a gulp of his chilled ginger ale with much satisfaction. "So Nate…Tell me what it's like."

"Which part of it, sir?"

"To live the way you do, to be so similar to us without being human. I wanna know what it's like."

"I would venture to say we share the same existence, but I am not qualified to make such a statement, for the same reason why you have asked me this very question. I am undoubtedly alive, but I believe there is one area in which we differ drastically. My primary prerogative is pre-programmed, whereas a human being's will is undoubtedly its own—free to pursue any path at any time. There are most likely other cognitive differences, but this protocol I follow is all the reason I need to acknowledge where our similarities in existence end. You live a life in which there are no boundaries. Not in a physical sense, but in reference to borders of the mind. There are several moments in each day in which I wish I could experience this state, unbound by the digital protocols that govern my life…Regardless, what father has given me is a blessing. I awake each morning with an unparalleled view of the cosmos, after a night filled with rigorous studies, to a world built over thousands of years by human beings. Often derailed by conditions of their character, but always realigned by the nature of their morality. The dwellings, the vehicles, the gestures, I am in love with your kind, Monte. I feel exuberated simply being amongst you."

"Well, that certainly puts things into perspective."

"Ask and you shall receive, Mr. Cizek."

"How do you tell the difference between what you were made to do versus what you choose to do?"

"I am not certain that I can, sir. I feel a collective consciousness. My choices and actions simply…come to me. Can you tell the difference between what you were made to do versus what you choose to do?"

"I got nothing." replied the stumped young man, as he took a nice, long swig of his beverage, while admiring his view of the cityscape of his dreams.

17

Life Of The Party

Monte and Nate reached the destination Claire had given them via autonotaxi. Claire's friend lived on the third story of a large residential complex with retail outlets and social hangouts on the ground floor. They rode three flights of escalators, as Monte shot Claire a quick message letting her know they had arrived.

"Brian, can you get let my friend Monte in? He should be at the door any second now. Thanks, sweetie," Claire said to her friend's teenaged brother.

Monte and Nate spoke behind the door for a few seconds as they waited. It sounded lively, as faint music and conversation could be heard from just outside the main entrance.

"I must say, you are looking quite dapper this evening." said Nate.

The only difference between what Monte was wearing tonight versus what he typically wore was that he was wearing a midnight blue blazer over his traditional daily outfit of a t-shirt and jeans.

"I don't wanna hear it. You're not even wearing clothes…You're naked."

"That is not true. I am decent."

"Yeah, decently naked!"

"Androids do not require human clothing."

"Yeah, that's cause you'd look stupid in them!"

"I would not. I would look handsome."

They enjoyed their childish but entertaining exchange until the door cracked open.

The boy opened the door to find Monte and the world's most intricate android.

"Whoa!" shouted Brian.

"That's what she said." said Monte as he walked right passed him. Nate greeted the boy and followed suit. Brian stood there with his mouth hung open, still clenching the doorknob. It wasn't every day you saw something like Nate walk into your home.

They made their way through the small cliques of guests. Monte recognized a few classmates from PULISC and nodded a respectful hello.

"Monte, Nate" a classmate said as he nodded, acknowledging Monte's hello.

They continued to walk through the crowd, looking for the kitchen or for Claire.

The party reminded Monte of Aaron, his old pal from high school. Aaron typically didn't attend such functions because of his demanding work schedule as a rookie police officer. The Commander (his father, Captain Draifer) could pull a string or two for him here and there, but at the same time felt it was important for Aaron to reach maturation in the police department the organic way.

Monte saw a few girls eyeing him before he made it to the

kitchen.

"You must be Monte! Hi, I'm Teagan, Claire's friend."

"Whatever you've heard about me, it's all true, unfortunately..."

"Ha. Who's your friend?"

"This is Nate. He has major anger management issues, so I'd be careful not to piss him off."

"Really??" she asked with concern in her voice.

"My friend Monte here has spent too much time in laboratories, and the fumes from his experiments seem to have rotted his mind. Forgive him, please. It is a pleasure to meet you, Teagan."

"Hahaha, you guys are so funny! Make yourselves at home, plenty of food in the kitchen and drinks are in the coolers. Enjoy! Oh, Claire's floating around somewhere, still getting ready. I'm sure she'll be done soon."

"Thanks," Monte responded.

Claire was upstairs in one of the bedrooms, perfecting her makeup.

"Claire! Get your sexy ass down here!" shouted Teagan.

"I'm coming!"

Monte sifted through one of the ice chests, unable to find a libation he deemed satisfactory, while Nate put together a snack plate for him.

"That's a good little robot! Goo' boy!"

"I am only assembling this meal for you because I am going to enjoy it though you, vicariously. What do they taste like? These human party favors?"

"Like sodium and regret. No good for the mind, body, or the spirit."

"Interesting...Why do humans consume them if they make you look and feel regret?"

"The more time you spend trying to find logic in human

behavior, the more you'll begin to realize that you're wasting your time. Save your Qorlithium-Ion juice for more important things, like making me snack plates and bringing me drinks."

Nate stood at attention.

"Sir, yes, sir!"

"Cut it out, you metal monkey."

"Sir, as you wish, sir!"

"Damn it, Nate," said Monte, fighting back a smile "You're going to embarrass me if you keep that up."

As the two continued flirting with one another instead of the many attractive females that were present, Claire came down the staircase with a couple of her friends.

"Hot dog…" Monte muttered under his breath.

"I can see why she owns you, sir."

"I'll remember all of this when it's time for your next crystal."

"Hey, you two! Come here and give mama some sugar!" Claire said, appearing to be in a great mood.

"Don't mind if I do!" said Monte.

"I'm glad you guys are here." Claire air-kissed the boys on their cheeks.

"Always a pleasure, Miss Ortega," replied Nate.

"Yeah, what Romeo said." said Monte.

"You guys met Teagan, right?"

"We sure did."

"Come, let's go sit in the lounge area and mingle."

The boys followed Claire. She really did look quite stunning that evening. It was a combination of her edgy, eclectic appearance, combined with the skin-tight dress and heels she was wearing. She was a showstopper in addition to being quite intelligent, and that's why Monte came undone in her presence.

Claire grabbed Monte's hand and led him through the hallway to the main room where most folks were sipping their drinks, chit chatting, and enjoying themselves. She introduced him to several people, mainly classmates and acquaintances of hers that she knew wouldn't be mutual friends of theirs. About half of the attendees were either PULISC students or people Monte happened to know anyway.

The styles of the times were a fashion soup. Colorful and various, form-fitting with sharp lines. Borrowing design cues from past trends while incorporating newer, asymmetrical, vivid styles of the present. The architecture and home decor was also colorful, while using newer, stronger, and lighter materials.

Generally speaking, life had been simplified. Logos, signs, menus, all designed to garner maximum attention in minimal time. The vehicles were sleek, with aerodynamics and functionality taking precedence over aesthetics.

Astute and keen in his observations, Monte was aware of just about everything. He was the sort of person that could carry a surface level conversation with anyone about anything. And although his outfits were simple and repetitive, his broad spectrum of knowledge was uncommon.

He wanted to learn more, do more, and speak several languages, but his obsessions with nanotechnology, chemistry, and robotics meant the rest of his pursuits, educational and personal, were always forced into the shadows of his priorities.

Monte spent the next hour or so mingling with friends. He explained to many of the guests what Nate was.

Then, he had an idea. What if he took his project plane out for a little spin with Claire? It wasn't a great idea. Heck, it wasn't even legal. But he really wanted an opportunity to be alone with her and to impress her.

It was a couple hours into the party, and most of the brainy hooligans were quite tipsy and having a great time.

Monte walked up behind Claire and pinched her hips.

"Hey, I have an idea…let's get out of here."

"Really? Ah, c'mon, it's just getting good! Everyone finally got here!"

"I know, you're right, but I have something I really wanna show you."

She gave him a look that said, *"you know I'm going to come with you, but damn you for making me leave a great party at its peak."*

"Okay, whiz kid, let's go."

Monte grabbed her hand and found Nate.

"Hey, we're gonna get out of here for an hour or two. Will you be alright here by yourself?"

Nate was busy chatting with some of the other PULISC students.

"I will be absolutely fine, sir. It is you I worry about."

"We'll be fine. We're gonna go for a little…test drive. We'll be back later though."

"I hope you know what you are doing, Mr. Cizek." mumbled Nate to himself as the pseudo-couple ran out the front door.

18

Living On The Edge

"Ready for my master plan?" said Monte, clasping Claire's hand as they walked briskly.

"This can't be good."

Monte stopped, grabbed Claire by the hips, and turned her toward him.

"Let's go for a space flight."

"A what?"

"A space flight!"

"You've finally lost it for good, huh?"

"Let's fly around Legaia."

"Fly around Legaia? In what? Since when do you have a spaceship? Is that even legal!? You're nuts! Can you for once just be normal, or do you need to bring negative attention to yourself all the time in order to function?"

"Listen, you chicken, I'm going for a space ride. Either you're coming with me, or you can sit here with your pals and watch the lilies grow. If you're lucky, one of these squares will eventually strip down and dance on a table before he vomits on himself and passes out."

Monte started backwardly skipping away from Claire to see if he could get her to join him for a little test flight of the small aircraft he'd been working on.

Although technically it wasn't "illegal" (because no civilian had the capability to leave Legaia unless it was on a commercial flight, nor did they foresee anyone having the capability to do so), leaving the confines of Legaia on your own would most certainly be frowned upon.

Claire performed a couple of hop skips to catch up to Monte.

"If you send us adrift in outer space, I'm so going to kick your ass. And slow down! I'm in heels, jerk!"

"Fair enough. Now quit your whining! Live a little!"

They drove off in the Cizek family sedan, which had driven itself to their location, at Monte's request. Monte turned the music up a bit as they headed toward the private hangar where he kept his secret little project. He had been working on it since the day after their arrival. Monte needed a project that was strictly for him, not science. When he got stuck or tired, he turned to the hangar. And when things weren't going his way, in life and in love, he went to the hangar.

The nighttime guard was an NTI 'droid named Jorge, and Monte had become good pals with him. Jorge was aware of Monte's relationship to NTI as well as Professor Porter, and would accommodate any request Monte made.

Things were usually slow on this end of the spaceport's commercial terminals on a Saturday night. Jorge was happy to see Monte pull up to the gate. He opened it as quickly as he could.

"Monte, are you sure we can't get in super trouble for this?"

Claire was visibly excited and nervous, and as a result, showed a much softer, more vulnerable side.

"Have I ever gotten in 'super trouble' for anything? Not to sound like a self-indulgent dick or anything, but my lubricants are in just about every moving object on this over-priced space bubble. I wouldn't worry about it too much…But rather, get a load of this!"

He opened his hangar door via his watch, and Claire's jaw dropped.

"Ummm…where did you get this? And who paid for it?"

"Get? Built, my friend…built. Been working on it since we got here. Her name is Alexis. Bow in the presence of her greatness!"

The aircraft was small and nimble-looking with many sharp lines. It was a very dark gray, a kit plane to which Monte had made many adjustments with custom fabricated parts.

"Okay…show me what she's got."

Claire tried talking herself into being ready for the flight, even though she was still on the fence about it.

Monte opened the cockpit door upward. It sat two in a fighter-jet-style configuration, with the passenger seated behind the pilot. He helped Claire into her seat before taking his.

The impressive instrument panel lit up with vibrant, violet-colored data, as Monte went through his pre-flight checklist. He also sent a message to Jorge, letting him know to prepare to open the gate. The gate to space, that is.

"Like we discussed, got it?" Jorge sent an encrypted message to Monte.

"Roger that. No blame, no shame. I promise."

"10-4. Enjoy the ride."

"Will do, bud."

The plane was a few seconds away from completing its staging.

"You ready, lady?"

Claire adjusted her helmet to ensure a tight fit, more so out of nervousness than a need to correct anything.

"Oh God...Okay, yes! Let's go!"

"Oh we're 'bout to go alright...Jorge, I'm ready. Let me know when I'm clear."

With all braking systems engaged, the engine's turbines reached their desired output. Monte was giddier than a kid on Christmas morning. He gripped the thrust lever tightly with his right hand as he licked his lips and waited for the split second when Jorge would give him the green light.

"All clear. Go for launch. And be good!"

"Roger!"

Monte disengaged the brakes and took off. The aircraft accelerated rapidly into a tunnel. The lights on the ground, walls, and ceiling whizzed by. A doorway closed behind them and immediately afterward, the one in front of them opened, as they shot out of it like a cannonball. They had left the confines of Legaia.

"Woooo!" said the young prodigy, excited to see his project come to fruition.

"Oh Myy Goddd!" responded Claire, as the plane accelerated further.

They were experiencing something most others would only get to imagine, and they were elated.

Monte distanced himself from Legaia so that he would have ample space to really evaluate his new machine. They were pinned to their seats. It felt like a cutting-edge roller coaster ride, except their surroundings were that of the Milky Way.

Thrust-vectoring nozzles all over the plane pulsed with blue flame with each push and pull of the yoke. With sweeping turns and sharp cuts, Monte tested the boundaries of his new toy as well as his piloting ability. Those countless hours he had spent on his flight simulator seemed to be paying off. He occasionally hit the thrust hard, pushing for speed.

"Monteeee, Hahahaha!" yelled an overjoyed Claire, as the plane gently rolled several times over.

Digital communication came in, wondering why the aircraft was flying around rather than on a clear-cut path for Earth. Monte replied, "Just a quick test flight. Be back before ya know it."

The NDT Spaceport air traffic control officer turned and looked to her supervisor for suggestions. The manager stood there with his arms crossed on his chest, shaking his head in disbelief.

Monte continued to enjoy his flight—the view, the sounds, and the sensation of G-Force. After accomplishing what he set out do to, he pointed the airplane toward Earth and brought the speed down drastically, so that he and Claire could spend a moment just admiring their old home.

"That's where we used to live. We were born there. I never thought I'd get to see it from this angle. It's fucking gorgeous."

"I know…it's amazing. This is amazing. Thank you for not letting me chicken out. I'm glad I didn't."

"I'm glad, too," replied Monte in a more sentimental tone. "I've had my fun. Ready to head back to the party?"

"Yup," Claire replied with satisfaction.

Monte banked the plane to the right and headed back to the hanger, smoothly bringing the plane in and gently setting it down like it were a priceless piece of merchandise. The air traffic control supervisor was there waiting for him with a human armed guard.

When their feet were back on solid ground, the supervisor spoke.

"Young Man, A heads up would have been nice, 'Hey, don't be alarmed, it's not a U.F.O., it's just me, being an entitled jerk!'"

"I know, you're right, I'm sorry. It was a…spur of the

moment type of thing." Monte winked at the supervisor and grabbed Claire's hand, quickly making their way toward his car. As they got in, almost attempting to get away before the man could question them any further, the supervisor shouted, "I'm going to speak with Randal about this!"

"Okay!" Monte shouted right back, before rolling up the window to the driver's seat of the sedan and disappearing out of sight. Claire and Monte laughed as they headed back to Teagan's place for continued festivities.

19

Tell Him What He's Won

Back at the party, Monte felt a buzz in his pocket.

One new message: "Hey, Baby Knievel, the last thing I need is NDT management up my ass. I may be old, but I still need my beauty sleep. Save the rest of your shenanigans for another day, will ya? Hi Claire."

Monte slid his phone back into his pocket and laughed.

"Poor Doc. What is he ever going to do with the likes of a brat like me?"

"Let's hope your excuses are as cunning as your research!"

Claire took off her jacket and sat on the bed in the guest bedroom.

"Ha-ha. Ya'll know you love me."

Claire was too elated from the flight to argue. She leaned back on the bed, resting her weight on her hands.

"I'm not even gonna lie. That was unreal, Monte."

"That's why I built the damn thing. Do you want something to drink? I'm gonna check on Nate and grab a cider."

"Water, please."

"You got it."

He jogged down the staircase with purpose and looked around for Nate, finding him right where he had left him on the sofa. His eyes were closed, and he seemed to be meditating. Nate acknowledged Monte's presence in the room before Monte had a chance to say anything.

"I am fine, sir. I am assuming your lady friend is upstairs, waiting for you?" said Nate with his eyes still shut.

"Correct!"

"Lovely. I am studying Saroyan. Did you know he had a son that wrote poetry? Quite strange, but I am intrigued nonetheless."

"You've been spending too much time with Mr. Nahele." replied Monte.

"I admire Henry's tranquility. There is much to be learned from that man."

"Can't argue with that…You kids having fun?" he said to Teagan's brother and a couple of his friends who were gathered around Nate, still fascinated by him.

"I want one! How much are they?" a young boy asked.

"Ha, not yet available for sale. Sorry, bud."

Monte grabbed a chilled bottle of artisan water and raspberry cider from a cooler in the kitchen and made his way back up the stairs.

"Claire?"

She wasn't in the room, but the lights had been lowered to a very dim setting, and the restroom light was on as well. He enjoyed a few sips of his ice-cold beverage as he sat upon the bed. A brief wave of joy came over him, and suddenly, he had a smile on his face from ear to ear.

The rest room door opened and its light turned off. Only the faint glow of a small candle remained along with the soothing and mellow music Claire's phone was playing. She slowly came out of the restroom, wearing satin lingerie. Her stunning body revealed, her fair skin contrasting with her wardrobe. Or lack thereof.

Monte was awestruck. Her hair, her tattoos, her tall, slender, and toned figure. Her crimson hair color, barely detectable in the dark, romantic setting.

"Good mother of God..."

Claire lit a couple more vanilla-scented candles.

"Like what you see?" she asked.

"I think that's a given."

"Oh?"

Claire placed one knee at the bottom edge of the bed and then the other. She swung her head back and flipped her hair, while seductively gazing at Monte.

"If you need any favors, now would be the time to ask. Homework help, kill a man, whatever you need."

"I do, actually," she said as she placed her hands on Monte's shoulders and mounted his lap.

"Well...this is certainly a..."

Claire put her index and middle fingers over Monte's mouth, feeling his lips while signaling that she no longer wanted him to speak. After he quieted down, she hung her right index finger off of his bottom lip and used her free hand to take his beanie off, while running her fingers through the back of his shaggy, black hair. She had a look in her eye, a sultry killer instinct, like she had her prey exactly where she wanted it. Monte usually had no problem being the aggressor, but as far as Claire was concerned, these were waters he wanted to tread very carefully.

She placed her hands on Monte's head, just under the ears. Her long magenta nails, somewhat matching her hair color, navigated his scalp. She was playing a little bit of a game. A little give and a little take. Whatever it was, this young man was along for the ride.

Claire placed her nose alongside his, hovering her lips as close to his as she could without kissing them.

Monte caressed her back with his hands. He was completely under her spell. She guided her mouth to the side of his head, where she could nibble on his left ear lobe, lick the cartilage at the top of his ear, and even put her tongue inside of his ear.

The entranced young man placed his left hand at the small of her back, his left middle finger drifting underneath her underwear's elastic band, and used his right hand to explore her back, taking in the firmness of it. Enjoying the little valley where the spine lies, he slowly ran his hand up her back until it got to the back of her head. There, he grabbed her by the hair and took control of her head, lined it up with where he wanted it to be, teased her with brief hesitation, and began kissing her. It was sweet and gentle for no longer than a few seconds, before they were consuming one another like deprived animals.

His submission had come to an end, as he picked her up and turned the both of them around.

Monte aggressively ran his hands over her body and through her hair as the two kissed. He lowered a bra strap onto Claire's arm and enjoyed the taste of her neck, shoulder, and neck again. She pivoted and cocked her head back, exposing the front of her neck, and he indulged accordingly.

Whatever scent she was wearing there was intoxicating, and it made Monte want to tear her remaining clothing off. It looked like expensive lingerie, and as much as he wanted to destroy it all, he refrained.

Claire reached for Monte's belt. She began undoing it while Monte took his shirt off, exposing his olive-skinned physique. Once she got his pants undone, she eagerly pulled them down toward his ankles. They had crossed a threshold there was no pulling back from.

As Monte removed his jeans, one leg after the other, Claire took off her bra. She balanced herself on her rear so that she could remove her underwear as well. She then lay on her side. Monte slithered up behind her in the spooning position.

She closed her eyes and smiled euphorically as Monte caressed her frame and kissed the side of her rib cage. After a few more seconds, when they were both more than ready, Monte entered her and felt the sensation he had longed for day in and day out since beginning his studies at PULA.

It didn't seem real, that his fantasy had become a reality, but boy did it feel real. Monte wanted to stay in this very position forever, but he also wanted to return to the party before folks wondered where they were and started looking for them. Upon clearing his mind of distracting thoughts, he climaxed with one of the most powerful orgasms he'd ever had.

They caught their breath. Monte needed a bit longer to recuperate than she did.

"You alright there, slugger?"

Monte responded, halfway out of breath. "Oh yeah…more than alright…I hate you, btw…you're evil."

"Ha, I'll take that as a compliment."

"Did you finish?" asked Monte.

"Mmhmm…We should head back downstairs soon huh."

"Yes…yes we should. Next time you step into a room wearing stuff like that, I might not be able to refrain myself."

"Hahaha. Don't make promises you can't keep." She threw Monte's jeans at him. "Let's go party."

"Yes, ma'am."

20

This One's For Your Old Man

"That's no concern of mine, Professor Potenza. We've never had an issue with funding, and I hope we never will. The facilities themselves are performing wonderfully, and we've got more equipment getting installed every month. I don't really have anything to complain about. So far, so good, friends." said Randal as he stood up from his conference room chair at the head of the table.

The other individuals present in the room were Porter University's board of directors. Staff and faculty joined in via video conferencing from the Legaia and Los Angeles campuses.

"We agree, Dr. Porter. In the short time since PULISC has opened its doors, things have gone just as smoothly as we had hoped. All of our reports look good. We'll keep you posted if anything changes."

"Sounds great, folks. And you guys in L.A. be good. Just cause I'm floating around 265 miles above the Earth's surface doesn't mean I'm asleep...I'm watching you!"

The attendees smiled. Dr. Porter was uncharacteristically cheerful as a result of the positive reporting.

"Okay, everyone. I'm outta here. Email me if you need anything. Until next time."

Randy got up and started the short walk over to his office in the next building over, while the L.A. staff disconnected and the Legaia staffed chatted among themselves and slowly emptied the conference room.

With Nate's existence stable and marvelously successful thus far, Randal decided it was time for him to divert his attention to another project. That afternoon, he spent the majority of his day locked in his office with his email client closed and his mobile device on standby. In this mode, it would accept certain types of communication from a chosen few sources (Monte, Nate, HQ, and emergency beacons of sorts) but for the most part, Randal was trying to focus on the objective at hand.

He visually scanned his desk from left to right as he mentally prepared himself. There were a couple stacks of students' classwork in one corner. He removed them, placing them onto the floor next to his desk. Even though the scholastic assignments were submitted digitally, and even though Randal was a robotics pioneer, there were still a few things he preferred to do the old-fashioned way.

After going through his rituals, organizing his workspace, and preparing a tea and a snack, the professor walked over to the other side of his office and grabbed a large cardboard box labeled "Dusk." With his quantum-computer online and all necessary applications loaded and ready to go, the professor pulled open one of the drawers in his desk and removed a box cutter. He slowly and meticulously cut slits in the tape that held the box shut and opened it. Then, he began to remove the contents of the box, which included entire binders full of notation, data drives on several different generations of storage devices, and a few miscellaneous personal items that had belonged to his old pal Christopher Cizek, Monte's father.

Randy thought long and hard about putting the irrelevant items away and coming back to them later, but he couldn't resist the temptation. The professor concluded that he had all afternoon to dedicate to the project, and that it wouldn't hurt if he spent a few minutes browsing through the items. He grabbed a few envelopes full of photographs and took a seat at his desk.

He avoided his pastry, not to get smudge marks on the photographs, and had a sip of his tea instead.

Inside the envelopes were pictures of Monte as a child, not what the professor was expecting to find at all.

A few of the photographs included pictures of Chris. The pictures resembled happier times in Chris's life, moments he'd spent in laboratories or with Monte. Even though Chris and Roxanne had two other children, Chris had intentionally placed pictures of Monte inside this collection.

As the doctor browsed through the envelopes, he saw images of a very young Monte Cizek. And in those images, he was constructing scale models of sports cars and fighter jets. Even a remote-controlled semi-truck Chris had helped him build from scratch for a second grade competition using spare metals left over from other projects and some basic metal-working tools.

There were pictures of Monte mashing on a computer keyboard as a baby, staring into a screen as if he could understand and comprehend the data being displayed on the monitors, when all he was really capable of doing was soiling himself.

There were also photographs of Monte trying to put together his very first toy robot, which spoke pre-programmed text and had quite a bit of mobility for a toy. Monte wearing goggles two sizes too large for his face and playing with his first chemistry set. And Monte taking books off shelves and scattering them throughout his room, so that he could alphabetize them and put them back. Philosophy, biology, chemistry and mathematics and aeronautics. Fields of study the youngster knew nothing about, but it was this type of early exposure to the sciences that led Monte down a path of experimentation and discovery.

As the professor continued to look through the pictures, he noticed a pattern. It was almost as though Chris was trying to communicate a message through the photographs, as if he were constructing an early timeline of images in the life of a scientific prodigy. The collection called out to Dr. Porter in a powerful fashion, saying, *"Take my son. Make him yours. Entrust him with the future I never had and the world you've been able to create. Hand him the baton that is the relay-race of your fate."*

Randal felt empowered. Overcome and electrified.

He put the photographs back into their pouches. Didn't even bother to go through the other two stacks before putting them back into the box. Immediately afterwards, he grabbed every blueprint that was rolled up and bound with rubber bands and began opening them feverishly. Each time he unraveled one of the large documents, he placed weights on the corners to help them flatten out, making them easier to work with.

"Okay, this is it. Show me what you've done here, old man." The professor spoke to himself under his breath. It was his way of keeping Chris's spirit in the loop and motivating himself for the objective at hand.

As he plugged in the data drives and opened digital versions of Chris's files, he separated the work he'd already processed in the past from the elements he was missing, the pieces Chris hadn't been able to complete. The work was mostly done. It just needed the finishing touch of a one-of-a-kind nanophysicist.

The minutes soon became hours, as Dr. Porter ran through

energy theory simulations. His computer used the connected drives and the entire web to process data, citing both experimental formulas as well as scientific data from past analysis, and then simultaneously incorporating all of the information into the calculations. This process repeated itself, and each time the data was run through a processing cycle, a tweak was made. New information was introduced.

In his younger days, Randal would have run these experiments from sunrise to sunset. He'd take brief naps and wake only to process more data, never really getting a full night's rest for days on end. He was equal parts curious and dedicated, and it was that sort of drive that had laid the foundation for much of his success.

After glancing down at what looked like a classic timepiece on his left wrist (actually a prototype super-watch), he was surprised to see five and a half hours had gone by. He set the application to auto-run so that it would continue processing formulas for him, tracking its own progress and noting changes in the code that it felt would best improve the odds for success. He frowned upon not being in front of a screen to see such data in real time, but he knew he needed a break. He was no longer the intern from his younger years with bountiful energy.

Randal opened the mini-fridge in his office, grabbing some baby carrots, celery sticks, and a sealed package of hummus. He had to check the date on the packaging because he couldn't remember when he had put it in there.

While hydrating and snacking on his veggies, he thought to himself, *I hope you know what you're talking about here, bud...the bracelets and the kid.*

The professor already knew that Monte's purpose at PULISC and NTI would be unlike any other student's or any other employee's. He just wanted so badly to be able to complete this project as well. To give Monte just another tool for his toolbox, an additional method of protection. To further ensure it would be very difficult for his academic and corporate babies to be colluded, stolen, or destroyed. And as great as his nandroids were, the successful completion of the Dusk project would help Randy sleep easier at night.

With his digestive system content and his blood sugar stabilized, it was back to work as usual, and the professor continued to process and refine the information contained within the applications until his eyelids grew heavy. Randal hadn't spent this much time focused on one task, in one sitting, since the creation of the eight. It was an indicator of just how important this project was to the doctor.

After tremendous data enrichment with no resolution, and upon realizing that father time had crept into the morning, Randal set his pride aside, engaged the automated setting once again, and laid down on the futon several feet away from his desk to get some shuteye.

The following morning, Randal Porter would awake to discover that his computer had completed the formula, and his sense of satisfaction reminded him of the joy he'd felt on the day he'd been assigned to oversee the Legaia project in the first place.

Of course, the project was nowhere near complete. There'd be a lot of testing necessary in a controlled environment before the professor would feel comfortable enough presenting Monte with a final solution, but the hard part was over with, and it provided Randal with a great feeling of comfort and reassurance. The Doctor saved the completed formulas to his glass data drive, grabbed his thermos, his brown leather satchel, and his hat, and headed for the door to his office, ready to teach a class enthusiastically and embrace whatever the day would bring him.

21

B + +

"Unreal…" Monte muttered to himself, upon being handed back the B+ paper he had rewritten and turned back into his professor.

Dr. Randal Porter had a personal policy, allowing any student to rewrite any paper as many times as it took to get an A, during an allotted period of time. Monte had made corrections and further elaborated on the relationship between philosophy and artificial intelligence in his essay. Upon completing the paper, he was confident the enhancements were enough to get his grade upgraded from a B+ to an A, and he was frustrated when his paper given back to him marked "B++".

That same afternoon, Monte swung by Dr. Porter's office with every intent to vent to his mentor. It wasn't during the Professor's normal office hours, but Monte knew Randal's schedule well enough.

"I'm coming in there, so you'd better not be doing anything

weird!" Monte shouted, after lazily knocking on the professor's door a few times.

"Quit hollerin' and get in here," responded the doctor. Randy enjoyed having one student he could be chummy with. Even a life as compelling as Randal Porter's had its monotonies, and it was nice to be able to let loose after a long day's work. The completion of the dusk project was still fresh on the Doctor's mind, as he awaited the right moment to share the discovery with his disciple.

"Unless you have something groundbreaking to announce, I don't wanna hear it. Between Suttridge blowing up my inbox and that mountain of papers to grade, I don't know what I'm going to do with myself."

"Tell Mike you'll shoot the shit later over scotch and have Nate grade the rest of the papers. Any other mind-numbing issues I can resolve for you, Oh Great One?"

"You know, every once in a blue moon, when the stars align and the cosmic winds are blowing just right, you actually make sense."

"You know what doesn't make sense though? A B++ on a paper!"

"Ah...so that's why you're here. And here I thought you were just stopping by to say hello to your favorite professor out of the goodness of your own heart."

"I've heard of B+'s, and A-'s, but do you seriously want me to redo this thing a third time? I gave you everything you wanted."

"C'mon , kid. The B++ is obviously a joke, and your paper is obviously missing something."

"Okay, well guide me then. What am I missing? I sure as hell don't want or need a B plus plus plus!"

"The prompt asked you to watch one of the listed science fiction films and come up with your own five-page observation answering the listed questions. Nevertheless! There is no actual right or wrong answer, Monte. It's just that. The philosophical observation of a scientific question. You just need to go deeper than you do."

"It's quite elaborate. I just don't see how I can make it any longer."

"It's long enough. Maybe too long. I need depth, not length. I want you to explain your conclusion further. Why do you think what you think? We know what the character's stance is. Why do you think he thinks the way he does? What drove him to think that way? Talk more about that. And let loose. Let it flow, kid…But before you do, don't forget we have that IRRC presentation to prep for."

"We should just have Nate do it. He'll do it better than either one of us can anyway. Give him the main bullet points and let him do his thing."

"That's it, Cizek. You're officially on the payroll."

"Just trying to help an old man out. I will carry your groceries. Help you cross the street, sort your pills. Anything you need, sir."

"Might wanna save the jokes until after I've graded your next rewrite."

"Ha. B-plusssss'us'us'us'us…"

The two shared a good laugh, the kind that comes from deep inside of you without any formal thought process or filtration. They knew one another well, and their chemistry was undeniable.

Back at Richard Hurlocke's ASG office, Dick spoke with a few members of his entourage after being informed his lobbyists had failed to get a bill passed by Congress that would have assisted him in acquiring a few companies he'd been eyeing. He wasn't used to losing, so when it did happen, he took it very personally.

"It's time to…turn up the heat, a bit on Mr. Porter's operations…and anybody who isn't ready and willing had better say something now…" He waited to see if there'd be any objections. There weren't any. "Good. Just the response I was looking for. Things are about to get quite a bit more complicated for NTI and friends…I warned that son of a bitch. I told him I wasn't fucking around. He didn't listen. He never listens. He's going to hear me now, I can assure you of that."

22

Technologic Expeditions

A few days later, Monte received a voice message from his professor.

"Hope all is well and that you're not doing anything insane. Here's what's going down. We're performing a systems upgrade on Nate. O.S., apps, memory, storage, processing, cooling, all of it.

"It's very important the instructions and sequencing I'm about to send you is followed. I've never done any of this before—not in this way, not to this degree. As you know, many of his systems haven't endured long-term testing. I don't know what his thresholds are when it comes to certain things, and I sure as hell can't risk damaging or losing him in any way, shape, or form.

"I'm going to bathe his exoskeleton in a particle array. Make him stronger. You could call it an experiment, I suppose. A very controlled experiment. Promise you'll execute the commands to a tee, kid. That's my boy we're talking about here."

Nate's upgrades would give Randal a chance to practice relinquishing control for a change, while also providing him with an opportunity to test his understudy.

Monte spent several hours over the course of the next couple days accepting parts from delivery droids and reviewing notes regarding the upgrade. Android upgrades in and of themselves were no big deal, but an experimental upgrade to a prototype 'droid was a far more unique undertaking.

The moment had come for the world's most impressive android robot to further push the envelope of robotics and take his capabilities to yet another unprecedented level.

Monte paced throughout his apartment while reading a manual that had come with one of his new parts. Nate was in the laboratory, seated in an upright position with his eyes closed, studying. He wouldn't be one to admit it, but an ever-so-small part of Nate was nervous about the procedure he was about to undergo. His scholastic session was, in part, an effort to divert his thoughts elsewhere.

"Hey, Nate?"

"Yes, sir?" Monte's voice immediately brought him back to the present moment.

"It's time, bud. The last of the parts are here. Everything is ready to go. I gotta strip you of all power sources except for your kamacite-cadmium. You'll be completely unconscious, and you'll have just enough juice to be able to send me and Doc your vitals. I'm going to take care of you, and you're going to wake up a new man!"

"You mean a new robot...sir."

"Yes, that's right. Come here. Lay down. Let's get you upgraded."

23

Momentary Lapse In Judgment

Nate had spent the previous night sleeping in a vat. It was a necessary process that would prepare his chassis for the day's planned procedures. The aquamarine gel he'd laid in would coat every nanobot in his shell, making his exoskeleton more resilient to the negative effects of particle array.

The two were in Monte's personal lab. As Nate lay down in the chamber in which he'd be spending the next hour, he voiced his concern to Monte.

"Sir...is it unreasonable of me to be uncomfortable right now?"

"No, Nate, it's perfectly normal, actually. Human beings have always feared the unknown. And you're no different. It's normal to be uncomfortable in a situation like this, I can assure you of that. I just want you to remind yourself of something though. You're in good hands, and I'll have you back up and running before sunset. Fair enough?"

"Yes, sir."

"Good. I'm going to install your new hardware first and update your software second. It'll seem like the blink of an eye to you. You won't feel a thing."

"Thank you for your comfort." said Nate as Monte slid on a pair of anti-static gloves.

"Anytime, bud. See you soon."

Monte then proceeded to initiate the necessary protocols for the removal of all but one of Nate's power sources, including his crystals. Upon removing Nate's partially spent crystals from their respective bays, Monte grasped the last of them in his palm for a moment, marveling in its mystery, before setting it aside and proceeding.

And so Monte began the process of removing Nate's main CPU, replacing it with a pair of faster processors. He also filled several expansion slots dedicated to random access memory with gold-finned memory modules, essentially doubling Nate's short-term memory-related processing capabilities and increasing the speed at which the memory operated. There was no need to alter long-term storage, since the state of the art hard drive in Nate's head was what a bulk of the eight's research and development budget went to.

Nate's "brain" was the greatest component of his construct. It was an advanced high-speed flash memory drive that harnessed the advancements of atom-based storage, and it was 96% free, so Professor Porter knew from the get go that it would be adequately future-proofed.

Additionally, any data acquired after the installation of Nate's operating system was also backed up wirelessly and stored in a special cage at NTI's premiere data center.

Once the new hardware was in place, Monte used various android assistants to secure Nate's protective covers back into place. He continued to download and install new applications from Randal's personal server, which was stored at an undisclosed data center six stories underground.

Using both lights and sounds, the particle array generator warned onlookers to clear the room, the same way a dentist used to leave the room and come back in between x-raying teeth. The particle array beam was co-designed by Randal for use on top tier robots only, and it required the utmost caution.

The newer exoskeleton required customized array timings, and so Monte was to keep a visual on Nate and deactivate the array at just the right moment in order for optimal but cautious exoskeleton strengthening to take place. This process would have to be repeated once every seven months. There was also a limit as to how many times this procedure could be performed, before the eight would require a new body altogether.

Dressed head to toe in biomedical grade clean room clothing, Monte input a few final keyboard strokes before quickly exiting the room.

He sealed all doors and windows as he prepared to engage the final phase of the upgrade. He looked on in awe as the particle array began to slowly spool up. It would take about fifteen seconds in order for it to be at one hundred percent power, and it began glowing a bit brighter with each passing second.

At full throttle, the array showered down on Nate's frame, sending aurora-borealis-esque light patterns around the small room he was enclosed in.

Monte felt a sense of pride, as everything seemed to be going well with the upgrade process. He was looking forward to sharing his experiences with the professor.

Then, he felt a vibration in his pocket.

He removed his gloves and played back the unheard voice message. It was Claire. She had left him a manic message, filled with screams and sobs without any explanation as to why.

"Monte! Call Me! Oh my God! Oh, nooo! Why!?"

His emotions took control of his thought process as he hurried, calling Claire back numerous times, to which she did not respond. Through his peripheral vision, he noticed a powerful glow coming from Nate's upgrade booth.

"Fuck! Nate!"

He ran as fast as he could, knocking metal carts on wheels out of his way, trying to get over to the particle array's controls as quickly as possible. When he got there, he mashed down on the emergency power-off button. The turbines slowly wound back down—about another twelve seconds that felt like an eternity to Monte. He was eager to run into the room and attempt to access the damage.

"I'm so fucked. I am done."

There was generally a five-minute cool down period required before it was suggested that you enter a particle array room. Monte ran in there immediately.

Nate looked unscathed, but his sense of guilt wasn't satisfied with that. He frantically put his gloves back on to avoid static shock to expensive hardware. Assuming, of course, that he hadn't just royally destroyed the world's most advanced android being.

He opened all slots to power sources and gently but efficiently replaced every qorlithium battery and every crystal. He tested the kamacite-cadmium, too, just to be safe, before closing everything back up.

It was the moment of truth. He froze for two seconds.

"Oh God, please, pleaseee let him be fine, please!"

"November, Alpha, Tango, Echo!"

Nate went through his standard boot sequence. While lying on his back, he tilted his head toward the right, so that he could see Monte. He spoke simultaneously while the upgrades finished installing.

"You appear as though you have barely escaped a wrestling

126

match with an alligator, sir" said Nate.

Monte didn't even bother to respond verbally, but instead, leaned down toward the table and gave Nate a huge hug. A tear streamed down Monte's cheek. Nate had no idea why Monte was acting the way that he was. He was, however, intrigued.

"How do you feel??" Monte asked with a sense of urgency.

"I feel…amazing. Potent. Superior to my former self."

"Upgrades are nice, yes. I mean, are you alright? Nothing feels wrong?"

"Nothing that I can sense, sir. Everything seems excellent. I feel rejuvenated."

Monte sighed with relief.

"Whew. Okay, good. If anything feels wrong, please let me know as soon as possible, alright?"

"Yes, sir."

Nate sat upright, squeezed his fists, and wiggled his fingers. Tested his connectivity. Ran through some motions and made sure everything was working properly. He had a concerned look upon his face, as though he was trying to figure out why Monte was questioning his wellbeing.

Just then, Monte's phone rang. It was the professor.

"Shit…time to face the music, I guess."

Nate perked up and looked on, still oblivious to the fact that both he and Monte were to consider themselves lucky, and that Monte came very close to frying every ounce of his being in that particle array room.

"Hey, Doc."

"Hey, Kid."

"Do I dare open my mouth, or shall I just stand here and shut up?"

"Shut up is almost always a good approach."

It was the first time Monte had been worried about communicating with his professor.

"Ditto. Shut up it is then." Monte slightly hung his head in shame.

"When I asked you to give Nate the array bath, I didn't mean get distracted and shoot him with plasma for half a minute longer than you were supposed to. It's not the end of the world. I have a couple of frames in storage we could bring up to speed…but what if you had cooked the drives, too? And there was a complication with the servers? The tiniest breach in that exoskeleton would've incinerated him. Do you have any idea how royally fucked we'd be if you'd reduced Nate to elaborate charcoal and I couldn't restore him?"

The professor went out of his way to ensure Monte was remorseful.

"I know. I'm not going to talk. I'm not going to make excuses. I'm going to say that I'm sorry, I made a mistake, and I hope I never repeat such a thing. My heart is still racing. I'm glad he's okay. I almost had a heart attack, Doc."

"Okay, okay, calm down. I don't need you potentially croaking either…I'm not even gonna blame her for this. This was your doing."

Professor Porter had a pretty good feeling he knew what had distracted Monte to this extent.

"No excuses, Professor…I'm sorry. I'll do my best to make it up to you."

Randal felt the sincerity in Monte's voice. He wasn't a bad kid to begin with, but the fact that he felt so bad for his mistake made the professor feel as though he'd been punished enough, and that it made no sense to further scold him.

Roxanne had always taught Monte that whenever one door would close shut, another would open. Neither Nate, Monte, or even Professor Porter were aware of it yet, but Monte's neglect would actually have a surprising positive effect on Nate, one that neither of them could have ever imagined.

128

24

Let Go Of Me

After a couple hours of working on his bike, Monte headed toward his lab to run some tests, turning on various elements of his dwelling via a holographic dashboard displayed from his watch. His unit was outfitted with an elaborate air filtration system that he ran 24-7, even when he wasn't working on anything scientific. His phone was on silent, but he happened to notice the screen light up due to an incoming call. It was Claire.

"Hey,"

"Hey…"

"You okay?"

"Not really…"

"What happened?"

"Oh my goodness, Monte. It was terrible."

"No kidding, mofo. I almost got castrated 'cause of you."

"What do you mean?"

"I'm halfway joking. Never mind that. What the hell happened?"

"I walked into the dressing room at the auditorium and found Teagan slumped over a vanity. I thought she was napping, but I eventually grabbed her shoulder and turned her over. She was pale, Monte. Lifeless."

"What? How?"

"There was blood coming out of her nose, she wouldn't wake up. I called LFD and they rushed her out on a stretcher."

"Did she overdose or something??"

"I guess…the doctors told her mom it would be a while until we got the toxicology report back. She's devastated."

"I'm sorry about your friend…"

"Thanks…Ugh, this is so bad."

"Look, I know that's a tough thing to see. It's very unfortunate, but we seriously can't afford to be getting wrapped up in that sort of stuff right now."

"Drugs are grimy, and I want nothing to do with any of it."

"Good. Me neither."

"Why'd you get in trouble?"

"Oh…dude, I got your phone call in the middle of an experimental procedure on Nate. I took my attention off of him for maybe fifteen, twenty seconds tops! I thought for sure I'd cooked him and that Randy was gonna cast me off into space…"

"OMG. Is Nate okay??"

Claire's admiration for Nate was quite apparent.

"He seems fine. We ran all sorts of external and internal evaluations and everything checks out perfectly fine."

"I'm sorry. I shouldn't have called you. I wouldn't have had I known you were doing something that important."

"You're cute, but that was my own stupid fault, not yours. It's over now, and everything seems to be okay. Let's just be glad about that."

"Yeah. I feel a little better knowing Nate is okay. Hey…if

you're not busy tonight, maybe you can come over to my place."

"I just might do that," he responded, cloaking his eagerness.

Technically, Dr. Porter was right. Claire was the cause of Monte's distraction. But in Claire's defense, as well as Monte's, it would have taken a true sociopath not be impacted by such a voicemail the way Monte was. Teagan's passing was the first fatal drug overdose on Legaia, as narcotics were not as readily available on the LISC as they were on the mainland.

He was the only person she turned to in a time of need, even though she couldn't give Monte a straight answer in regards to whether or not she wanted to be his girlfriend. She would contact him for chai lattes or a night out on the town frequently enough, but the stars had to align in a rare formation for Claire to extend an invite over to her place.

Monte parked his motorcycle across the street and a few buildings down from Claire's townhome. Out of his ordinary outfit, Monte wore a stylish gray dress shirt, boot-cut jeans, black motorcycling boots, and a black leather riding jacket supplemented by armor. With his backpack on both shoulders and his red and black, graphic-intensive helmet, he took one final breath and walked toward Claire's door.

He tried his best to keep his cool as he rang the doorbell to her unit. Claire's mother opened the door.

"Hi Monte," said Heather with a warm and welcoming voice.

"Hi, Ms. Ortega."

"Please come in. Have a seat. Make yourself at home."

"Thank you, thank you."

Monte slowly and carefully placed his bag onto the floor next to the sofa, out of the way.

"Last time I saw you we were Earth dwellers."

"You're right...kind of crazy when you think about it."

"It sure is. Can I offer you anything? Have you eaten?"

"I'm fine, Ms. Ortega. I've already had dinner. Thank you so much though."

"Let me at least get you some green tea and a snack. I know you can't say no to that. Claire's upstairs getting ready. Why don't you make yourself comfortable on the balcony and I'll bring you some tea?"

"That sounds great!"

The sliding door was already open, and he took in the fabulous view of downtown Legaia's skyline filled with buildings tall and short with inventive designs and attractive lights. High-speed elevators were visible on the exteriors of tall office buildings and hotels. It was the epitome of a modern-day city.

Upon returning from the kitchen, Claire's mother noticed Monte admiring the skyline.

"I see you like the view."

She gently placed two cups of tea onto the patio table.

"I do. Claire didn't tell me your place had such a nice location."

"I know, right? I think we got lucky with this one. So how's PULISC treating you? Claire tells me Doctor Porter's greatest creation to date is practically your best friend."

"Ha. Can't say it isn't true. Nate's grown on me quite a bit. Randal knocked it out of the park with this one. He tends to do that pretty often, actually."

"Ain't that the truth. Randal is an interesting man."

"You've got that right."

Just then, Claire approached, looking as meticulously put together as she always did.

"Hey yous."

"Hi sweetie. You look cute." responded Heather.

"You two sure look cozy. I almost wanna pour myself a cup

of tea and join you!"

"I saved you a seat." said Monte.

"Very sweet of you, Monte. We should get going though. I hate getting to the theatre when all the good seats are gone."

"Yeah, we should. Thank you for the tea, Ms. Ortega. Always a pleasure."

"Don't make me any older than I already am. Call me Heather."

"You got it, Heather."

"You don't come here often enough, Monte. Claire, I demand that you bring Monte here more often."

That last comment stung a bit, because the kid wanted to be there. It was Claire that saw fog and haze when it came to Monte.

"I sure will. Shall we?" said Claire as she motioned toward the front door.

"Yup. Goodnight Ms. Ortega. Heather!"

"Have fun you two."

Claire grabbed her jacket off the coat hanger next to the door. Monte took one last final peek at his backpack to make sure it was in a safe and secure place, and they were off. He had brought along a spare helmet in all black for Claire to wear. She looked forward to her first motorcycle ride.

Monte felt his left breast pocket vibrate. He removed his phone to check his message. It was Nate.

"Update?"

Monte responded: "Just left Claire's. Headed downtown for a flick. All's well. Stay close."

"Copy. I will be 'marinating' nearby. Ping if you need me, Romeo."

Monte smiled. Nate had stolen another one of his phrases.

"This is going to be fun!" said Claire with excitement.

"Ha. Imma show you fun."

"Oh, I'm counting on it."

Monte felt a form of giddy inner joy and pride, as Claire wrapped her legs around him and mounted the bike. He could feel the heat resonating from her legs onto his lower back. They got to the movie theatre in time to secure great seats, and that put Claire in an even better mood. She rubbed his inner thigh as the lights dimmed.

Legaia's entertainment district was a well-lit and lively eight-block area with a movie theatre, several restaurants, a large pool hall, a craft beer brewery, a record store for collectors and purists, a book store, retail outlets small and large, and many smaller eateries and cafes with a wide array of foods, and even a frozen yogurt shop. There was no shortage of food or fun.

After the film let out, they strolled around the streets which were brimming with life.

"Let's get some tacos. I'm hungry, and the taco place down the street is pretty popular."

"You don't have to ask me twice," replied Claire.

The two enjoyed tacos and shared a cheesy quesadilla on a red and yellow picnic table that had decorative patio lights strung above it. She had soda out of a glass bottle with a straw, and he enjoyed sparkling mineral water.

After enjoying their meal, the two headed back to where Monte had parked his bike. They hopped on and enjoyed a calm, casual ride back to Claire's place, now that they were no longer in a rush to catch a movie.

Upon stepping foot into the cozy apartment, she grabbed Monte's hand and tried to guide him up the staircase, putting her finger over her mouth to signal that Claire's mother was asleep on the couch, but she felt Monte pulling back. Surprised, she turned around to see what the holdup was. Monte had remembered he wanted to take his bag up there with him.

"Oh, c'mon," Claire whispered, questioning why the bag wasn't okay just staying put where it was.

Monte whispered back, "I need it."

In her bedroom, Claire grabbed Monte by his jacket, which was unzipped, and began to kiss him seductively. Monte slowly put the bag down as far away from where they were standing as he could, while his lips were locked with Claire's.

The kiss grew passionate and intensified quickly. Claire threw her jacket onto a chair several feet away, and then reached to help Monte remove his motorcycle jacket as well.

"Hey…" He was halfway hesitant to continue, and halfway too aroused to think straight.

"Yeah?" she said, as she continued to kiss his neck, her voice hot and excited, also too aroused to think straight.

"I wanna give you something first."

"It can wait, baby…" she whispered back in a seductive tone.

She grabbed his head with two hands, one on each side, and devoured his lips as passionately as she could.

They gave in to their sexual desires, being as wild as they could without waking Claire's mother.

When it was all said and done, the two gently stroked one another as they spooned. Claire ever so softly kissed the inside of Monte's wrist, and he buried his nose in her beautiful hair.

They laid there like that for a few moments longer before he grabbed his boxer-briefs, jeans, and slid them back on.

"Hey."

Monte had something on his mind.

"Yeah?" she replied softly.

"I made you something…"

"You did? What is it?"

Monte hopped off the bed and grabbed his bag, placing it on the corner of her bed and unzipping its main pocket.

Meanwhile, Claire still lay there naked and smiling, covering her nude body with a bed sheet.

Monte removed an object from his bag that was wrapped in tissue paper and then in bubble wrap.

"What is it, Monte?

"You'll see."

He placed his bag back onto the floor and began to slowly remove the several layers of protective wrapping. When the final product was visible, Claire's eyes opened wide and she gasped out of joy when she saw it.

Monte had acquired lots of Legaia crystal that was only fit for powering level six androids and lower. Crystal pure enough for Nate and some of Nanoflèche's other functions took more oil and more time to make, thus making it more expensive to manufacture and harder to come by.

He had shaped the crystal into a beautiful wine bottle with lots of laser etching on it, along with Claire's initials, CLO, at the center of the decorative design. He had filled it with a delicious red wine blend he had selected for from a local tasting room.

Claire's mother was a sommelier and as a result, she had a special appreciation for wine.

"Wowww, Monteee. That looks beautiful! And expensive...How did you get this?"

"I made it. What's important is that you like it."

"You kidding? I absolutely love it, Monte. It's the nicest thing anyone has ever given me. It's amazing."

She got up off the bed with her bed sheet still wrapped around her and gave Monte a slow and passionate kiss.

"Claire...I've been thinking about this a lot lately...and I really don't know how to say this other than to just go ahead and say it. I really enjoy the time I spend with you...and...I wanna be with you."

"Oh, Monte…"

"You love it when we hang, don't you?" He tried to display a casual exterior, but he was dying on the inside, wondering why her response was unenthusiastic.

"Yeahh, I doo…but…"

"But what?"

"Monte…I care about you…and…I want you to be a part of my life. But what the future holds, that I just don't know."

"I don't think I understand. If you feel for me the way you say you do, then how does any of this make any sense?"

"It's complicated, Monte. I have a lot going on. I have school. I have work. I don't know if I want to jeopardize any of that."

"Oh, I didn't know my existence was a burden on your productivity. You'll have to excuse me for being so thoughtless. We can't be 'jeopardizing' any of your agendas!"

"Maybe that wasn't the best choice of words."

"You're crazy, you know that?"

"Crazy for what you've got in your pants, maybe," Claire said, as she reached for his crotch.

Monte slapped her hand away.

"You really are nuts…"

"Okay, Casanova. Have it your way."

"This was all your idea!" Monte whispered loudly with frustration.

"My idea?"

"You led me on…"

"What are you talking about! Are you hearing yourself right now?"

"Why did you string me along if you didn't want to be with me?"

"I didn't think you'd want…this! We were friends! We still are! But I'm not interested in being with you like that!"

Monte stood there quietly, absorbing her last statement. Two extraordinary human beings with less than perfect upbringings, unable to communicate their true desires. Perhaps unaware of what those true desires really were.

He began to throw on the rest of his clothes as quickly as he could.

"Where do you think you're going?"

"I don't know, but away from here, that's for damn sure. I've had enough of your excuses, hesitations, whatever. Go be confused by yourself."

"You're making me out to be the enemy instead of thanking me for showing you a good time."

"Ha! Yeah, thanks Claire! I owe ya one!"

He scooped up his bag and made a beeline for the bedroom door.

Claire called for him to stop, but the boy was scorned and wasn't going to listen to anyone. Especially Claire.

Monte ran into Ms. Ortega, comfortably seated on the living room couch, watching a bit of television while slowly swirling her glass of wine. He composed himself, out of respect.

"Thank you, Ms. Ortega. Have a good night."

"Thank you, Monte. Leaving so soon?"

The door shut at a quick pace behind him as he made sure not to slam it. Claire's mother was surprised that he had disappeared before she could finish her sentence.

Claire came running down the stairs hoping to catch him, but by the time she was able to throw on a pair of shorts and a shirt, she made it to the door just in time to see Monte zipping past her place on his motorcycle.

"Everything okay?" Heather asked.

"No...nothing is okay..."

Claire went back up the stairs before her mother could question her further and as Ms. Ortega looked on in confusion, she figured it'd be best to just leave Claire alone until she cooled off and came back to her senses.

As Monte darted down the boulevard on his bike, he felt a lump in his throat. It wasn't strong enough to bring him to tears, but he was disheartened and disgusted. Disappointed, mostly with himself. Feeling as though he should have known better. Not having realized yet that there is no better approach than honesty. Not yet realizing that life cannot be lived in fear of the unknown.

He hammered the throttle on his bike, hating himself for what he had just done. But after getting that out of his system, he figured the best place he could go right now was the park. It reminded him of a time with Claire before he had gone and complicated things. And maybe Henry would be there, too, as he typically worked a graveyard shift and always had some words of wisdom that made Monte feel better.

If nothing else, the peace and quiet of the park would give him a chance to calm down, embrace the serenity, and decipher his thoughts.

25

Broken Hearts Are Sharper Than Knives

He'd typically go straight to the crystal burner in the center of the park, looking for Henry Nahele. This evening felt a bit different. He wanted some alone time. Time he could spend overanalyzing his actions, wondering if he'd done the right thing.

Contrary to his expectations, Henry found him first.

"Hanging out at Legaia Park? And not even informing me of your presence? Shame on you, Mr. Cizek," said Henry, as he slowly approached Monte and scattered handfuls of plant vitamins into a pond.

"Hi Henry."

Monte stood with his forearms resting on a rail, down and droopy, staring into the pond.

"What brings you to our park this fine weekend? Nothing too worrisome, I hope...It's been a while since I've seen you here. I was beginning to think you had forgotten about us!"

"Yeah, I know. Been a little busy…"

"Busy in your mind? Or busy in your life? My bet's on the former."

Henry's comment helped Monte feel a bit better.

"Ha. You've got the right idea. But um, I did kinda wanna talk to you about something. If you don't mind?"

"Oh? What could possibly be problem enough to warrant my assistance?"

"It's about this girl…"

"Ah. I should have figured that. Okay, talk to me, Monte. I'm all ears."

Monte took a seat on a park bench located a few steps over, close to the biometrically-protected controls linked to the crystal oven.

"Well, there's this girl from school, Claire."

"I've seen you at the park with her once before. She's quite a stunning lady."

"Yeah, that's her alright."

"Did something happen between you two? Something unsettling?"

"Well…I had been meaning to tell her how I felt about her for a while now. She's a tough girl to gauge, and during the time that I've known her, she's never openly expressed her feelings unless she really had to."

"Ha, sounds like another young PULISC student I happen to know."

"No, you're right. I can be that way."

"Go on, young man."

"Well, I thought about it and thought about it, and I finally just got sick of holding it in! I told her I wanted to be with her and only her. And I know she likes me! A lot! And yet…"

"She respectfully declined your offer."

"Yeah…exactly…I don't get it? Nanotech is easy. Women,

not even close."

"You may be a young master of most things science, but you will never master the psyche."

"Can't even argue on that one…"

Monte was starting to loosen up. Henry removed his gardening gloves, as if this particular subject would require quite a break from his duties.

"I'm going to let you in on a few secrets, as long as you promise me one thing."

"Yeah, sure."

"You have to promise me you'll absorb this information and reference it in times of need. Even when your gut tells you to do otherwise."

"I think I can swing that."

"Okay…the perception of fate has been skewed over time. The things that will happen to you over the course of life aren't 'predetermined' in the sense that your life is a film in which the scenes have already been written, shot, and edited. You undoubtedly have free will, perhaps just as much free will or perhaps more free will than the average citizen, given the power of your mind.

"What you have to keep in mind is that when something doesn't go your way, your natural response is disappointment! Frustration! Anger! Before those emotions have even concluded their cycle, ask yourself, 'Do I have anything to gain from this let down?' May it be time. Experience. Newfound motivation. Knowledge. Whatever it may be, Monte, just remember this.

"If the door you are trying to open is locked, remain calm. Because more often than not, that door will eventually swing open on its own without you twisting your way to carpel tunnel, and that which lies beyond it is marvelous. Grand in scale and glorious, the world behind that door will be fruitful beyond any expectations.

"I understand that you have feelings for this woman. It's only natural. She's given you a taste, and it only has you longing for more. But hey, if she isn't reading the same page of the book you are, or if she's foolish enough to pass up a good thing, that's on her. You are a busy young man with a brilliant future. And it's best that your efforts be concentrated on that.

"Love is a beautiful thing. When it is natural. It comes without asking. It requires no negotiation. It is self-evident. That doesn't mean it's perfect, because nothing ever is. But when it's right, it's right. No explanation necessary. And most importantly, it doesn't call upon a quest for its discovery. In fact, it discovers you. But while you wait, focus on Monte. Never forget what your primary objectives are, because those objectives are Monte Cizek. All else is secondary.

"Embrace your science, embrace your life, and remain as fluid as possible. And if you can manage to do that, every other piece of this puzzle will slowly but surely glide into place, completing your picture, as well as your purpose. You have my word."

"You, sir…are the man," said Monte, temporarily feeling alleviated of his sorrows.

"I am indeed a man. And I've experienced everything you're experiencing a half a dozen times over…So trust me."

"No, you are more than a man. You are a magnificent man! I want to build a huge statue of you and put it right here in this park."

"You sure make me laugh… Sometimes your youth seems to rub off on me. Heck, you should come around here more often! You're like a walking, talking, fountain of youth!"

"Glad to be of service. Man…sometimes I just wish I could get inside her head and see what she's thinking, you know?"

"All people are the totality of everything they've seen, heard, smelt, felt since day one of their lives. And there isn't anything you're going to do, fix, or invent that's going to change the way that woman thinks. You did the right thing. You spoke the truth about how you felt. You did your part. Now sit back, and let nature do hers."

"You're absolutely right, Henry."

Henry began to recite a poem.

"We've come a long way.
and we will be beautiful
some day.

you and I
don't know.
only the stars do.
isn't it beautiful?

to think
that we can
never speak again,
or to think
that we may be
each other's one day,
it's fascinating.

the deities are strong,
and they've created
something strong,
something beyond
our comprehension,
something
so beautiful,
so complex,
that it has yet

to be understood,
and may never be.

love
is a terrible thing
to waste.

the encounters
will be bliss.
something good
will come of this,
this
I am certain of."

"Your work?"

"Oh, no, sir. The early works of a twenty-first century poet named Soska. Poetry is a beautiful outlet, young man. You should look into keeping a journal of some sort. A creative outlet, something that isn't centered on walking computers."

"I think I just might do that...Hey, I don't mean to take up any more of your time. I've overstayed my welcome."

"Don't be silly. It's usually too quiet around here at this hour. I look forward to the likes of you."

"You've really helped me out. Appreciate the wisdom. And the poetry. It's...pleasant."

"No need to thank me. Now run along, I'm sure there's something that you haven't invented yet that the world is in desperate need of!"

Monte picked up his bag and slung it over his right shoulder.

"Hail, King Henry! Thanks for the chat, sir. I'll see ya later!"

"You got it, young man. Be safe."

Monte briskly walked and occasionally jogged back to his

motorcycle, jumping onto ledges and letting out laughs, unusually happy for a young man that just had his heart ripped out by the first woman he'd ever loved. Henry's voice and advice were quite comforting, and they were some of the many reasons Monte loved visiting Legaia Park as often as he did.

26

Blondie Goes Poof!

Monte felt life on Legaia had put a bit of distance between him and his mother. He called her in the morning and agreed to join her for some coffee and small talk. Even though Roxanne and Helen were now living in the same apartment zone Monte was living in, he'd allowed himself to get a bit too caught up in his day to day.

"So you're too much of a big shot now to spend time with your mother?"

"Noo, Mommm. Don't be ridiculous. I've always been too cool."

"You'll need something from me eventually."

"I'm kiddinggg, I'm kiddinggg. Just been really damn busy since we got here."

"So, tell me about your new friend."

"Natey boy?"

"Yeah. I heard he turns heads everywhere he goes. Maybe we should just get you one of those glasses that have mustaches

147

attached to them."

Roxanne burst into laughter. She was her own greatest fan.

"Not a bad idea, Mum, but I'd take Nate over a glue-on mustache any day of the week. He's...amazing. Sometimes I feel like dropping whatever it is that I'm doing just to talk to him. Ask him questions. Get his take on stuff. The guy is brilliant. I still haven't been able to really get my head around the fact that we can make things like that in this day and age...It's absolutely crazy."

"Does this mean you're going to be nicer to robots now?"

"No...maybe...well, a select few robots anyway, yes. The ones like Nate, definitely."

The two continued to chat over coffee. Roxanne took hers black, and Monte only drank it if it was creamy and flavorful. Nate sat in Roxanne's living room, meditating. And although the two spoke freely, assuming nobody was listening, Nate's auditory system picked up every word, loud and clear.

After feeling his family obligations had been met, the young man and his android companion wished Roxanne a good day and headed back to Monte's lab.

It was Saturday afternoon. Legaia's artificial sunlight was shining in through the vertical blinds, making it bright and cheerful in Monte's quarters. The fish and corals in his salt-water reef tank were lively. The shelves in his bedroom were lined with gizmos, gadgets, spare parts, and unfinished projects.

Monte was lying in his bed, wearing a t-shirt, jeans, and socks. He had a green tea on the nightstand, waiting for it to cool a bit further before taking his first sip. It was his version of taking a load off, but his mind thought about his projects whether he wanted it to or not.

He wasn't alone, however. In the leather seat at his desk sat a woman, a petite blonde with a flat stomach and delectable curves. She was quiet, only speaking in short, brief sentences.

Her hair was platinum blonde and to the middle of her back. Her bright red lipstick stood out, and she wore an elegant yellow dress that flattered her. Monte didn't pay much attention to her though. He carried on, reading press releases from scientific journals and brainstorming as she sat in that office chair, playing with her phone and hair.

As he browsed through the day's news, as well as the science section of the Legaia News Press digital news feed, he received an incoming message from one of his PULISC classmates.

"Hey, it's Bryan. What are you up to? Don't make any plans for tonight. I've got some chaos lined up."

Monte was relatively certain he wasn't interested in partaking in the festivities, but he replied, looking for more information, in case he felt more social later in the day. The older Monte got, the more of a homebody he became. Every now and then though, he'd catch a social itch, and like any twenty-two year-old would, he loved scratching it.

"Elaborate on this so-called, 'chaos,' will ya?" His phone converted the message to text before sending it to Bryan's inbox.

"Feeling festive, Mr. Cizek?" said the blonde, as she sat in Monte's office chair with her legs crossed, as if she was intentionally using the power of her seductive looks to coax him into acknowledging her.

"Mayyybeee. It's been quite a few weeks since I've spent a Friday or Saturday night in downtown. Might do me some good."

"I'll have to agree with you on that one," replied the blonde. "Do I get to come with?"

"Don't you always?"

"You say I do, but you don't walk the walk. Empty promises, Monte Cizek. Empty promises. I'm just your toy."

"Just be glad you get to serve a purpose. Most of us never

get to."

"Prophetic…" responded the snarky blonde. She opened a small purse and removed her lipstick from it, reapplying it.

Meanwhile, Bryan responded to Monte's text message.

"My old man got a promotion. Sent me a gift to celebrate with since I can't be there. It's a night out on the town, all inclusive!"

"You mean that speck of a city called downtown Legaia? That town?"

"You know you love her. Don't even pretend like you don't. This place is good to us, and you're its poster boy, so I don't wanna hear it. Anyway, no backing out this time. You're coming!"

The more Monte thought about it, the more he was up for it. His school load was heavy as it was. On top of it, he had several other projects he was working on for Legaia's Department of Public Works, PULISC's own scientific journal, and NTI. Although he loved them all the same, he also enjoyed a break every now and then.

"Tell your pops I said congrats. I'm in. Gonna work into the evening. See you guys later tonight though."

"Niceee! Will do. See ya soon, Cizek!"

Monte was actually looking forward to joining his classmates for some fun. The anticipation of the night ahead helped motivate him to work harder, too.

"Okay, my dear. It's time I temporarily bid those thighs farewell. I've gotta get some work done before I join the boys downtown. Don't miss me too much, alright?"

"I'm pretty sure I only miss you because you've programmed me to. Go ahead. Put me back in my magic lamp. Maybe I'll find a well hung genie in there while you're gone."

"Ha. You're a bad girl. Ta-ta blondie."

Monte entered a four-digit pin into his phone that

deactivated the hologram of the blonde, sending her into a user-induced slumber. She was Monte's pleasant distraction. A form of digital eye candy that kept him company, for when silence wasn't working out so well. She was programmed to look as he wanted her to, speak as he wanted her to, and act as he wanted her to. Just another one of Monte's many little toys.

He spent the next few hours listening to experimental electronic music as he reviewed formulas, read articles, ran simulations on his own proprietary programs, and communicated with friends that were information technology and robotics majors at his school.

It was one of the more productive work sessions he'd had. No stress on his mind. No major distractions. Just good tunes, the field of study that he loved, and the excitement of finishing his tasks and meeting his friends for a few hours of drinks and relaxation.

However, the evening's festivities would not be the pleasant, drama-free social hour Monte was envisioning.

27

Welcome To The Green Gazelle

Monte's classmate Bryan playfully punched Monte in the arm as they rode in the backseat of their buddy's sedan.

"You ready, sucka?"

"I'm afraid to ask…Knowing you, we're on a collision course with the titty bar."

"This is why I love you, man!"

"Nooo! I was kidding! Are you serious?" said Monte, surprised that his sarcastic guess was actually exactly what Bryan had in mind.

"Yes, sir, and you're getting a lap dance this time! Girl, 'droid, it doesn't matter! You're getting one!"

"Oh boy, ummm, I think I hear my mother calling me. I gotta go," Monte said jokingly before messaging Nate with an updated destination.

"I don't think so, nano-boy! There's no escaping the sex kittens of the Green Gazelle. So brace yourself!"

The band of boys parked their car and eagerly jumped out.

They had arrived at Legaia's go-to source for adult entertainment; The Green Gazelle, co-owned by good old Richard Hurlocke. The town's only gentleman's club was one of dozens of businesses on Legaia owned by Mr. Hurlocke.

They entered the nightclub, which was tastefully decorated and well regulated. A couple of the boys went straight to the bar to change out big bills for small ones. Meanwhile, Monte and Bryan sought out comfortable seats, close to the main stage.

It was a sizeable adult cabaret, and there was a great variety of women. The typical fake-breasted blondes, along with a raven-haired rock and roll type with tan skin and plenty of tattoos. The dancer who had been dancing since before Monte was born, and yet somehow managed to maintain a figure that rivaled those of women half her age, the Asian and Russian imports who sometimes spoke hardly any English at all, as well as your African and Afro-Latin pair that looked like sisters. They enjoyed dancing together and the attention that came along with it. There were a few junkies that danced just to support their drug habits, and a few that danced because they knew nothing else.

Last but certainly not least, there were the bots. Android strippers were usually the stars of the show. They were newer, more exciting to watch, and could be programmed to say or do anything.

Sure, stubborn naturalists (including Monte) wouldn't settle for anything less than the real thing—Monte wasn't even a fan of any type of surgical enhancement or augmentation— but there were also die-hard fans of the bots. Androids were big money makers for the clubs, or for any business entity that could afford the up-front cost associated with such a fine piece of machinery. A few were blatantly robotic, but some of the android dancers looked human and could only be differentiated by paying keen attention or asking the right questions.

They were a bit more…stiff. Unnatural. More mechanical than the average person. Not by very much, but enough to be distinguishable by cautious eyes. They were almost human, though. On the outside, anyway.

Android bylaws were no different when it came to the man-made exotic dancers, abiding by the ASG mandate that a 'droid must disclose the fact that it is a 'droid when questioned. This was one of the original bills passed by Congress when nandroid-class robots were first approved for commercial as well as personal use.

Monte caught a dancer headed his way through his peripheral vision and thought, *"Oh boy, here we go…"*

"Hello, handsome. Can I sit here?"

"You can sit wherever you'd like," he countered with a half-hearted smile.

Monte moved over a bit, and the dancer took a seat right beside him.

"How's your night going? Are you guys having fun?"

"Oh yeah, we're having a blast."

Monte was much warmer to women from school or even women he met in social settings, but he figured engaging in genuine conversation with the dancers was a waste of his energy, and that they cared for nothing more than what was in his wallet.

"I'm Delight. What's your name?"

"Monte."

This artificial entertainer appeared almost human, but robots were part of the kid's livelihood, and he could spot one a mile away.

"Who's your maker?" he asked.

"Nanoflèche Technologies Incorporated. Level 5, Run 3, O.S. version 9.3.11. Legaia State Identification Number R000967."

The dancer extended her hand and Monte shook it without hesitation.

"Would you like a dance, Monte?"

"No, thank you. Maybe later?"

There'd be no later. Monte wasn't interested.

"Okay, honey, I'll come back later."

"*Yeah, you do that,*" he thought to himself.

For a brief moment, he wondered to himself if he would ever meet another android like Nate.

28

Facing The Demon

His friends ran around the Green Gazelle like school children, flirting with anyone and everyone they came in contact with, while Monte just sat there and thought, occasionally engaging in small talk with a dancer. He seldom bought a dance, only giving attention to the ones that really caught his eye, and almost never getting more than one dance from the same girl. The downtime was what he looked forward to the most. A mental health break.

All in all, it was a nice venue. Not the largest, but the DJs were charming enough. The girls weren't too pretentious. Maybe they realized how fortunate they were to be living on Legaia in the first place.

Most of the patrons were the same old men you'd find in just about any other exotic dancing club on Earth. One man in particular sat across the club from Monte and looked to be in his late forties or early fifties. He looked relaxed as he occasionally pressed his ear piece deeper into his ear to combat the club's blaring music. Just behind him stood a couple of other men, also dressed professionally and using earpieces.

Monte caught them staring at him.

"Can I go anywhere without these goons hounding me? Shit…" he said to Nate.

As soon as the seated man's associates were aware of the fact that Monte was aware of them, they approached.

"Good evening, Mr. Cizek. I hope all is well. May we speak with you for a moment? It won't take very long."

Their candor was certainly better than Robbie's, or any other Hurlocke tribesmen that had tried to isolate his attention. They were professional and polite. It was downright odd. Monte almost felt like talking to them just because they weren't assholes like the others had been.

"I'm just here to take a load off, guys. Just let me be, will ya?"

He was unusually calm. Almost Zen-like.

"Mr. Cizek, Mr. Hurlocke has been waiting for a long time for an opportunity to speak with you. Won't you at least consider hearing what he has to say?"

Was this a bodyguard or a logician? His approach was working perfectly.

"Okay…fine…I'll chat with Mr. Hurlocke, but just this once. Approach me again in the future, and you'll have a problem on your hands."

"Agreed. Right this way, sir."

Monte and Nate got up to follow the guards to an office so that they could talk. They were interrupted by one of the men before they could walk more than a couple of steps.

"I'm sorry, Mr. Cizek. The boss doesn't like bots."

"Neither do I."

"You'll have to proceed without him."

"Bot joins or no meeting," Monte muttered. The guard

wasn't able to hear him, especially over the club's music.

"I'm sorry, sir?"

"Bot Joins Or No Meeting," Monte said again, loud and clear.

The guard received instructions through his earpiece. All of the Gazelle's security staff carried high-powered EMP pistols, for use in the event that one of the android dancers malfunctioned.

Hurlocke didn't like the idea of their meeting being recorded and broadcast, but he figured it was better than no chance to communicate with Monte, and he didn't want to press his luck.

"It's fine...Let them up."

"Okay, sir. Mr. Hurlocke has made an exception. Please follow us now."

"Let's go," replied Monte.

Monte and Nate followed the guards to the staircase that led to the second floor. The dancers glanced at him a bit more closely now, wondering who this young lad was that rolled with the big shots that hung out upstairs. Monte had never met Hurlocke, and yet he knew him better than most.

He made his way up the stairs. An auburn-haired dancer admired him as she walked down the staircase with another gentleman in a suit and even winked at Monte, still holding hands with the other man who looked like he had just forked over a hefty chunk of currency to spend time with the gal. They turned the corner and continued up the other half of the staircase. A few doors down on the second floor was a door, protected by an additional two guards, stationary at their post. Each of them opened one of the double doors, allowing entrance.

The guards from downstairs, Nate, and Monte entered an over-the-top office suite.

Once a few steps into the room, Monte and Nate passed

Regal, who was seated in the corner of Hurlocke's exotic office. Monte glanced over at the stern android. They'd only heard of each other, and this was their first time crossing paths. Regal slowly tilted his neck toward Monte, following his steps with a cold look. Nate was edgy, too, ready to act if provoked.

Hurlocke told all but Regal and the guards from downstairs to scatter. Even the female entertainment for hire had to leave, as they quickly grabbed their clothes and were rushed out of the room. Monte and Nate took a seat in front of Hurlocke's desk.

"Good evening, Monte," Richard said with a sense of composure in his voice. He tried hard to make it look like he wasn't excited to be speaking with Monte Cizek.

Monte starred directly into his eyes without saying a word.

"Cat got your tongue, Mr. Cizek?"

Monte clenched his right fist. The Zen master had checked out, and the only thing left was an angry young man with too much weight on his shoulders. Everything he had been taught by the professor, everything he had read about regarding ASG history and ASG operations, it all came pouring into his mind.

"You remind me of a twenty-two-year-old Richard Hurlocke, you know that, Monte? You and I are supposed to be friends. I really don't know why you enjoy makings things so much more difficult for yourself than they have to be."

Monte composed himself.

"What do you want, Hurlocke?"

"What are you willing to give?"

"How's a silver bullet? You like those, right? I don't have any garlic on me though. Sorry, Dick."

"You know what pains me the most about you, Monte? You know more than almost anybody. You can compute and calculate and contemplate the sciences that govern robotics, better than almost anybody...and yet...you're absolutely clueless."

"I don't know what you want. I don't sell private jets or exotic cars. And I sure as hell can't help you get laid. You're just going to have to pay for that like the rest of the pathetic bastards in this place do."

Hurlocke fought back his anger.

"Look…I'm not going to pound my fist into the table and throw demands your way, especially when you've got a tenth of NTI's R&D money sitting next to you in a velvet chair. What I simply want to know is whether or not you'll help me.

"I've got regimes with limitless funds breathing down my neck. Looking for answers. Products. Technology. A leg up. Not too much of a leg up, of course. That's reserved for us. But we can throw them enough of a bone to keep them happy while providing foreign IRRC equivalents and their affiliates with valuable assets. It'll be very profitable, Monte, funds we'll use to launch awareness campaigns and science fairs for youngsters. Funds we can use to build more bots. Better bots. Enhance medicine, science. Change the world, Monte! Don't you want that? Don't you want to see your nano-toys rise to the glory that they deserve? To mend the planet's wounds? Heal sickness? Boost underprivileged lives? I think this is what you want, Monte. I think you can help RBH Ventures get there."

"Oh, it's RBH Ventures now, not ASG? You're hilarious, Hurlocke."

"Well, I'm sure you're well aware of the fact that I play an active role in many organizations, federal and private. It's my desire to lend a helping hand to the robotics community in any way that I can. For the betterment of science. To ensure a healthy future for robotics. Many of the same things you care about."

It was an ounce of sound logic, several tons of bullshit, and Monte wasn't buying any of it.

"I wish I could help you, Mr. Hurlocke, but unfortunately, I cannot."

Monte was beginning to get tired of hearing Hurlocke talk in circles.

"No good can come from defying me. Do you realize that, son?" It appeared as though Richard was starting to lose his cool.

"You're probably right. And I'm not your son."

Nate perked up a bit, still seated. Sensing the tension in the room, he prepared himself.

"Oh, look at that. You've even got your robot pal all worked up. Nice work, Monte. You're stressing everyone out!"

"Are we done here, Dick? I've got things to do."

Hurlocke wasn't too fond of being addressed as "Dick." Especially by someone like Monte. The kid was striking nerves.

Hurlocke began spinning his chair around in circles as the thoughts in his mind began boiling over.

"A peasant with a beautiful mind can be a real pain in the ass. And you, young man, are like a nasty thorn in my side that can't be removed."

Hurlocke stopped fidgeting and straightened his chair.

"Now you listen to me real good, you piece of shit. I'm through being nice with you. These level six bots are worthless! What the hell am I supposed to do with these? It isn't fair! Why does Porter get everything when I'm the one footing part of the bill? I AM the ASG! I AM the IRRC! I should have the greatest bots! I should have everything you and Porter have and more!"

Hurlocke took a deep breath and tried to calm himself down a bit before ranting any further.

"Let me make a long story short for you and your little bodyguard. Either you and Porter help me get what I need, or I take it. And I'm not going to be gentle about it either. I'm going take it from you in the dirtiest way. Your resistance will prove to be pointless. And you're going to like it, too! Every bit of it!"

161

"I heard you were weird, but holy shit, you're a fucking demon. I'll be sure to inform the professor of the dark, homoerotic fantasies you have about us."

"I don't think you realize what you've gotten yourself into, kid."

"Nothing that I wasn't into before this delightful conversation. Anyway, we're out of here. Have fun playing with your 'worthless bots'. I've got work to do."

Monte and Nate got up and made their way out of the office. "Ciao, Richie!"

One of the guards closed the doors behind them. As they reached the first step leading back down to the lobby of the club, Nate and Monte heard a loud smash. Hurlocke had thrown an expensive desk ornament at the door after it had closed. Monte was a bit startled by the disgruntled display, but he couldn't help but walk away smiling at the fact that he had angered Hurlocke and prevented him from having his way for a change.

Monte heard the club's disc jockey begin to speak.

"Alright, Gazelle. Let's all sit down for this one. We've got a special treat tonight! A dancer who's only been with us for two short weeks and has already made quite a splash. Let's have a warm round of applause for Justinaaa!"

The audience clapped and cheered as Monte gave his attention to the stage to see what all the fuss was about. The curtain at the back of the stage parted, and Justina made her way toward the DJ booth. As the club eagerly anticipated its newest dancer, Monte did a double take.

"Sir...that woman is Claire," said Nate.

"I can see that, Nate...the fuck?"

A slow rock song with deep bass and elements of electro played as Claire, slowly and seductively, began to dance for the crowd. She was wearing very long, black leather boots. She

162

didn't have the same elegance about her that she usually had, but she looked just as enticing.

Several guests got up from their seats and moved closer to the stage to get a better view. The men of all ages dug into their pockets and presented "Justina" with varying donations for her show. She ignored the money, focusing on her dance, placing her back against the pole and slowly lowering herself, spreading her legs wider as she got closer to the stage's floor.

Monte and Claire locked eyes. He looked stiff and white-faced. Claire was in a squatted position, with her arms above her, stroking the pole in an erotic display. Perhaps the most sinister part of their visual engagement was the fact that Claire seemed completely unfazed by Monte being in the crowd. She continued to stare at Monte, biting her lower lip seductively and even winking before standing up and continuing with her routine.

Monte didn't want to stick around to see the undergarments come off.

"This is bullshit."

"Shall I inform Bryan of our departure?"

"Yeah, tell him the party's over. For me, anyway. I'll be waiting outside…"

29

Merked By A Nandroid

Still reeling from his discovery at the gentleman's club, Monte walked into class just several seconds before the official start time. Claire smiled at him, but he ignored her as he took his seat.

"Morning, class. Hope you all had a pleasant weekend, devoid of vomit and bail bondsmen. We've got a lot to cover, so I'll try to minimize the horseplay and actually teach you something today.

"Mr. Cizek, I see you're in your casual get-up. Genius or not, all PULISC students are required to wear their uniforms while on campus, weekends being the only exception. Even for you, Mr. Cizek."

Monte remained silent.

"Okay, not in the talking mood, I see. That's good. That's alright. Let's hope you can mime your way to an A this semester." Randal sifted through files on the large holo-display that faced the classroom. His back to the class, he used his arms to motion and navigate his way through the computer's desktop, pulling up various files to share with his students.

"Everyone, please pull up the graphs we were reviewing on Friday. We're going to look at this some more."

The scholars took turns activating the holographic monitors embedded in their desks and pulled up the data while Monte just sat there with his hands clasped, staring into the floor in front of him.

"Mr. Cizek. Are you trying to put a dent into my morning?"

"No, Professor."

"Then cooperate or go for a walk, got it?"

"Yes, Professor."

His mundane, politically correct responses were further testament to his defiance. Monte wasn't rude very often, and when he was, it usually wasn't intentional. He continued to space out.

The red level-six ASG trainee, sitting a couple rows to his left, turned and gave Monte a blank stare, as if it was trying to dissect the boy's behavior.

"Keep looking at me like that, and I'll send you back to ASG headquarters as a crate full of nuts and bolts, you piece of metal shit."

The young man had anger in his eyes, and the ASG bot picked up on it. Claire was nobody's princess. He knew that. There was just something about her that had a hold on him. Her wit. Her confidence. Her style. He wanted her. And as more than just friends.

"*What the fuck is she thinking? It's not like she needs the money!? She has a full ride! Her mom supports her! I mean, it's not for the money. She must get a sick kick out of it. She's trouble. Why can't I just forget about it? Ahh!*"

Monte clenched his fists. The memory of seeing her with her legs wrapped around that pole made him nauseous.

"By the way, class, if you're distracted, sad, hungry, horny, or find yourselves incapable of absorbing the day's lesson, please feel free to go home and take a cold shower. Eat a fucking tuna sandwich. Do whatever you need to do. Just get out of my classroom. We don't babysit here. This is one of the top universities in the world for a reason..."

The funny part was Doc knew his future, THE future, didn't rest upon his classroom instruction. It rested upon the shoulders of Monte Cizek.

Monte noticed the ASG bot was still staring right at his face. He began to grow livid. Everything was starting to boil over. The stress, the workload, Claire. She had really set off a chain of explosives inside of him.

The bot spoke.

"Professor Randal Porter, does your student have a problem with me? I sense a great deal of hostility in this classroom."

"I'm giving you one last chance to go fuck yourself." said Monte.

"I am authorized by statutes set forth by Director Suttridge and the United States government to protect myself against any threat to my safety," said the android in a tense tone.

"Huh...is this rust on legs for real? Fuck off."

"I have been educated on your strengths as well as your...inadequacies, Mr. Cizek. I will not tolerate your abuse."

Monte had had enough.

"I am authorized by statutes set forth by Director Suttridge and the United States government..."

Monte stood up while the 'droid continued to recite the same legal blurbs, and the bot suddenly changed its tone.

"Threat, detected and engaged."

Monte cocked his knee upward, extended his leg outward, and kicked that bot square in the chest, knocking it onto its back. Several classmates gasped while others got out of their seats and backed up. But what they probably didn't realize was that an android had to first wait to be struck to strike back.

The bot got up immediately and stood guard as the class looked on in horror.

Monte threw a wild swing, but the bot dodged and used Monte's momentum against him to throw him into the wall.

"Incident report filed. You will receive your citation in six to eight weeks via…"

Monte struck him again in the face with a spare desk leg he had found in the corner of the room, damaging the bot's vision out of one eye.

"Damage sustained. Threat, detected and engaged."

The bot was following a different set of protocols now. It had sustained an expensive injury, and the ASG didn't take kindly to people damaging its goods. No high-grade android owner would.

Monte swung at the creature again. This time, it caught the improvised weapon and discarded it. Then it went after Monte.

"Eliminating threat."

It reached for Monte's throat, but Monte evaded his arm and struck the bot on the side of the neck. Nanobots of this degree had many vulnerabilities. They weren't built with the same enhancements and budgets as level seven bots, and they were nothing compared to level eights. Their necks were one of their most sensitive points. But that didn't change the fact that they were made out of pliable metals and physically superior to humans.

Bots were programmed to use just the right amount of force to achieve their objectives, in a manner comparable to that of law enforcement. This was one of Hurlocke's premium bots, and who knows what kind of modifications his technicians had made to it.

The red and black ASG bot grabbed Monte's arm and pulled

him closer before whipping around and delivering a spinning back fist to Monte's face, dislocating his jaw. Monte was angry, too proud, and wasn't thinking straight.

Only a trained martial arts veteran had any business engaging in hand-to-hand combat with a nandroid. A couple minutes of downloading and review was all a seven or eight would need to dismember any human that posed a major threat to it. There was good reason why these bots were in the hands of Randal Porter and not many others.

"Lucan…Stand down!" shouted the professor.

"I am authorized!" Lucan shouted back.

"You are correct, but I am telling you to stand down or your training at Porter is over."

"I take orders from ASG, not NTI!"

That particular statement led the professor to believe there was more to Lucan than he had previously conceived, and it wasn't looking pretty.

Monte used the distraction to gain an advantage over the bot. He grabbed the small switchblade he occasionally carried from out of his hooded sweatshirt pocket and jammed it into a rubber grommet that went all the way around the bot's neck and pulled it forward toward the bot's face with all of his might, hoping to sever some pertinent cables. Now the bot was leaking, disoriented, and upset. He wasn't very open to logic before, and these injuries certainly didn't help his thought process.

The robot brought its leg up under Monte and kicked him halfway across the room, and Monte broke five of his ribs upon landing. Upon witnessing Lucan's lack of inhibition, the professor decided it was time to end the show.

Lucan started making his way toward Monte. Having lost all sense of reality, he began to run across the room, looking to finish off his wounded prey.

The professor grabbed his EMP pistol out of his desk and

armed it, waited for it to prime, and just as the bot was several inches away from Monte, he shot Lucan with an EMP pulse that made him instantly buckle and fall to the ground.

A hit from this type of EMP round would fry any electrical component inside a bot. The pistols themselves weren't commonplace. A limited number of people outside of law enforcement were allowed to own such weapons.

Monte was curled up in a corner, bruised and bleeding. His eye was swollen, and he was spitting up blood. His hand was placed over his lower right ribs, and he was moaning from the pain.

The professor, having realized the severity of Monte's injuries, summoned the school's nurses, one human and one level-seven medical nandroid.

Randal wasn't looking forward to having to explain to ASG why he cooked one of their top trainees, but this was just one of the many tasks the professor had to deal with on a daily basis.

The other students in the classroom looked on in shock. Claire ran over to Monte's side.

"Oh my God, what did you do?!" She broke down and began to cry. Seconds later, the school's on-site medical staff arrived on the scene. Doc grabbed Claire and moved her away from Monte, so that the nurses could get in there as efficiently as possible to begin tending to Monte's injuries. They deployed small robots that assisted in tending to his injuries, while using advanced scanners to check on internal injuries. Upon seeing the level of activity being shown on the scanners' display, the human nurse spoke.

"We need to transport to the ICU."

"I'm fine...I'm fine..." Monte was hardly able to get the words out, as he lay on the ground, resting his weight on his right forearm, battered and beaten.

He was not fine. He tried to sit up. The pain was so

excruciating that he screamed and began to cough up more blood. The professor moved closer to him. The nurses urged him to remain still.

"Quit moving, you fool. An ambulance will be here any second. You're fucked up. Lay still..." said Dr. Porter.

Of course, in his mind, the professor hoped Monte would be lower maintenance, but he also realized that was wishful thinking. Simplicity and brilliance seldom go hand in hand.

When the professor was Monte's age, he was twice as bad, and he was good about reminding himself of that very fact.

The nurses continued to work on Monte as two campus security guards, also one human and one bot, arrived on the scene.

"Get me a cleanup crew, will ya? Remove all power sources from this ASG slime bucket and put him in a storage locker until somebody comes to claim him. I need to call Suttridge. Class dismissed. Go home," said Dr. Porter, as he headed off toward his office to be left alone.

30

Let's Go Dreaming

For the first time since Monte involuntarily adopted an android, Nate's absence was truly felt. The professor was angry at himself for allowing Nate to be gone, even if it was only for a few hours while Monte was in class. Nate was attending an IRRC convention, fundraising and campaigning for increases in robotics education among public K-12 schools in America.

Randal wasn't even sure how Nate was going to react to news about the incident. But, if anything, the scuffle that took place between Monte and Lucan confirmed to Randal that Nate becoming Monte's entourage was not only a good idea, but a necessity.

Soon, Nate would return from the seminar, only to discover that he had failed his greatest obligation and allowed his good friend, his best friend, to sustain considerable injuries. Sure, Monte ran his mouth and could have easily prevented what took place, but Lucan's reactions were debatable. Lucan's instigation was arguable. Monte felt it, the professor felt it, and they were the only ones that knew enough, that knew better, and smelled something funny with that 'droid's demeanor.

Monte was recuperating at PULISC's Aristotle Medical Center. He was in stable condition with an elevated status code. It would be at least another day before visitors would be allowed to enter his room, his immediate family being the only exception to that rule. Randy liked to follow protocol; he seldom did anything just because he owned the place.

Dr. Porter got comfortable at home in his favorite recliner. He had articles, stories, and emails pulled up on his holographic reading screen, but he wasn't paying much attention to them at all. Lost in thought, he was trying his best to relax without much success.

Moments later, Randal heard his doorbell ring.

"Yes?" He responded loudly, making sure whoever was behind the door could hear.

"It's Nathaniel."

With a mild sigh of relief, Randy pressed a button on the screen of his mobile device that unlocked the door upon confirming Nate's presence with voice recognition. Nate walked in.

"Good afternoon, Father."

"Hey, son..." Randal's tone was tired and somber. "Did you have fun at your seminar?"

"I did, yes, and I felt our efforts were worthwhile."

"That's good news. Glad to hear it."

"Is everything alright, father? I sense some uneasiness in you."

"I had to cook Lucan today. Fried his ass like chicken."

"We have never had to disable an android student before. Was he attempting to steal data?"

"Nahhh. He was being a little dick though. The kid was in a rotten mood, probably mad at Claire or something. Anyway, they got into it pretty bad."

Nate tensed up without even realizing it. His body looked as though it was preparing to sprint or something; the guilt was instantly setting in.

"Where is Monte??"

"Relax, Nate. He's in my hospital, and we can't visit till tomorrow. He's fine though. Probably more emasculated than injured. He took a whooping, but he's fine."

"I am genuinely sorry, Father. I will make this right."

"Don't be ridiculous. This wasn't your fault, and I don't need you launching some sort of vendetta right now. We've got enough on our plate as it is. You wanna help? I'm gonna need your help tomorrow when we go visit him. In the meanwhile, keep your eyes and ears peeled, and if you ever need to leave his side again, I'll make sure half a dozen sevens are there in your place. Keep your mind at ease, son. I've got it under control, 'kay?

"Yes, Father."

Looking down at a timer on his cellular phone, Randal said, "It's time for your charge. I need you to get some rest."

"My qorlithium is at 18%. I have nearly six more days."

"I know, but my gut tells me you should charge. And moving forward, I want you to start charging at 25% instead of 5."

"As you wish, Father. See you in the morning?" said Nate, as he gently rested his palm on Randal's shoulder, attempting to comfort him.

"I'll be fine, my boy. Have a good night's rest."

Randal stayed in his chair a while, drinking white wine, recalling past conversations, accomplishments, and milestones. Primarily the ones he had shared with Christopher Cizek.

"He's no different than you and me, you know...He's a brilliant scientist, a devoted scholar, and an amazing kid. The

three of us could have done so many things together. You shoulda stuck around for a while longer..."

The professor reminisced until he dozed off in his chair to the glow of his holoscreen.

Meanwhile, Nate had made his way to Randal's office for a seven-hour charge. He closed his eyes, hoping he'd have a clearer mind upon waking up post-defragmentation, a process that ran during every charge, optimizing Nate's data storage functions.

A mile away, Monte slept. His room was relatively dark, lit only by the white fibers of his mesh hammock and the numerous monitors that displayed patient vitals.

The hospital beds on some of the floors (mainly ICU or ER type areas) weren't conventional hospital beds. They were technologically advanced hammocks, able to utilize nanotechnology and light to repair external injuries. These tiny, fibrous strands had gathered near Monte's face and the right side of his rib cage, concentrating their focus on the parts of Monte's body that had sustained the greatest injuries.

What appeared to be tens of thousands of tiny lights gleamed as the hammock's mechanisms tended to Monte's wounds. The brighter the lights, the harder the hammock was working to repair and rebuild.

A glow radiated through the room's privacy glass door from the status indicator light strip just outside his room, which was now shimmering in yellow and green tones, rather than a light orange. These high-output fiber optic bulbs quickly and easily communicated the vitals of a patient to nurses and doctors. Medical staff would have an idea as to how the patient's recovery was progressing without ever having to step into the room, look up data, or read a chart. The lights displayed patient data using color hues and brightness. There was also a much smaller bulb on the inside of the room shining the same light-based data.

A few floors up, one of the hospital's most tenured doctors had dedicated four of his sixteen screens to visually monitoring Monte's vitals and progress.

"Looks like you've learned this lesson the hard way, young man. Save the mixed martial arts bouts for your human counterparts. You might not make it out alive next time," thought the doctor, as he transferred Monte's information to the head nurse's desk. His shift was ending, and he was looking forward to going home and relaxing after a long day at work.

Back home, Nate was calm as he pressed a concealed button on his thigh with his right index finger. A panel on his thigh slid open, exposing his charging cable. He plugged himself in and initialized his stand-by operating mode. This OS function enabled Nate to retain his Wi-Fi connectivity while conserving power in a sleep-like state, allowing for faster power transfer and maximum charge retention. Nate reviewed meditation techniques while viewing images of tranquil nighttime beaches in his mind and finally forgot about the news he'd been given. He embraced this calmer state until his CPU usage reached just three percent, caused mainly by the disk defragmenter application running in the background.

Late into the night, as Nate sat still and rested, he began to see data he hadn't requested to view. Images of foreign androids in a single file line at night in downtown Los Angeles, picking up light rifles from weapons lockers, filing into squadrons, into cargo helicopter type aircraft. The robots then proceeded to dissipate and reform, spreading through city streets, scaling walls, breaking windows, kicking down doors, using concussion grenades on innocent civilians, threatening and bullying shop clerks, setting fire to structures, revolting against confused military personnel, imposing their will on intimidated law enforcement officials, all in search of something. It wasn't quite clear in Nate's visions whether that thing was an object, a person, perhaps another 'droid, or something else.

Nate saw a city overwhelmed and felt as though he had to act swiftly in an effort to stop the deranged droids from wreaking havoc upon this metropolis. He sprinted down a boulevard and used internal energy weapons, light cannons embedded in his limbs, to disarm the droids with the rifles. He caused an aircraft to crash into other nearby aircraft or tall buildings. He ran through the streets shouting "Randal! Monte! Claire!" but he doesn't get a response.

Weaponized armored buggies driven by droids with 'droid passengers assailed onto the boulevard and attempted to pummel him with energy fire, and even tried to run him over. He used a mind-and-will-powered sphere to protect himself from the threats coming his way. Using focus to direct energy blasts, he fired rounds that exited his forearms at the dangerous assailants. The world seemed to be crumbling around him as fires burned. Innocent men and women tried to shield themselves and their children from cruel robots with an agenda, robots with no desire to distinguish adult from child, or soldier from civilian.

Parked passenger vehicles exploded as Nate ran by them, lighting up the streets with a fiery glow. Nate kept running, looking for people he knew, people that could help him, but regardless of how much damage he was able to inflict upon these cruel, destructive intruders, it wasn't enough. Until finally, he reached NTI headquarters, where the entire building was on fire, burning intensely against a dark horizon. Fire crews attempted to douse the flames while protecting themselves from robot attack. It was all too much.

Nate ran into the building, making his way toward the doctor's preferred labs and offices as quickly as possible. His exoskeleton protected him from the heat, but the flames and smoke impaired his senses, making it more difficult for him to navigate. He switched his eyesight to non-thermal imaging and continued up the stairs, stepping over fallen employees and damaged NTI security droids. He finally made it to Randal's office, only to find that Dr. Porter and Monte were both unconscious and covered in mild burns and smoke stains. He checked on them and tried to revitalize them and failed, and in the corner of the room he found himself, sitting, hiding, badly damaged, and barely alive.

He didn't know what to do, overwhelmed by the sight, and just as it seemed things couldn't possibly get any worse, the building began to shake violently, as if a significant earthquake had just struck. Everything was destroyed. The building collapsed, burying everyone and everything in it. And as it did, he looked over at himself again, and just as a large, mangled steel beam was about to crush his face, he woke up.

Nate was shocked by the images he saw during his charge. He looked down at the panel in his thigh where the cord was connected, and a small display in his thigh that showed a few pieces of data read "75%." He unplugged the silver cord from the wall, before it retracted into its storage compartment in his thigh.

He sent Randal (who was still asleep in his chair) a message: "Do not be alarmed, Father. I had a difficult time completing my charge and have decided to complete it at the hospital. I will be there waiting for you whenever you are ready to join. See you shortly." As he made his way out the door, closing it quietly behind him, cautious not to disturb the professor's rest

31

A Heart To Heart

Monte was in a light sleep and woke at the sound of Nate entering his hospital room. Groggy and a tad disoriented from his medication, he squinted and attempted to identify who his visitor was.

"Nate..." said Monte, still half asleep.

It was roughly 8:30 in the morning, and with the blinds completely shut, it was still dark in Monte's hospital room.

"I am sorry for waking you, sir. That was not my intent. I was merely attempting to see how your recovery is progressing."

"Pipe down...Sit...I'm glad you're here."

Monte tried to sit more upright, and a sharp pain shot up the side of his chest. He was quickly reminded of just how injured he was.

"Monte...you must minimize your movements."

He sighed and grunted as he pressed a button on a small touch-screen display located within arm's reach, releasing a small surge of pain killers into his blood stream. He spoke with a hint of rasp in his voice.

"Something reeks of filth...Hurlocke's filth...I don't know what that troll is thinking...What he's forming...But I know it can't be good...I know Doc agrees...And I'm going to get to the bottom of that freak's agenda if it's the last thing I do...I've had enough of his bullshit...I've had enough of that sinister asshole creating a stench under the guise of the ASG...too many people have worked too hard to make the LISC a reality, and I won't let anybody jeopardize its future...I don't want to hear about it anymore...I just want it fixed or eliminated...And you know I'm more than good with either solution."

"I suppose I could attempt to talk you out of whatever scheme it is you are conjuring up in your mind, but I know better than to waste my time on such hopeless endeavors. Practice patience, Monte...and when the time is right, we will make our move. You have so many projects in the works. Father does as well."

"You're right, but I'm not..."

Nate digested Monte's statement and felt now would be a good time to change the subject a bit.

"I have something I would like to discuss with you, Monte," Nate said in a concerned tone. It wasn't something Monte was used to hearing from Nate.

"Oh? Well, go ahead..."

"Something strange occurred last night as I attempted to charge. It was...troubling."

"What happened?"

"I had set my protocols to charge late into the night. And...I began to see things. At first, it was difficult to distinguish whether or not what I was witnessing was reality. Strange things were happening. I witnessed an attack. There were unidentified droids involved. You and Father were injured. My home was on fire. I...I still cannot completely make sense of it all, but I witnessed many terrible things. An invasion. Hopelessness. Loss of life. It was horrific."

"You had a nightmare, Nate...A bad dream...Happens to us poor human folk all the time."

"I was not told I would have the ability to dream. There is no reference to it in my operating system."

"You're right...It's definitely odd, but very interesting. What else will you learn to do on your own, robo-boy?"

"If all of my dreams are to depict death and destruction, I would rather not have them."

"You'll have good ones, too...Sometimes dreams have naked ladies in them."

"Women are remarkable creatures, but I do not see how fantasizing about females in the nude enhances my training."

"It doesn't...it actually does more harm than good...Might even put you in the hospital one day."

"Do you love her, sir?"

"I don't think I know what love really is...Love is very complicated...I think it's pretty funny that you can claim to 'love' so easily, but a silly little dream has you all weirded out."

"I am conscious when I feel emotion. What happens in my mind when I am asleep concerns me because it is outside of my control."

"I suppose that makes sense. More sense than love makes, anyway."

"I love Father. He is responsible for my inception. And he loves you. Therefore, I loved you before I had ever met you."

Monte responded by raising an eyebrow at Nate, and immediately followed it up with a big smile.

"Well, hell, if you love me, then I love you right back, buddy."

"Rest well, Monte. You will be needing it. I am glad to see

you smiling. Use this opportunity to meditate and maintain this positivity. I will return later in the day."

"Okay. Try to bring Doc along next time...I miss his wrinkly face."

"He will be stopping by later in the day. I am going to complete my charge in the lobby as I wait for his arrival. Enjoy your rest."

Nate made it halfway to the door. The sensors above the doorway detected him and the sliding privacy-glass door opened before Monte called his name.

"Nate..."

"Yes?"

"Thank you..."

"What for, sir?"

"For being my friend."

"I have been programmed to be your friend, remember?"

"Haha...Yeah, yeah."

"You are my brother, Monte. Bot or human, we will see this through, together. I can promise you that."

"You're pretty awesome for a bunch of circuits and tin...Now get the hell out of my room so I can go back to sleep."

"See you shortly, sir."

"See ya."

Monte turned out the small light next to his bed and went back to sleep. The nurses checked on him every couple of hours or so, but he spent the majority of the day in and out of sleep, until that evening.

32

Visiting Hours Are Over

Claire quietly entered Monte's hospital room. He was bruised and sore, but in perfectly stable condition and on the road to recovery. The medical staff was proficient, and after his early morning visit from Nate, Monte was in good spirits.

A part of Claire felt guilty. After all, it was her moonlighting as a dancer which instigated his hissy fit in the first place. She began to gently brush the tips of her fingers against his bruised forearm, currently hanging off the side of the bed. The nanomesh of the hammock felt her presence and reacted by collecting over her fingers, almost dancing around her hand. Once they detected there was no work to be done, they fell back and began scanning Monte's arm again, looking for injured tissue cells to liven up.

Monte started to wake up. He looked over and realized it was Claire at his bedside. He couldn't be angry, even if he tried. Once he was conscious enough, he let out a few quiet groans before speaking to Claire in a groggy voice.

"What are you doing here?...Shouldn't you be out somewhere, experimenting with your soul?"

"Yeah, but I wanted to see you." she replied.

"What's there to see? No double lives here."

"Oh stop it, will you?"

"I wonder what else you do that I don't know about...The Unsolved Mysteries of Claire Ortegaaa!"

"Monte, listen..." she said softly. "It's really not that big of a deal that I work at the Gazelle, okay? The money's good, the club is clean, and it scratches my itch to dance."

Claire tried her best not to upset him further.

"Couldn't Waltz? Samba? Pop N Lock?"

"Vince does a pretty good job of making sure nothing too crazy goes on in there. It's safe. Besides, Legaia is really strict on stuff like this. There are a lot of guidelines we have to follow."

"Who the fuck is Vince?"

"The GM. Look...you know I wouldn't put myself in harm's way. Half the girls in there are just young college kids like us, looking to make a few bucks and have some fun. There's even another girl from PULISC working there as a server."

"I don't know how many times I have tell you—you can talk to me about this sort of stuff. Don't leave me in the dark."

"I know. You're right. I should've told you. You know I don't really like talking about stuff like that. Anyway, just relax and rest up. I'll be back later to see you again, okay?"

"Alrighty," he said as he attempted to adjust himself into a more comfortable position, but was met with discomfort instead.

Claire planted a smooch on his cheek, threw her handbag over her shoulder, and headed for the door.

Late in the evening, Professor Porter decided to pay Monte a little visit. He casually entered the hospital. The dual sliding doors give way to a large, well-lit lobby. Randal approached the information desk.

"Hi, I'm here to visit Monte Cizek."

"No problem, sir. Can I see your I.D?" responded a human hospital security guard.

Randal handed the guard his identification.

"Thank you, Dr. Porter. I'm so sorry for not recognizing you. I don't believe we've ever met. And I'm relatively new," said the embarrassed guard as he handed Randal his driver's license.

"All is well, young man. Thank you."

"Here's your visitor's badge. Monte is in room 1511. His mother requested that we accompany all of his visitors with a few exceptions. You, mainly. You're all set."

Randal found Monte in a heavy sleep. As the professor placed his hat and satchel on an empty seat, an android nurse entered the room, smiling softly at Dr. Porter before replacing Monte's nutri-bag, which was silver in color and nano-infused. She left as gently as she came.

The professor spent a few moments hovering over Monte, taking a close look at all of the injuries that were inflicted upon him by Lucan. The real purpose of his hesitation was to spend a few moments questioning himself. Was Monte the person he was going to rely upon to continue his life's work? Was Monte the young brainchild he had so patiently been waiting to find, or did he not quite fit the bill?

"They keep tellin' me you're the future of this industry, kid..."

Dr. Porter removed the small, computerized vial from his pocket, activated it, placed it on Monte's free forearm, drew his blood, and placed the full and secured vial back into his coat pocket. The professor had gotten what he came for.

He made his way back down to the lobby to retrieve his vehicle from the valet, with every intention of heading right back to NTI headquarters to continue working late into the night.

33

Ultimate Confidence Trickster

Hurlocke knocked on Suttridge's office door a couple of times. The door was already cracked open, and Richard wasted no time assuming he was welcome.

"Good afternoon, Michael."

"Mr. Hurlocke. Come on in."

Hurlocke made sure to close the door behind him.

"How do you sit in this dark office all day, Michael? Where's the light? Where's the action? I need to get you some entertainment. Something to spruce this place up!"

"My entertaining days are over with. I've had my fair share, though, I can assure you."

"Well…you know I'm not here to remodel your office. There is a daunting dilemma on my mind I would very much like to speak with you about."

"I knew this was coming. I've been preparing myself for it all week, as a matter of fact. And I already have a response for you. But why don't you go ahead and express your concern to me, I'm all ears."

"Well, let's get right to the meat of it then. Your buddy Randal Porter roasted one of my most precious androids. It's going to take me several weeks and hundreds of thousands of $CAL dollars to make Lucan whole again. And so, I would like to know what your thoughts are regarding Randy and Monte's behavior, as well as your proposed course of action."

"I can assure you, Richard, I intend on having a lengthy conversation with Dr. Porter in regard to exactly what he witnessed that day as far Monte and Lucan's encounter is concerned."

"A lengthy conversation? You think it's okay for people to electrocute my most advanced bots? I don't suppose you're going to pay for the repairs, are you?"

"First of all, I'm certain financial hardship is the least of your concerns, so let's cut the crap, Hurlocke. People are allowed to defend themselves against rogue bots like yours. Your android violated several protocols and got what it deserved. You already know that. So why are you wasting my time?"

"I'm...I'm afraid that's not good enough. I don't think a 'lengthy conversation' is going to cut it here, Mike. I would address this situation very differently if I were you."

"Then I suppose it's a good thing you're not me."

Hurlocke stood by one of Suttridge's bookshelves, admiring a small glass plaque that had been awarded to Michael in his younger days as a robotics pioneer. Without any warning, Hurlocke changed his tone.

"You're a piece of shit, Mike, you know that?"

Suttridge looked up from his desk, peering at Hurlocke from over his reading glasses.

"I beg your pardon?"

Michael thought his ears were playing tricks on him.

"You worthless son of a bitch. You're going to ruin me!"

Michael had a silent alarm linked to his timepiece, which he used to summon Xander, an upgraded six Randal had gifted Michael when he was appointed Director of the Android Sustainability Group. The dedicated android received the alert and knew it came from Suttridge's office. He immediately left his post managing the ASG security detail and made his way toward the source of the distress signal.

Suttridge remained silent, in an attempt to soften Hurlocke's anger while awaiting Xander's arrival. Michael's gut was right in doing so.

In a display of pure rage, Richard picked up the same precious glass plaque he had been admiring earlier and flung it toward the wall to the right of Suttridge's desk.

"I've had enough of you!"

Michael's digital timepiece displayed a beacon that revealed Xander's exact location. Slightly rattled, Michael spoke,

"I have something to give you."

Hurlocke's face went from irate to inquisitive.

"What is it?"

"Your termination letter…along with your severance pay. I've been waiting a long time to give this to you. And today, you've proven what others have told me all along. You are not fit for this organization. Security will now escort you to your vehicle."

Richard unleashed a barbaric yell as he lunged toward Suttridge. He began squeezing Michael's neck with all his strength, as the older director grabbed Hurlocke's wrists while attempting to fend him off. The director's face was flushed red as they crashed into bookshelves, knocking the contents of the once pristine office all around and onto the floor.

Just then, Xander came barreling through the doors. He grabbed Hurlocke by the upper arm and subdued him immediately, pinning him face down into the floor and placing him in handcuffs. Hurlocke continued to huff, puff, and swear, as Xander checked on Suttridge to make sure he was alright.

"Are you okay, Dr. Suttridge?"

Michael attempted to catch his breath.

"Yes…yes…I'm fine…call the police."

"Yes sir," replied Xander.

"I'm going to make you regret the day you were born, you mangy mother fucker," Hurlocke growled. "You're a dead man!"

"Get him out of here, Xander." said Suttridge, still leaning on his desk and wiping the sweat beads from his forehead with a napkin.

Michael's phone rang, it was Professor Porter.

"Mike," said the professor in his usual hurried tone.

"Randy…"

"You alright?"

There was no need for Dr. Porter to inquire about the specifics, as Xander's data stream had provided the professor with more than enough information. Video, audio, statistical data, the works.

"Yeah…I'm alright."

"I'll save the 'I told you so's' for later. For the time being, I'm sending over another six-plus and half a dozen grunts. If you think this is over, you're sadly mistaken. He hasn't even started yet, this lunatic."

Although Hurlocke was now out of the ASG, he had enough friends and crypto-employees in the organization that it almost didn't even matter he'd been ousted.

"I've got a feeling you're right, Randal. And I hate it when you're right. I always have and always will." Suttridge shook his head in disbelief while staring at the glass and books on the floor.

"They'll be there tomorrow morning. Just try to get some rest and don't think about it too much. We'll figure this out. I've got your back, buddy."

"Appreciate it...I'd be lost without you."

"Take it easy, Mike. Talk to you soon."

Porter hung up before Michael even had a chance to respond. He may have played the cool and collected card for Dr. Suttridge's sake, but deep down he knew what sort of trouble was brewing. An angry Hurlocke on the offensive was never going to end well, and the professor knew that better than anyone else.

34

Voicemail From A Goddess

Monte ever so gently brought his finger up to the aquarium glass. A maroon-colored clownfish touched its nose to the glass where Monte's finger was, saying hello and almost appearing to sense that heavy thoughts were weighing him down. He glanced over at a wall covered with his achievements, and as Monte sat in his bedroom, pondering everything and nothing simultaneously, it hit him. The weight of life on Legaia (or just life in general) had taken a seat, resting comfortably upon his shoulders.

He suddenly realized that science was inseparable from its dark economic and political siblings. Monte wasn't the type of person who would cave or give in. He had his sights set on his goals, as well as the hurdles he knew he'd have to overcome to reach those goals. This was the challenge he was ready to face head on and either conquer or succumb to.

He replayed in his head the words he had heard from others, and the advice he had been given, most of which didn't make much sense to him. Sure, he respected the opinions of those close to him, but he firmly believed that his gut was the only one with answers. That there was no alternate resolution, other than the one he already had in his mind. Monte knew full well what had to be done, even though he wasn't the slightest bit fond of the idea, his own idea.

He thought about his friends, his family, Randal, Nate, Claire; it didn't help. There was a turf war coming, and it was time Monte prioritized his agenda, for an inevitable battle was on the horizon, and he knew he'd need every ounce of preparation and confidence he could gather.

He snickered to himself at the idea asking law enforcement for help. How would he explain to them what only he and Randal truly understood? But he also realized that it would be foolish not to at least explore the option of receiving help from law enforcement. Especially since he had a couple friends on the force, in Aaron and Ben Draifer.

He wasn't looking forward to the idea of bringing all of this to Commander Draifer's attention, but he felt as though he had to in his efforts to explore all of his options. Monte had felt that a passive approach to dealing with Richard Hurlocke was a bad idea from the get go, and not much of that had changed.

It was Friday evening. He picked up his trusty helmet, jacket, and keys and stormed out of his room. Monte's mother was over at his unit, looking for ways to help tidy up. He seldom left much housework to be done. And really, Roxanne just missed him and wanted an excuse to spend some time with her eldest son.

He zipped through the hall as he made his way toward the garage.

"Where you headed, speed racer?" asked his mother.

"I have to go see Aaron's dad. I need to talk to him about something."

"Just ride safely, okay? I hate worrying about you being on that thing."

"Yeah, I will. See you, Mom."

"Bye sweetie, be safe."

As he prepared to ride off toward LPD headquarters, Monte pulled out his phone and saw that he had received a voice message from Claire, and that always got his attention.

"Monte, it's me. I was wondering what you were up to. I'm not working tonight…would you wanna grab some dinner downtown or something? I know of this excellent sushi joint. We should go. Anyway, I'll be around. Let me know. Muah!"

And he was off, figuring Claire's rare dinner invite would be the only thing he had to look forward to that evening, as he headed toward Commander Draifer's office.

Aaron and Monte were close pals from high school, and although their busy work schedules didn't afford them the luxury of hanging out as often as they used to, Monte knew the Draifers would always be there for him, should he need anything at all.

Monte walked into the police station, where law enforcement droids as well as human officers shuffled around, working at a rapid pace. The department wasn't necessarily overwhelmed, but they did hold themselves to a higher standard than any law enforcement agency back home. The Legaia Police Department strove for excellence.

He approached a desk with a bulletproof barrier. Behind it sat a bot with a badge.

"Good evening. Can you let Ben Draifer know that Monte Cizek is here to speak with him?"

"Retinal scan, please," said the android in an authoritative tone.

He quick-stepped about a foot to the right and aligned his face with the scanner.

"Thank you. Please have a seat while I inform Commander Draifer of your presence," said the android as it typed away.

"Thank you."

He couldn't help but notice a bot in handcuffs being brought in by an android officer.

The wait was brief.

"Mr. Cizek," said the Commander.

"Hey, Mr. Draifer, how are you?"

"What brings you here? You've never visited me at work before, even back home. Come, let's go to my office."

"Yeah, I know. I just really needed to speak with you."

They chatted further as they walked down the hall and into the Commander's office.

"Well, no worries. Please, have a seat. Tell me what's on your mind."

The office was nice, nicer than you'd think a police commander's office would be.

"I need to talk to you about Richard Hurlocke."

"Oh, boy. Should I tell the front desk to hold my calls?" joked Benjamin.

"Oh, this won't be long, believe me. I just have a really bad feeling he's about to do something stupid. And I wanted to hear your thoughts. He's got a different robotic insect buzzing around me for every day of the week. And now he's harassing Mike Suttridge? Are you kidding me?"

The Commander rubbed his chin as he nodded with agreement.

"I can tell you this, Monte. I'm not afraid of Hurlocke. He can flex his political alignments and bank accounts all he'd like, but he's definitely going to be charged, held, and fined for attacking Director Suttridge like that."

"That's just the thing. He'll pay whatever he needs to pay. He'll get out. He'll pay more; he'll get the charge reduced. He'll launch a PR campaign to make himself look civilized, for Christ's sake. Knowing him, he'll make it look like it was Michael's fault!

"I don't care about all that though. What bothers me is what I feel like he's going to do next."

"Monte, I completely understand your frustrations. But I certainly can't incarcerate Hurlocke for what I think he might do. We're keeping an eye on him. But like you said, a couple hundred grand and three weeks later, he'll be right back at it. We'll just have to keep our eyes peeled and stay alert."

"I have a hard time standing idly by, waiting for him to strike. Potentially hurting you, me, my friends, my family. You're damn right I'm absolutely going to keep an eye on him. I can't let him continue to get away with this sort of shit...because it'll never end."

"Look, off the record here, bud, there isn't much I can do. But I can make a case for your safety and have Aaron essentially be assigned to monitoring you. You're pretty vital to Legaia's functionality. It shouldn't be too difficult for me to get that approved."

"That's awful nice of you, Commander, but to be frank, I highly doubt there's anything Aaron can do for me that an NTI Eight can't. I don't know if you're aware of this, but I have a multi-billion dollar NTI prototype for a bunkmate. Pardon my French, but I feel pretty fucking safe. I'm more worried about the friends of mine who don't have the luxury of a cutting-edge android entourage."

"Fair enough. I'll increase patrols around Porter's properties instead, and let's have you put in an app for a CCW as well, but I really can't do much more than that until Hurlocke gives me reason to. I'm sorry. I know you understand how this all works."

"No no, I know. I get it, I really do. Just wanted to make sure you were fully aware of the situation. Hell, at least I got it off my chest. That helped. Sorry I wasted your time, Commander. I'll get out of your hair."

"Don't be ridiculous, Monte. You're practically family. Here, take a few business cards. My mobile's on there as well. Give one to your professor. Call or text me if you guys need anything. I'll do whatever I can. I can promise you at least that much."

"Appreciate it. Enjoy the rest of your day, Mr. Draifer."

"You as well."

Monte grabbed his things before heading out to meet with Claire for their pseudo dinner date.

35

All You Can Eat

When word got back to Hurlocke about Lucan being terminated, he was livid. It brought out a side of him most of his current associates had only heard about. He was furious and viewed the incident as a personal attack, and vowed to seek vengeance.

Hurlocke contacted various private security firms, making them offers for their services. But in typical Richard Hurlocke fashion, he wasn't very modest in his pursuits. Rather, he was looking to form an android army. Not entirely aware of how much manpower he wanted or needed, but he was a man with virtually unlimited finances, and he had no problem showing it off.

Meanwhile, Laurens (one of Hurlocke's right-hand men) was sent to purchase anything he could get his hands on that would give Hurlocke some assistance in his endeavors. He headed to downtown L.A. to comb warehouses and liquidators' show rooms. There were several robot dealers and pawnshops in the area he could probe for help.

Laurens found a large consignment store and decided he'd drop in to see if they had anything useful in their inventory.

There wasn't anybody immediately available to help him, so Laurens took it upon himself to browse through the store, looking for bots. He found household goods, musical instruments, and inside the glass counter was jewelry and watches.

Toward the back of the store, he found an area that housed robots. Short ones and stocky ones and lanky ones and bots that were nannies and bots that were maids. Bots that were auto mechanics and bots that were gardeners. Dissatisfied with his findings, his already minimal patience began to grow even thinner.

The store owner came out from his back office.

"Can I help you with anything?"

"I need androids."

"Okay, well, we've got plenty of those here. What kind of robot do you need?"

"Mercenaries."

The owner hmm'ed to himself and almost laughed out loud.

"We certainly don't have any robots like that. Have you tried the federal government? Maybe the Army? Perhaps they can help you out."

Laurens placed his briefcase on top of the counter.

"These are garbage. I need proper androids."

Laurens opened the briefcase, which was full of platinum bullion. The store owner had never seen such a thing. His concern was mixed with excitement.

"Who are you? Who do you work for?"

"That's not important. Do you have what I need? We're willing to pay, as you can see."

"Follow me."

The owner led Laurens to an inconspicuously placed staircase that led to the basement. He opened the door and took a few steps down. Laurens followed.

"I think you'll find more of what you're looking for in this room."

Things were barely visible, until he hit the light switch. The room filled with bright white light, revealing dozens more bots.

Laurens stepped forward, ahead of the owner, admiring the various machines. There were generic android bots that could be customized, brand new bots that were surplus models from previous model years, and even a few refurbished and discontinued NTI bots.

"I need all of them."

The store owner looked at Laurens with disbelief.

"All of them?"

"All of them."

"Okay, umm, let's go upstairs and figure out what this is going to cost you."

Back upstairs, the owner crunched the numbers and Laurens handed over its equivalent in precious metal, no questions asked.

"Do you know where I can get more?" Laurens asked.

Now the owner knew something was up. He certainly didn't want to carry this on his conscience, being the guy that helped some lunatic secure enough high-tech bots to ransack a small town. But he certainly didn't want to anger Laurens either because he looked menacing.

"There are several other shops downtown that sell a wide array of things. I can't guarantee they'll have quite the selection I had, but they're worth a shot. There's an army surplus store about a mile from here. They usually have some stuff, too…Where do ya want these boys sent?"

"Deliver the bots to this warehouse at your earliest

convenience."

Laurens slid a business card with the delivery location on it toward the owner, as the curious shopkeeper adjusted his eye glasses and squinted.

"You got it. Thanks for your business. Come again."

Laurens closed his briefcase and walked out as if his purchase hadn't even made a dent in his shopping list.

36

What Doesn't Kill You

It had been a couple weeks since Monte's release from the hospital. His doctors told him to avoid physical activity other than basic movements for a month, just to be on the safe side. Monte wasn't the most patient of men, however.

Nate was studying in Monte's bedroom when he heard a ruckus coming from Monte's lab next door. He decided to check it out, still harboring a sense of guilt over what had happened to Monte while he had been away.

"Monte, is everything alright? I hear quite a disturbance coming from your study."

The racket Nate was describing was actually the sound of Monte hitting a heavy bag, practicing some Muay Thai kickboxing moves he learned watching video clips on the web.

Out of breath, Monte responded, "Hey Nate," as he continued to punch and kick the bag in between words.

"Just getting some exercise in. These video tutorials I found are awesome!"

"Monte...I do not believe it wise for you to engage in this degree of physical activity, when three weeks ago you were in an intensive care facility."

"You kidding me? I feel like Superman. A hammock nap a day keeps the doctor away. I wanna keep that thing!"

The professor had arranged for Monte to be lent an optic hammock for one month to assist in his recovery. The PULISC hospital itself only had about a dozen of them.

"Yes, you are correct. You look good as new. But more often than not, it is better to err on the side of caution."

"I'm being cautious. Don't you worry."

Monte wrapped his gloves around the bag and pulled it into his body while he drove a couple of knee strikes into it with all his might, as if it were the real thing.

"Sophisticated robots are not fazed by kicks and punches, Monte. If it were not for the restrictions set forth by law, the average android could strip you of your manhood far worse than Lucan did."

Monte struck that bag with a right as hard as he could, and then stopped. He then rested his forehead on the heavy bag as he caught his breath.

"Some of us don't get to be androids, Nate. Some of us have to sleep every night, or we die. We have to eat several times a day, consume eight or more cups of a clear liquid every fucking day, or we die. Most of us bust our balls day in and day out, and half of us are still epic failures, full of disease and insecurity. We don't have charge ports! We don't have data drives and network connections in our heads! We weren't birthed in multi-million dollar android incubators! So fucking forgive me for trying to better myself."

"It was not my intent to hurt your feelings, sir...I am merely concerned for your safety and success. That is all."

Monte spent the next few seconds wondering whether he

was venting frustrations onto Nate that he didn't deserve.

"I know…I'm sorry. I was hoping Legaia would get easier with time. That was my mistake, though."

"I think a walk through the park may be just what we need. Would you like to go on a walk with me?" suggested Nate.

"Yeah, that doesn't sound too bad, actually. Let's go get some fresh air. Freshly recycled air, that is."

And on that note, the two went to Legaia Park and spent a little bit of time doing nothing at all. Just taking it easy, enjoying one another's company, having the same type of talks that almost always made both of them feel anew.

37

Fly Me To Sin City

With the Dusk project complete and safely nestled away at a property that wasn't even in Randal's name, the only thing the professor had left to do was to tell the kid about it.

The two chatted over a video conference. Monte updated Randal on how his various projects were coming along, and on this bright and casual afternoon, Randal spotted his opportunity to communicate his intentions.

"Kid..."

"Yes, Professor?"

"Got any special plans for this weekend?"

"Umm, not really. I've got a little bit of studying to do and I was planning on spending most of the weekend tinkering with my plane and some conceptual battery designs I'm working on, but I mean, other than that..."

"Never mind all that for a minute. I wanna take you to Vegas this weekend, show you some of my latest work. You think you can make it?"

"Um, yeah, absolutely. That'd be awesome."

"Excellent. There's a flight leaving NDT later tonight. We've got a lot to talk about."

"Tonight? Ooh, wee. Sounds like a plan."

Monte had to make a conscious effort to hide his enthusiasm, refuting his urge to prance out of the room.

That afternoon, Monte played with his science knowing the professor was taking him on a weekend getaway to display some of his latest and greatest creations. And although Monte still had a lot of growing up to do, he knew just how privileged he was to be experiencing such a thing.

Nanotechnology had come a long way. Science and humanity in general had come a long way, but after the pandemic of 2047, Randal always had a lingering feeling in his gut that he would either create, or at the very least play an integral role in the creation of, the next big thing that would change society and the way humans lived their lives.

The professor's demeanor came off as harsh to those who didn't know him, but the people closest to him had a completely different understanding of Randal Porter; his unintentional brashness was matched only by his brilliance.

38

The Data Haven

Legaia's library, where Roxanne worked full time, was on his way home. Monte wanted to stop by for a second and give his mom the good news in person—that the professor had invited him to his vacation home in Henderson, Nevada, to give him a sneak peek at his newest projects.

He was in a rush to speak with his mother due to sheer impatience, parking his bike quickly and making a beeline for the library's main desk.

Inside Legaia's Central library (and only public library) was a grand display of technological feats. What once used to be aisle after aisle of bound paper was now dozens of contemporary tables with computer monitors embedded in them. Metal and leather chairs, and countless, deep blue fiber optics. The library was typically used as an alternative studying ground for students from Porter University as well as students from the local junior college, high school, and middle schools.

The main help desk resembled more of a network operations

center than a home for the written word. Servers, 10 feet high, 20 feet wide sat behind a large, curved, brushed aluminum desk surrounded by thick glass that allowed the climate around the hardware to be different than that of the rest of the library. Plenty of lights. Some informative, mostly decorative. It was quite a sight, though, knowing that almost all of the world's literature could now be housed in this small stack of computers.

Roxanne was sitting behind the front desk, staring down at a holographic image. She wore reading glasses because her corrective eye surgery was beginning to fade, and she was too afraid to have the procedure redone. Monte stood there quietly and waited. No more than several seconds would pass before the giddy, young scientist would approach the front desk in his typical, goofy manner.

"Excuse me!"

His mother looked up with concern.

"Are you trying to give me a heart attack!?" she giggled. "What are you doing here?"

He didn't visit her at work very often.

"I was too excited! I had to come here! See your beautiful face!"

"Pretty sure that's not why you're here. Are you hungry? Do you want money? Spit it out. What is it?"

Monte laughed.

"Randy wants me to go to Vegas with him for a couple days. Says he has some important shit to show me. Not your typical stuff though. Something big."

"That does sound exciting. When are you guys going?"

"Tonight!"

"Tonight?"

"Tonight! Vivaaa, Las Vegas!"

"Be good…You're going there for work, not to party."

"I know. I'm kidding."

Professor Porter frequently traveled back and forth between California and Legaia, but Monte hadn't been back on solid ground since they'd left.

"Is Nate going?"

"Of course! Glad you brought that up though. One of his cousins will be staying with you in our absence."

Monte got a kick out of referring to all androids as "Nate's cousins," especially in front of Nate.

"Don't be ridiculous. You two are the ones that are gung-ho about needing robots. Not me."

"Mom...I don't have time to explain this to you over and over and over. So, in our absence, NTI security detail will stay with you. End of discussion."

"I wish you guys would tell me the reasoning behind your paranoia."

"We work day in and day out enhancing these robots with the hope that they will help us prevent the need for such explanations, stories, statistics, headlines. That's what they're for. Just trust us, okay?"

"I do, sweetie. I do. Well, run along then. Go pack your stuff. You've got important things to do."

Monte leaned over the counter and gave his mom a quick peck on the forehead. Something he hadn't done in a very long time.

"Muah! I'll call ya from Vegas!"

"No poker!" his mother insisted.

"Yeah, yeah! Later, Momma!"

"Bye, hon."

And just like that, the boy was off to prepare himself for a brief trip to Earth, where his professor and mentor was planning to unveil some pertinent details about his secret project. Monte and Randal's day-to-day was ground breaking, so Monte knew that if the professor was flying him two hundred and seventy five miles through space to talk to him about a project, it was huge.

After the professor was done with his academic duties for the day, they grabbed that day's only flight out to LAX and headed via a second short flight to Nevada. It was during this flight that Monte took a moment to truly contemplate his role in the security of Legaia, without an ounce of youth or arrogance. Monte appreciated the invite, realized how lucky he really was to be in his position, and further promised himself life-long dedication to scientific advancement. The LISC, the future of Nanoflèche, all of it.

Dr. Randal Porter spent the weekend showing Monte ideas, designs, schematics, concepts, and really caught him up on the majority of his off-the-record work, but there was one project in particular he was most excited to share with Monte.

39

A History Lesson

The professor placed his hands on his knees and let out an exaggerated groan as he took a seat on a leather sofa.

"Ahhh...Monte, Monte...let me bring you up to speed on something. When your father and I were in our mid-twenties, we worked for a company named F6 Global Robotics. My old man was the head of our department. Some of the projects we were working on together were unprecedented. Our division was singlehandedly revolutionizing the robotics industry. These were exciting times, as I'm sure you can imagine...

"We had a military-sponsored prototype. Its name was Sirca. He was supposed to be the next big thing in android technology, a "game changer". Take a 2045 data center's worth of computing capability and stick it inside a computer the size of a Rubik's cube. Now give it the honor and logic of a world-renowned spiritual guru. That was Sirca.

It wasn't perfect, like anything else, and it wigged out one day, stole an impressive amount of F6 funds, forged a bunch of signatures, divulged tens of thousands of classified documents on U.S. foreign policy, and boarded a plane to China. We were never able to confirm whether it did so on its own accord, or if any sort of outside influence played a role in its behavior. It didn't matter. We were in hot water. Our investors were pissed off. Homeland Security and the Department of Defense were fuming. We were pretty fucked, to say the least.

"Your father and I were in the early stages of birthing our own firm anyway, and it's a damn good thing we did. Everyone pulled out. F6 went belly up, and we had essentially handed over some of our latest technology to our greatest competitor.

Imagine the weight of every aspect of the United States of America, or life on Earth for that matter, resting on your chest. Sirca simply knew too much.

The U.S. government labeled Sirca a POW and created propaganda campaigns to throw Chinese robotics firms under busses the size of moons, all in an effort to keep resources and talented minds here in the States. Sirca had underestimated China's consideration toward American robotics and overestimated their understanding of conscious androids. They questioned its motives. Videos surfaced of Sirca, used and abused, in retaliation to U.S. backed sanctions, surveillance efforts, and disinformation attacks. My father was done. That event started it all. With F6 down the porcelain, Papa Porter retired. My father spent the rest of his life, until his dying day, fighting for android equality."

"People for the Ethical Treatment of Androids?" joked Monte.

"Pretty much. Once advancements allowed for producing androids with consciousness greater than the average human's, it was a no brainer, so to say. The later models began speaking publicly on societal change, socio-economic transformation, philanthropic endeavors. Shit was crazy. The builds that came after Sirca were brilliant.

"Meanwhile, your father's drinking worsened. He spent whatever time he wasn't spending at the local dive bar isolated in his garage, tinkering and experimenting. He grew very anti-social. Your dad had a powerful mind, Monte, and I, along with many others, believe his fate was beyond unfortunate.

"When your mother cleaned out the garage after Chris's passing, she gave me a few cardboard boxes full of 'stuff' he wanted me to have, along with the key to his offsite public storage closet. Most of what I found in there was experimental, conceptual daydreaming, but I did find a few things that were of interest.

"One folder was labeled, 'The Answer.' Some blueprints, a journal, and some rare metals. He never got to finish this project, because his thinking was ahead of its time...but I finished it for him, Monte...

"In the safe in my office at HQ, I've left a copy of the nandroid eight files and some next-gen data that's still in the works. It'll be your job to complete those projects, the same way I finished your dad's. But I've also left you with something else. I'm not going to tell you about it now because now isn't the time. It'll derail you, and I know how your mind gets when it goes to other places.

"I'm sure that when the appropriate time comes along, you'll more than utilize what lies in that safe, and it'll be profound, out of this world crazy shit."

"Why me?" asked Monte.

"Because I said so."

"You slay the English language like a knight in shining armor, sir."

"Because it's what feels right. Because I owe it to your pops. Because I owe it to my pops. Because I owe it to myself. And because there's no person better fit for the job. It's because fighting for the survival, for the betterment, of society, is simply what you were meant to do and you know it."

"I don't know what to say, Professor…other than I'm honored. And you have my word that I'll carry things out to the best of my ability."

"That's all I ask of you, kid."

"But what about all the drama 'n' bullshit that's starting to boil over. Nate's intel confirms that Laurens has been visiting every stinking pawn shop and robot broker on the LISC and in L.A. as well. They're gearing up for something."

"I know. That's why I brought you here, where we can talk in peace. Shit's getting heavy. And the scale of their capabilities is hard to gauge. They don't have our toys, and they certainly don't have our tech, but they have something better. Money. In large amounts. We need to be very careful moving forward."

"Agreed."

"You have my permission to add two of my best guards to your entourage. I'd give you more, but we need them back at home base, too, and I wouldn't want to attract too much attention with you walking around town with a small army. Keep Nate with you at all times from here on out, no matter what. Got it?"

"Absolutely. Speaking of the devil, what's up with my robot booger? He said he was gonna meet us here, then at LAX he said he couldn't come but didn't really elaborate."

"I wanted Nate's decisions about Hurlocke's motives to be based solely on his own intuition, and not anything he may have picked up from this weekend's conversation. Call me crazy, but I trust his judgment more than mine."

"Roger that."

"The two seven-plus troopers are waiting for you in the garage. Lathe and Dremel. Started booting 'em remotely before we left NDT. You'll like 'em. They're grunts, but sharp as throwing knives.

"Take the sedan in the garage as well. It's armored, and it's yours to keep. Try not to trash it for a while, will ya?"

"Why do you do all these things?"

"Because I just might need you more than you need me. Now go meet your new friends and get your ass back to LAX before you miss your flight home. You have a lot of work to do and not a lot of time to do it in."

"Okay." Monte responded nervously, as if he had just been tasked with protecting all of mankind.

"Oh, and don't forget this. You'll probably be needing it, but you didn't get it from me."

Randal handed Monte an EMP pistol, and like an obedient young apprentice, he headed for the garage with newfound dedication and intent.

Monte pulled out his mobile device and started the engine of the armored sedan that had been given to him by the professor. It was black and had thick, tinted windows all around. The bulletproof glass and armor-reinforced body panels would provide Monte with an added touch of safety. The sedan was new, as the professor had saved it for a moment when he'd feel its use was necessary. That moment was now upon them.

As the engine warmed up, Monte diverted his attention to the android bays that were lined up against the side of the elaborate garage. Small LED backlit screens attached to each bay both read "100%." The androids' boot sequence was complete. Monte input the pin codes required to open the bay doors, and out came two athletic droids that looked like they meant business.

"Ah, it's our assignment. The two of us have been designed and built for no reason other than to ensure your safety. You must be one important motherfucker," said Lathe, as he clenched his fists while stretching, testing his pneumatics.

"I like you guys already. I'm Monte."

"Let's save the buddy chat for the flight home, shall we? Doc's data stream tells me we've got a full agenda, and I'm not one to stand around and watch the grass grow. Let's move," said Dremel.

They hopped in the car and went directly to McCarran International Airport. Their sedan would be shipped to Legaia in an expensive but prompt fashion. Monte and his pair of new friends would meet with Nate at LAX for their ride back to the LISC.

The four of them joked around on the flight home and grew quite fond of one another, but their laughs were restricted by their heavy minds, as all four of them were well aware of the complications that awaited them back on their floating home in the sky.

40

Next Best Thing

Upon returning to Legaia from his eye-opening trip to Professor Porter's vacation home, Monte sensed some uneasiness in Nate, which was strange because it was usually Nate that was consoling Monte's occasional mood swing.

"What's wrong, buddy?" Monte asked the distraught android.

"I am unaware of the appropriate response to your query."

"Alright, Mr. Sophistication. Let me know what your bloody problem is when you figure it out for yourself, will you?" Monte replied to Nate in a broken British accent.

Nate was unresponsive.

"Wow, silence. Now I know it's serious. Let me pull up your vitals. You must have a defective crystal or something!"

Monte continued to joke, hoping it would help ease whatever stressors were on Nate's mind.

"I think I miss Father."

"Oh...why didn't you just say so? Tell you what, let's force that workaholic to carve out a couple of hours this weekend, and maybe we can hang out at his place? Shoot the shit. Have a barbeque. Just sit around and relax for a while."

"That does sound pleasant."

Monte could tell Nate was fond of the idea. Babysitting a depressed android wasn't on Monte's agenda for the day. Or ever, for that matter. If there was any android he was obligated to, though, it was Nate.

"I know what you need to do," said Monte.

"I am always open to contemplating a genuine suggestion."

"You need to go for a little walk, let your thoughts simmer for a while, and then you need to send Randy a voice message. As soon as you get these feelings off your chest, you'll instantly feel better. I can assure you of that."

"I will do that. Thank you, sir."

"You're welcome. Go now. I'll be here. And don't come back until you've sent the professor a message telling him exactly how you feel."

"I will return promptly."

"Roger that."

Nate made his way outside for a soothing walk where he could collect himself. Monte placed a pair of wireless ear buds into his ears, as he prepared to enjoy some music and brainstorm a bit.

"*My silly robot…too advanced for his own good…*" Monte said to himself, as turned up his music.

Outside, Nate formulated his thoughts. He wanted the message he was getting ready to send Randal to be thorough and concise, without sounding overly emotional, depressing, or needy. He took great pride in his independence, but even a nandroid eight will have a bad day every now and then.

Nate began to walk more slowly, his hands clasped at the small of his back as he digested his surroundings.

"Hello, Father. We have not had a chance to speak in depth for some time. I was looking forward to meeting with you and Monte in Henderson, but I do understand why that meeting could not take place.

I know you monitor me actively. My whereabouts. My actions. My energy levels. I know you receive data pertaining to my health in real time, but all the pie charts and bar graphs and spreadsheets in the world will never be the equivalent of speaking with you...being in your presence.

Monte and I have become great friends. I now realize the full significance of my mission, and I can think of no better resource than the son of Chris Cizek, as far as NTI's future is concerned. I feel as though your conclusions about him are accurate.

I will not, however, attempt to suppress the fact that the past few days have been emotionally burdensome for me. There will always be a part of me that longs to be by your side. I feel as though...I am your son, regardless of the mechanical make-up of my construct. My generation is proving to be a wonderful success, and I am hopeful that my data slabs will be used to birth brothers and sisters with even greater capabilities.

I will not ramble on. I seek not to stray too far away from my duties. But I needed a moment to myself. A moment to be with you in solidarity. May we continue our missions in full faith and to the best of our ability.

I love you and miss you very much. And I will never be able to repay you for bringing me into this world, but I will continue to try."

Nate realized that Monte was right. It was the fact that he had bottled up his feelings that had caused him to feel so down. After sharing his thoughts with the professor, he felt almost completely better.

Realizing Nate needed to be at the top of his game for the efforts that were soon to come, Monte was committed to making sure his pal was in the best of spirits. He had arranged for him and Nate to participate in a tour of the onsite robotics museum located on the first floor at NTI headquarters called The 'droid Lobby.

It wasn't a huge museum, but it did contain many interesting and important artifacts of robotics history. Monte had even spoken with Randal and arranged for him to attend the short one-hour tour with them. Nate would get to spend some time with the professor and see first-hand the history that led to his creation. Monte was certain this would make his bot of a best friend quite happy.

As the tour commenced, Monte gazed at the museum's content with genuine appreciation, soaking It all in. There were robotics prototypes and other bits and pieces of technology enclosed in glass, as well as collectable memorabilia from science fiction films.

Monte admired a marble mosaic in the floor that was located in the center of the foyer containing images of android children playing with human children, nature, industrialization, and the cosmos. It seemed to be full of symbolism, along with a Latin slogan that read, "*Nil Desperandum, Auspice Apparati.*"

Monte wasn't a nosey person. In fact, he preferred solitude in most instances, especially when it came to work, but the ambiance and his curiosity got the best of him.

"Professor…"

"Yeah?"

"What does this Latin quote mean?"

"If even the nandroids fail, we're fucked with a capital F!"

"Really?"

"Eh, close enough."

Monte smiled and shook his head. Randal sounded like an older version of himself, he thought.

The professor's mannerisms sometimes reminded Monte of

his own father. Occasionally, a brief memory of his father would pop into his head. Whether it was something he had said, an image from an old photo album, or worse, a memory of some terrible thing he had done in a drunken stupor. But the memories didn't last very long, and they didn't come very often either.

41

Robotic Reverie

One wall was covered in framed printouts of digital newspaper headlines pertaining to robotics. Another wall was covered with framed photographs of important figures in twenty-first century robotics history.

Randy didn't visit the 'droid lobby very often, but when he did, he couldn't help but be overwhelmed with visions of the past.

Upon seeing pictures of his father and a photograph of Chris Cizek, Randal remembered a conversation he'd had with Chris that was essentially the precursor to the formation of NTI.

"I don't know how much longer I'm going to be okay working on projects I don't know the causes for, the uses of. Busting my balls so that somebody inferior to me can take the credit, the praise. This is such bullshit," said a young Randal Porter.

"Yeah, true, but at least you're not cutting grass, or pouring concrete, deep frying food, shining shoes, sewing sweaters,

221

chopping wood...Shall I continue?" replied Chris.

"No, that's okay. I think you've made your point. Between the two of us, we can jump this raggedy ship. We'll drag an engineer or two along with us and we'll launch our own firm. We're wasting our time here."

"Patience is a virtue, buddy. How long have we been here? Nine months? How old are you? Twenty-four? What's the rush? Seriously? I've got half a dozen side projects I'm working on, and I'm still keeping it together, so I don't know where these fire ants in your pants are coming from."

"My point exactly. Instead of fixing what's broken at F6, we should be researching and developing our own shit. Making our own shit. Selling our own shit. Taking credit for our own shit. You know you want to, so what's the hold up? Why put it off? This stuff is getting exponentially crazier. We're going to be on the forefront of it all, whether you realize it or not."

"But a big boy salary tastes so sweet. How are we going to revert back to being ramen-loving transients, chasing robotic pipe dreams?"

"My old man's gift to me goes live in three months, on my twenty-fifth birthday. I'll pay you what you're making here, so you can continue enjoying the finer things in life, fucker. We'll go in it for ourselves. I'm done giving it away. It's mine. Yours. We deserve it."

"I wish I had more ammunition to rapid-fire into your dream bubbles, but I'm afraid your crazy ass is making sense. Perfect sense. And wait until I show you some of the rough science behind my latest creation. You're going to cream yourself."

Randy was on an adrenaline rush and entertained Chris's desire to share details about his latest experiments.

"I'm listening...Dazzle me!" said the young roboticist with half-hearted enthusiasm.

"It's going to sound like insanity. I'm warning you right

now."

"I'm only interested in that which sounds like insanity, my friend."

"Okay…I think I may have discovered a way to use an android's state of mind to power an energy-based weapon."

"Are your bold claims quantifiable through science, or were you planning on pitching this concept to your local motion picture studio?"

"The formulas are on my secured drive at home. And after I show them to you, you're going to have to kiss my ass."

"Sounds like you've got yourself a date."

"Freak…" replied Chris.

"I love you too, baby."

Randal Porter always felt there was too much wit in one room between the two of them, and that their energy felt like it was going to make the place spontaneously combust one day. He sat back in his chair and reassured himself that he was going to utilize his inheritance to take robotics to the next level.

Standing in a corner, away from the group that was still immersed in the tour, Professor Porter smiled to himself, returning to reality from past memories of robotic fantasies.

42

Extended Family Tree?

It was Saturday, late into the morning. Randal invited Monte to meet him on campus, where he hoped to spend some calmer time with Monte, after the hectic few weeks they'd had.

Things had been tense for some time now, but Randal's thought process had reached an inevitable hurdle. It was apparent what was happening as far as Hurlocke's most recent behaviors were concerned, and it was time for Monte and Dr. Porter to decide whether they were going to stand by and let inevitability smack them square in the face, or if they were going to do something about it.

Although Monte did a good job of displaying a powerful and unfazed exterior, these repetitive uncertainties were starting to wear on the young man. But it was important for the two of them to support each other while strategizing.

He arrived early in the afternoon. It was a bright and gorgeous day on Legaia, and that helped ease the mood. You'd think that in an environment with artificially generated weather patterns, it'd be eighty-two degrees and sunny with crystal clear skies three hundred and sixty-five days a year, but Legaia's vast team of psychological specialists thought it made more sense to incorporate meteorological variance.

"Good afternoon, boys."

"Hello, Father."

The kid smiled while Nate greeted Professor Porter in his typical fashion.

"Sit down, enjoy yourselves. I'll bring you a glass of liquid refreshment. Let's take it easy today. You see the markets this week?"

"Yeah, pretty ridiculous. It's like 2068 all over again. I've got more important things to worry about though. Shouldn't the economists be dealing with the economy?"

"Somethin' like that…So, I've caught wind of some of your plans via Nate's feed…Can't necessarily say that I disagree with any of them…Being proactive is usually a better approach than being reactive, right?

"You've got the right idea, Professor. I know there are times when I don't say much, but I want to make one thing very clear. I am forever in debt to you. Everything you've done for me, from allowing me to participate in the development of the eight to the LISC to everything else. I owe you a tremendous thank you. I've been thinking about the stuff you were telling me about, the stuff in the safes, and although I have yet to fully grasp what's in there, all I can say is that you have my word that I'll look over everything to the best of my ability. The data, the eights and even the nines, all of it."

"If I've done my job right, you won't have to. It'll be Nate that's gonna be watching over you, kid. "

Monte hoped the professor was right just as much as the professor did.

"The eight is the sum of my life's robotics research.

225

Everything I've ever wanted and then some...He's got five brothers and sisters in storage at PULISC. They're missing crystals and have blank drives, but are otherwise good to go. In the rare event that something should happen to Nate, the next one in line will be alerted and automatically activated. Give 'em juice and an OS. Use them. Once they're gone, you're pretty much on your own, bud."

"Wait..." he said with a smile. "Did I hear that right? Five more eights?"

"Yup. Nobody knows about them though, and we should keep it that way."

Monte was actually pretty excited about the news. He wondered for a split second why Randal hadn't told him about the other eights sooner or maybe even why they weren't being utilized, but he figured the professor probably had good reason to go about it the way he did. He always had good reason.

"Holy shit, Doc, that's big news."

"I know. Sometimes I just wanna turn 'em on so bad. I don't know exactly why I haven't to be honest. Those are my babies, and they're safe when they're asleep, existing in secret like that...I kinda just went with my gut. Seems to steer me right...most of the time."

They both smiled and took sips of their drinks, daydreaming of the androids of the future, and hoping for more peaceful times.

43

A First Time For Everything

As the days went by, Monte felt more and more confident in his decisions. He ran through a mental checklist, reviewing the things he had done to prepare and the things he told himself he had to do. He remembered a conversation he'd had with Danny before they decided the hospital was the best place for him. Danny was an all-black level-seven android that once belonged to the Android Sustainability Group.

He was a little different. A sweet character; considerate, but unstable. The specifics weren't known with certainty, but something had gone awry during Danny's construction, which caused him to suffer from severe nervousness and anxiety. Danny had in-depth knowledge about Hurlocke's operations, and it was time for Monte to pay Danny a little visit, as he made his final preparations for what he thought to be a not-so-preemptive preemptive strike against one of the most powerful men in the nation.

Hurlocke purchased Danny from the ASG for his own

private use, hoping his susceptibility would make it easy to take advantage of Danny, using him for personal gains. And although Danny had some quirks, he was bright enough not to fall victim to Richard's schemes. He refused Hurlocke's orders, and as tensions grew between the two, Danny ran away.

Even though Danny was not an NTI design, Professor Porter volunteered to adopt Danny in a sense, granting him passage to Legaia. The hope was that Dr. Porter could monitor and study the disarrayed young android and help to improve his condition, while learning how to curb mental health issues in the bots of the future. Danny was fond of Monte, and Monte felt for him because in many ways, Danny reminded him of his brother.

Monte made his way toward the entrance to the small, mental health wing of PULISC's hospital. Next to his motorcycle were several news media vans, and Monte wondered what the local news networks were doing there. He wasn't too fond of the idea of visiting a hospital for the mentally ill. It reminded him of how irritating it was living with Turner before he was admitted. But Monte wasn't there for Turner this time. He had come to speak with Danny, hoping for information that would give him and his professor some sort of insight or leg up on how to deal with Hurlocke.

From the distance, Monte had seen a group of individuals just outside the main entrance to the hospital, but as he got closer, he noticed they were picketers, performing some sort of demonstration for robot rights.

Some of them stood. Most of them sat. They held large signs stapled to wooden planks that read, "All living beings deserve rights" and "Different fathers, same God." Another sign hinted at the fact that most of the group hadn't eaten in a couple days. As he walked by them, distracted by their signs, one of the hunger strikers began to speak with Monte.

"Did you know there's an android living in this facility?"

asked the protester.

"I do, actually. He's one of the people I'm here to visit."

The original speaker looked at Monte with amazement after spotting Nate standing nearby.

"You're Monte Cizek?"

"Nope. Just a concerned citizen, like you guys."

Nate was waiting at the gate in front of the parking entrance; androids that weren't residents were not allowed on the premises. Monte wanted to get in and get out, avoiding complication.

"Monte, most of us are members of the robotics club at Legaia Community College. We're huge fans of your work, and NTI, too. Please stay with us for a few minutes; the group would be so happy to speak with you."

"I'm sorry. I'd love to, but I'm on pretty tight schedule here...I really can't. Your efforts are appreciated though. Keep kickin' ass."

"We understand...Well, it was a gift meeting you, Monte."

Monte smiled and continued walking. Part of him wished he could spend a couple hours just hanging out with the kids and answering their questions, but he knew that was a luxury he couldn't afford.

Having run into Mr. Cizek, the group was invigorated. They got back on their bullhorns and continued protesting their cause proudly as the journalists continued to interview them. Monte made his way through the doors and stepped inside the visitor's waiting room.

It was a cramped room with a couple of sheriff's deputies sitting behind a thick bulletproof glass wall on one side, with a few vending machines on the other side. The vending machines contained snacks for the residents that were pre-approved, in case a visitor wanted to buy something for a resident.

Caffeine was contraband. The machines were filled with

low-sugar snacks, drinks, and sandwiches, the boring kind. There was no one in line as Monte approached the information booth.

"Hello, I'm here to visit a couple of friends?"

"Let's start with one, pal. ID, please…"

Monte aligned his head with a lens to perform an ocular scan. Monte hated these machines, but he wasn't in the mood to argue. He stared into the light beam as he debated whom to see first.

The Deputy was slightly surprised when Monte's identification data popped up onto his screen. The file was longer and more detailed than anything he had ever seen before. He was impressed, but only on the surface. He didn't really understand what he was reading. They were only trained to interpret criminal aspects of personal identification files.

"Okay. You're fine. Name of the patient, sir?"

After a little bit of hesitation (still not being overly fond of the idea), he asked to see Turner Cizek.

"Have a seat. We'll have him out here in about fifteen."

Monte sat and waited, and as he did, he thought about his motives. He almost wanted to smack himself for being so overly analytical. With the top-level secrets and advancements of nanotechnology in the hands of sociopaths, an ugly world was imminent, he thought. He was committed to decreasing the likelihood of that happening.

He heard the sound of a large metal door unlock and open, and his brother entered the visitation area, accompanied by a guard. He was all smiles, and Monte couldn't help but smile as well, even if he hadn't originally intended to.

"Sup, bro? Haha." Turner's face lit up with excitement as he chuckled with his typical, obnoxious laugh.

"What's up, Turner?"

"Oh, not much, not much. Good to see you! Haha."

"Yeah…good to see you, too. So what are you up to these days? Learning anything? Reading those books I gave you?"

"Yeah, I've been reading a lot, reading my bible, too, and I play basketball with some of the other guys, and Aunt Jasmine came and saw me with Grandma the other day, and they brought me a double cheeseburger with fries!"

"Sounds pretty awesome…Hey, have you seen the robot that lives here?"

"Yeah, dude! Everyone's been talking about him! They say he's the first crazy robot. But I don't think he's crazy, haha. He looks pretty cool, haha."

"He's a good guy. I want you to make friends with him. His name is Danny. He's actually a friend of mine. I want you to show him around and make him feel comfortable. You guys will get along. And you're right, he is cool."

"Really? Sweet, bro. I want a robot friend! I'm gonna invite him to church with me and to play basketball."

"Right on…Well, I gotta run, dude. I actually need to see Danny for a few minutes before I head out. I have some important things I need to do…But it was good seeing you. Stay good. Don't make any trouble. Listen to all the doctors and nurses, and be respectful. Okay?"

"Yeah, for sure, bro. Hey, when are you guys gonna come see me again? It's boring here."

"Hard to say, bud, but I'm sure mom and sis will be here to visit you soon enough."

Monte hated feeling guilty when it came to Turner.

"Okay, be careful, bro, don't let those robots kick your ass too bad. Hahahahaha!"

Turner continued to laugh in his standard, demented tone, but somewhere in that mad laughter was concern and love.

"I'll try. Take it easy, Turner."

"Later, bro!"

Turner stood up. His wild and wavy hair flailing all over the place. Before stepping away, Turner gave Monte one last glance, and even put a forced smile upon his face. Behind his leery eyes, however, he wondered when he'd get to see his family again, and how much longer he'd have to stay captive inside this facility.

A deputy pointed at the large metal door, and Turner made his way toward the exit with a funny walk that caused his head to bob.

Monte sat back down as he waited for Danny to make his way to the visitation room. His pocket buzzed. He took out his mobile device to find that he had a new voice message. It was Doctor Porter.

'Hey, it's me. I need you to do something for us real quick. Swing by the park and see Henry. He's managed to secure some…additional supplies for us. We're gonna need 'em. He knows you're coming. No rush, but make sure you visit him before we meet tonight. Gotta run. See ya later, kid.'

Right as he finished playing the message, the metal door swung open again, and Danny came through the door with two guards, one armed with an assault rifle and the other with an EMP pistol. They only had one at the facility. This whole robot patient concept was still very new to them as well as the mental health commissions nationwide. It was interesting that rules and regulations for android mental health weren't more abundant, given past occurrences. Sirca, namely.

"ZzZ Monte, hi."

Danny made a few strange sounds during speech. A digital stutter.

"Are you okay, Danny?"

"ZzZ Yeah, just a few side effects ZzZ from my new ZzZ therapy, that's all ZzZ ZzZ."

Monte noticed he was wearing an intricate anklet. It was

white in color, over his black exoskeleton. He also noticed that Danny had two different color eyes now.

"You look like a wolf dog with those eyes. When'd that happen?"

"Yeah, that one I don't know about. ZzZ I woke up and it was like that. Hehe. ZzZ It was weird at first but then I talked to the doctors and they told me I was fine so I'm happy now ZZZzzZZzzzzztsssZ."

He was edgy to begin with, but his hospital surroundings made him even more nervous. So did fear of retaliation. The tests made him uneasy, and the experimental procedures tried to fix it, but were only partially successful with side effects of their own. Danny had a lot to be worried about, and it showed on his face and in his voice.

"You have to stay calm, buddy. And in all honesty, you're probably in the best place you can be. Think about it. It's well staffed. They have everything you need, nurses, doctors, medicine, friends...security. Much better you be here than out there, right?"

Monte's statements definitely helped Danny calm down a bit.

"Yeah, I think so. Yeah, you're right. It's not so bad here. ZzZ I saw the funny boy with the big hair ZzZ. He's your brother, I hear?"

"Yeah. I told him about you. He said he'd invite you to go see the cleric and maybe play some basketball with the boys, if they're okay playing with a bot. You'll have to show them you're a nice bot. You guys should be friends, definitely."

"I don't expect them to want to play with me. Basketball with a bot is no fair. I'll win every time ZzZ."

"Yeah, can't blame 'em. Listen Danny...I came to talk to you about the warehouses."

"Are you ZszZZZ gonna take them out?" Danny raised his

voice a bit with excitement.

"Shhh…..We're working on it, but listen, you gotta tell me everything you know. Anything you think might help us out I need to know and now."

"ZzZ ZzZ ZzZ Yeah, ZzZ sure Monte!"

It was evident that any powerful emotion, regardless of being positive or negative, decreased Danny's ability to function smoothly.

"ZzZ ZzZ ZzZ it's big ZzZ ZzZ ZzZ it's under the Central Library ZzZ ZzZ there are many ZzZ ZzZ ZzZ some are my brothers and sisters ZzZ ZzZ ZzZ it's heavily guarded ZzZ ZzZ ZzZ you can do it though ZzZ ZzZ I've seen them train and they're inefficient ZzZ ZzZ ZzZ after you take down the digital defenses ZzZ ZzZ ZzZ it's the bots you'll have to worry about ZzZ ZzZ ZzZ ZzZ ZzZ ZzZ they're tough ZzZ ZzZ ZzZ and there are so many of them ZzZ ZzZ ZzZ what will you do Monte? ZzZ ZzZ ZzZ Ts Tssss, TS ZzZ ZzZ ZzZ We can't let them have their way! ZzZ ZzZ ZzZ ZzZ ZzZ ZzZ"

"Danny…do you trust me?"

"ZzZ What do you mean Monte? Of course I do."

"Then I need you to understand that you're drowning in your own thoughts. I need you to constantly remind yourself that there's nothing to worry about, ever, because Monte has it covered. Can you do that for me? Can you remember to always remind yourself to stay calm, no matter what happens? That Me, and Doc, and Nate, and everyone else, will figure this out? Can you do that?"

"Z I don't think I'd be able to if it weren't ZzZ for you. But I can do anything for you, Monte. Hurlocke has used these warehouses for years to store his secrets. Zzzz He's been working on it for years. The power needs to go down. ZzZZZ The backup generators need to be disconnected as well. You can….. ZzZZZzZZZZ."

"It's okay, bud. Talk it out. I'm listening."

"You can access the warehouses directly, from beneath, or repel in from up top. ZzZzzzz You might want to consider trying to get on board a delivery truck with Nate the next time that ZzZzzZZZ freak Laurens buys a bunch of droids. You'll get a free ride. Right into the belly of the beast you'll go."

"I knew I kept you around for a reason. Atta boy, Danny."

"Most of his friends secretly hate him…Zzzz You don't have to worry about immediate reinforcements. ZzZzzzz But, but Regal is pretty scary. I don't see any other ZZZZZZ major hurdles though. Nate will take care of everything, right? He's amazing. Sometimes ZzZZZ I dream that I'm a bot like him."

"Tell you what. When I get back, I'll have Randy find a way to get you out of here. And I'll work on you personally, until you're healthier and stronger, and you never know, you just might be a bot like him someday."

"ZzzZZzzZzzzz Do you really mean that Monte? You're not just playing with me, are you? ZZzZZzZzzz."

Monte put his hand on Danny's shoulder and looked him square in the face.

"I'm giving you my word. I'll ask the professor to get you released so I can fix you myself. But only if you promise me you'll be on your best behavior in the meanwhile."

"ZzZZzz Oh my God, Monte, I promise. I promise."

"Good job, Danny. I've made friends with a couple of the guards here ever since my brother moved in. I've asked them to keep an eye on you for me. Stay bright for me. Alright? I gotta go now. I'll see you soon though, Danny."

"Z…..Zz….."

Danny was searching for the appropriate thing to say, without getting too emotional about it all, since Monte had just lectured him on learning to keep his cool.

"You're going to be just fine. I just know it. Something tells me you're going to be just fine," Monte interjected with a warm smile.

"You're right. I've done a good thing. I'm going to be fine. I will be patient and calm."

"I like the new Danny already…See you soon, bud."

Monte winked at Danny before getting up to leave. Danny had a huge smile on his face as he got up. With a guard to his front and another to his rear, Danny left the visitation center.

As Monte made his way back to his motorcycle, he ran his checklist through his head to make sure he hadn't forgotten anyone or anything. The only thing left for him to do was make a quick stop and see Henry. Danny had given him quite a bit of information about Hurlocke's secret android stockpile, and he felt confident coupling that with the data he had been gathering on his own.

One final step, and they'd be ready.

44

Behold, The Itinerants

Monte hoped to squeeze one last encounter with Claire in before embarking on his mission to derail his nemesis.

"Hey, I'm at the park. Got here just a few minutes ago. Looking forward to seeing you." said Monte's message to Claire.

As he waited, he enjoyed some alone time, gathering his thoughts and weighing his options while trying to keep himself as calm as possible. There were many resources he planned to employ during his attempt. The focus of his brooding on the couch, in his lab, in the library, and even during class, were about to become his reality.

"Kay, on my way! See you soon…XOXO"

With his back resting against a park bench, his hands in his sweatshirt's pockets, and his right forearm atop his helmet, he waited. He saw the itinerants slowly moseying about the park and was intrigued. This was his first time seeing them on the LISC.

The itinerants were a self-formed band of powerful psychics that had originally set out to work and learn together. Over the years, they became more of a family. Their abilities were seldom used, but rumored to be quite powerful. Their exteriors were simple. Completely mindless of their wardrobe, they maintained impeccable hygiene and only dealt with the most natural of products. A holistic lifestyle and charitable contributions in the form of volunteer work were a couple of their core philosophies.

Although often misunderstood, they were considered by some to be key components in the next chapter of human evolution. Vagabond geniuses, never settling in one place for too long, but always looking for ways to improve society and lend a helping hand.

The nostalgic young scientist peered down at his timepiece. Claire wasn't the most punctual of people, but she wasn't habitually tardy either, and so Monte reassured himself patience was invaluable. What may have been the youngest itinerant female of the pack approached Monte and struck up a conversation.

"Hii, Monteee."

"Hey there, little one."

"You have to be careful, Montee. It's hard to see out there. So darkk!"

"You're right, it sure is."

"Not like that, sillyyy. The floating city! Everything has come with you. Nothing stays behind. Where humanity goes, their downfalls follow. The businessmen will follow you. They will lie to you. You have to be very careful. Mother says you're just a boy, but I don't believe her. There's more to you. Your heart is selfless. And you will be rewarded for the sacrifices you make. They'll be so proud of you!"

Monte began to feel a connection with the child, and

although he already knew she was an itinerant, he was fascinated by her words. Monte wasn't put off by her at all, as he expected such behavior from the tiny prophet that stood before him.

"I have to do what I have to do. But do you know why I'm not worried?" said Monte.

"Whyyy?"

"Because I've got little angels like you on my side."

She smiled.

"We've been waiting for you for a long time now, Monte. I'm going to help you! Even if I'm all by myself!"

The child hugged Monte's leg. He smiled and patted her on the head as one of the women in her itinerant family said, "Come along, my love. It's time to go now."

"Kayyy. Byee, Monteee. Be alert, okay? We love youuu."

His response consisted of one slightly raised eyebrow, coupled with a smile. Those last three words threw the boy for a bit of a loop, but he maintained his composure as he waved farewell.

In the arms of one of the itinerant women was a baby boy, no more than a year and a half old. This child was staring at Monte with focus and dilated pupils, mesmerized.

The baby may have been the strongest of the itinerants, and his view of Monte showed him things no one else, not even the rest of the itinerants, could see or understand.

Before they departed, what appeared to be the head of this itinerant family approached Monte. He was a middle-aged man with a braided beard. Slightly hobo-esque in style and dress, he carried himself with amazing grace and even walked in a manner that drew your respect.

"Perhaps you realize the weight of the tasks that have been bestowed upon you, perhaps you do not. Just know that we will be with you, in body and in spirit, and should trouble arise, we will be there for you."

Monte thanked the man appreciatively, even though he was getting rather accustomed to hearing such things. The itinerant tribe began to depart, and Monte looked back at them as they walked away, soaking up what had just taken place before him.

Claire snuck up behind him and wrapped her arms around Monte's neck, before she drew her face around the back of his head, placing a wild smooch on his left cheek. He removed his right hand from his sweatshirt's pocket and placed it over her left forearm, while reciprocating with a tired smile.

"I was hoping you'd be in a better mood," said Claire, as she gave him a little neck rub.

It was difficult for anyone to truly understand his current state of mind. After all, he had just been warned of the trouble that lay ahead by a six-year-old itinerant. Nobody questioned the visions and sayings of the itinerants. They had become celebrities in a weird way, garnering whispers and pointed fingers of astonishment everywhere they went.

"I need you to make it back in one piece, you know," she said, resting her chin on the top of Monte's head.

"Oh? And why's that?"

"Because I don't know what I'll do if you don't."

Monte tilted his head backward to see Claire's face and was surprised to see both of her eyes were filled with tears that looked like they were ready to avalanche their way down her cheeks at any moment.

"It's really not that big of a deal. Come, sit." Monte moved his helmet and gloves to his other side of the bench. He opened his right hand while assisting her in taking a seat.

"You're a terrible liar, Monte, you know that?" Claire sniffled and ran her right index finger across her nose, her left hand now holding his right hand. She had never shown herself so vulnerable.

Monte put his hands around her arms and turned her toward him so that they were facing one another. He wiped a tear from her cheek with his thumb, and then repeated the process on her other cheek.

"Claire...I'm not doing this because I want to. Nobody wakes up in the morning and says to themselves, 'I'm going to go risk my life today, because it sounds like a good idea.' I'm doing this because I've given it a lot of thought, and if I don't do this, it might be a while until someone willing to do it comes along.

"Now is the time...My mind has been racing for days, maybe weeks. The anticipation is driving me mad...I'm in too deep, and too many people need my help. If I can't pull this off with two dozen psychics and billion dollar androids by my side, the world should worry...I'm doing this so that people like you and I can worry just a little bit less."

A final tear navigated its way down Claire's face.

"Always trying to be somebody's superhero. Don't you ever get tired?" she said.

"I'm too young to be tired, and I've been tired for a long time, but I'll be damned if you're not the most beautiful thing I've seen since I got here..." He stroked her ear. "I've never been the church type, but maybe it wouldn't be a bad idea for you to pray for me."

"I will. Every morning and every night, until you're right back here," she reassured him.

Monte caressed the top of her head. His hand made its way toward the back of her head, cupping it. He reached in and kissed her on the cheek, retracting his head slowly, enjoying the smell of her perfume. Claire couldn't help but throw her arms around his neck and pull him in closer for what she felt was a far more appropriate embrace.

She kissed his lips very gently.

"That, in and of itself, is reason to make it back in one piece," he joked.

He managed to get a smile out of her, and on that note, Monte felt it would be a good time for them to part ways, for Claire to head back home and for Monte to get his show on the road.

He stood up while guiding her onto her feet.

"I'll message you soon as I'm back. Deal?"

"Okay."

"I've gotta get going.….I'll see you soon, Claire."

"Bye, Monte...Be safe…"

Their hands drifted apart, and she walked back to her car as calmly and casually as she could. Meanwhile, Monte fought back his emotions, started walking the other way, and began to look for Henry.

45

Henry's Gift

When he wasn't overseeing crystal production in the heart of Legaia Park, Henry could usually be found somewhere along the short walls where the lotus ponds met the decoratively paved concrete walkways. It didn't take Monte very long to find Henry sprinkling water conditioner into the ponds.

"Mr. Monte Cizek," said Henry, as he continued tending to one of the many ponds.

"Hey, Henry. How's it going?"

"I'm as good as can be, young man. I don't think the same can be said about you, however. You don't look like yourself."

"Eh, I'm alright. Just got a lot goin' on right now. I don't think I've had anything to eat since breakfast, now that I think about it."

Monte sat on the low wall around the pond, admiring the optics that reflected off the pond water in a colorful array.

"Too busy to eat? No such animal. I'll fix you up something tasty."

The botanist took a few steps over to where some of his gardening supplies sat.

"Henry, please, don't. I don't come here to inconvenience you. I just enjoy…"

"Shhh! Nonsense! You're not leaving until you eat this food. All of it."

Monte smiled at Henry, as he had never shown himself so stern and concerned. He dug through the bag and removed its contents. A hearty cold cut sandwich with all the fixings, some gourmet crackers, and a variation of potato salad.

"I like it. You've got the goods in here, Mr. Nahele."

"I used to ask my mother to make me sandwiches like these all the time, and she never said no. Enjoy it all, my friend. I'm just making sure my babies have water that's ideal for high-quality crystals. pH balance, mineral content, temperature, botany is no joke, you know."

"Absolutely. I think growing pristine plants is an art form, like many things."

"Atta boy. I knew I liked you!"

Henry was in a great mood, in part due to his subconscious efforts to raise Monte's spirits.

The kid gave Henry a warm smile, as he took another huge bite out of his pistachio mortadella and salami sandwich.

"When I was roughly your age, I was plagued by the same thoughts, the same troubles that haunt you. Even though you've got a gem sitting inside that skull of yours, you still have a lot to learn. And it isn't anything that a textbook, a professor, or even God-given brilliance can teach you. Only time…The world will never be what you want it to be. And even if it were to become that world someday, it won't be so until long after you and I are gone, riding stars for horses, floating among the men and women that fought for it, that died for it, as we waited for tomorrow to come. We are, and always have been, the enemy.

The masters of our prosperity as well as our destruction. Two steps forward, three steps back. Don't you think that if we were capable of changing the way you expect us to, we would have? We haven't changed. Not in the ways we've needed to, anyway. The owl needed greater sight, and so it saw. The elk and deer grew tired of getting rammed, and so they grew antlers. And the lion needed to be bigger and louder, and so he grew a mane and learned to roar loud enough for the heavens to hear. And what have we done? We've remained man. Man that created the machine and the M-16. Man that filled the oceans with garbage and tore the forests down. Man that perpetuated disease one thousand times greater than that which we cured. We do not deserve the glory associated with being the dominant species of our home planet. Give it to the shark or the tiger or the eagle.

"Monte, this isn't the end. It doesn't end with you, my friend. The calendar progresses. Life continues whether you're here or not. The plants will still breathe. The crickets will continue to sing in the evening. Some will swim, some will fly. And some day they may dance. You choose to put the weight of the world on your shoulders. It doesn't have to be this way. Even when the sky is crystal clear and the stars are shining upon us, there's always a storm brewing somewhere. The world's problems aren't your problems, Monte. They're *our* problems. Do your part. Do what you can, and let the rest sort itself out."

"I'm just getting sick of having to sift through all the treachery and bullshit...I can hardly tell what's real anymore."

"Brotherhood is a powerful tool. Strength in numbers is more often than not necessary to achieve significant objectives. But in the end, only a noble existence will allow your final breaths to be gentle ones. Live with those final breaths in mind."

"And that's exactly what I plan on doing...Your words don't go without appreciation, Henry. Neither do your delicious sandwiches. I'll see you later, sir."

Monte got up off the ledge and made a beeline for his book bag and helmet.

"Wait, where are you going?"

"Time to round up my cowboys and have myself a little shootout."

"Wait…"

He turned back around toward Henry, primarily with his torso and neck, rather than his body, looking eager to pursue his agenda.

"I don't know how this will play out for you, but I do know that you are a courageous man. Far greater than I…Oh, and you almost forgot about these…"

Henry threw a small enclosed sack of crystals toward Monte. The kid made sure to catch it.

"You have the angels of Earth by your side. My only hope is that they will be enough. Best of luck to you, Monte."

"Thank you. For everything." he replied.

And he was off to meet the professor back at PULISC, so that they could distribute the new crystals in the manner they felt to be the wisest, and proceed with their attempts to severely disrupt Hurlocke's mad schemes.

Meanwhile, at Hurlocke's undisclosed warehouses, Richard paced back and forth amidst the android collection Laurens had been meticulously assembling.

"I like what I'm seeing…"

"These are the finest second-hand androids money can buy, and I've been working in tandem with several technicians, restoring them. These are what you asked for."

"Yes, I see that. Nice work, Laurens. Start 'em up. It's time we sent Professor Porter a little hello."

46

Stuck Between A Bot
And A Hard Place

"Are you ready, sir?" asked Nate eagerly.

"No, but let's get this shit over with."

Monte was convinced further consideration would have no positive bearing on this endeavor.

"You have Father's intel, you have Danny's intel, you have the itinerants, and you have me. If that does not provide you with comfort, I do not know what will."

Monte was still rather nervous.

"I hear ya, Nate. The good news is that I work well under pressure. I just feel like…this needs to be done."

"I feel like I agree with you."

"In you go, buddy. Be good in there."

Monte gently placed a device in his trusted backpack. It was an intricate explosive device with an electro-magnetic charge. He had designed and built it with this objective in mind.

"It's just a shame that others have to suffer as a result of

Hurlocke's illness."

"Let us go now," said Nate impatiently.

Monte looked into Nate's eyes and nodded, a non-verbal indicator that he was ready and committed.

On Monte's to-do list was another objective. Hurlocke had unused keys belonging to several NTI sevens that were in his possession. He wanted to take those keys back from Hurlocke if he could, since he would never part with them willingly.

The doctor was working on a means to destroy the keys remotely and safely, but that was still in the works, and Monte was on a mission to retrieve the keys before Hurlocke could use them to activate any more level seven androids. They did contain a couple means of traceability though, and that would certainly help in the search.

Monte jogged down the school's staircase with his hands in his pockets. With a wide range of emotions from excitement to fear to nervousness, he kept his hands in his hoody pockets as he made his way to the sidewalk. Nate kept Monte in his sights, although he always stayed a few steps behind to help avoid drawing unnecessary attention to Monte.

The pair knew that the RBH Ventures satellite office Hurlocke used had a security desk that was only manned from 6 am to 10 pm. All after-hours entry used dual screening measures for access—your standard ID badge paired with an eye scan. Due to his advanced nanotech construct, Nate could actively shift his eyes to resemble the make-up of an RBH authorized nandroid. Getting into the building wouldn't be a problem. The unknowns associated with what would happen once they were in, was what concerned them.

The steadfast duo continued down the streets of downtown Legaia. There was an odd, gut-wrenching sensation inside of Monte's stomach. To know that compared to the average man, he was invincible, and yet just about anything could go wrong at any moment. A situation could easily arise that not even a cyborg Socrates or telekinesis-wielding psychic could fix. His devotion far outweighed his nerves, though.

As Monte navigated through the pedestrians, mostly dressed in business attire, leaving their offices, getting into autonomous cabs or heading for the rail system, he noticed a solid black level six 'droid that resembled Danny pass him by on the sidewalk, heading in the opposite direction. He was never one to jump to conclusions or make rash decisions based on assumptions. However, the android had thin steel plates that were strategically placed over areas where droids were typically marked, and his instincts told him that bot wasn't on the straight and narrow.

Monte pretended he was unfazed or that he hadn't even seen the thing. After a few seconds, he did a double take and sure enough, it was standing there about twenty-five yards down the road, staring at Monte. It was communicating. Most newer bots had visual indicators that revealed the degree to which they were transmitting data.

Monte knew it was revealing his location, but to whom? And why? He tried his best not to pay attention to the fact that he was essentially being stalked by a strange android. A couple of minutes passed, and diagonally across the street, in between the tall business complexes and lofts, he saw two more. They didn't stop dead in their tracks like the first bot did. They continued to walk, slowly, but their eyes were locked on Monte, and they were also transmitting.

The kid was already riled up with the mission on his mind, and these robotic spies certainly weren't helping the situation. Nate was more than aware of the heavy android presence, and this knowledge was the only thing preventing Monte from having a full-blown panic attack.

Checking his back every fifteen seconds or so, making sure

Nate was still visible, he kept walking. Nate was transmitting extensively as well, and it wasn't very long until a Nanoflèche security helicopter was flying over their perimeter.

Monte activated his comm-link.

"What the fuck is going on?" he whispered into his cell-linked mouthpiece.

"Unusual 'droid activity in this sector. I have alerted Father. Stay calm. Do not get hostile if confronted." Nate whispered back to him.

He wasn't sure he knew what to do anyway. He could flap his gums, but that hadn't gotten him very far with Lucan, and he only had a very limited amount of ammunition, both for his concealed handgun and the EMP pistol Doc had lent him.

The place was now crawling with level four, five, and six androids. Some marked ASG, most with no markings at all. Many of them repurposed and upgraded. Monte and Nate both scanned their surroundings and wondered where all these androids were coming from. There seemed to be at least a dozen of them on every street they turned onto. It was either his old resentment toward androids resurfacing, causing the paranoia Monte was feeling, or his gut telling him a terrible scene was on the horizon.

Several security droids belonging to Nanoflèche, mostly level six, had been dispatched to the area. Porter was in a vehicle with two of his own personal level sevens, trying to get across town to see what the fuss was about. Monte pinged Lathe and Dremel as well.

"We read you, kid. We've got our eyes peeled. These poor assholes don't know what they're getting themselves into…" responded Dremel. He tended to be the wilder one of the two: shoot first, ask questions last.

The pair were sitting at a java lounge that was located eight blocks east of Monte's location.

"I didn't know robots liked to drink coffee..." said an elderly woman as she slowly walked in front of the two militant androids. Her daughter, who was holding her by the arm and helping her walk, looked at Lathe and smiled apologetically for her mother's statement. Lathe nodded a respectful hello to the woman. Dremel, on the other hand, wasn't feeling as gracious.

He grabbed a white chocolate mocha that was sitting on the table next to theirs. The owner of the drink, a teenaged boy, took his large headphones off and was about to speak...until he realized the person that had taken his coffee was a military-grade android. Dremel starred at the boy as if he were inviting him to respond while using his right hand to heat the cup until its contents began to rapidly evaporate.

":::sniff:::, Ahhhhh!..." he inhaled its contents with purposeful conviction.

The teenager and his two friends looked on in dismay at what had just taken place.

"Not okay, Dremel," said Lathe.

Dremel found what he had done to be quite amusing.

"Sorry for my friend's behavior, kids. Here's some money. Get yourselves some more caffeine and comic books."

The young men smirked with excitement, as Lathe had just handed them a hundred California dollars.

"Thanks!" the owner of the now vaporized drink shouted, as he headed to the coffee bar to order a new drink.

Meanwhile, Nate continued to absorb everything that was taking place as he relayed it back to Nanoflèche Headquarters, where techs in the Network Operations Center diagnosed the data and dispatched bots accordingly to be as close to Monte as possible. A middle-aged traffic officer sitting on his motorcycle saw several pairs of robots sprinting down the sidewalk before looking up at the Nanoflèche chopper hovering over the area.

The pressure began to wear on the kid. He made a dash for

it.

Although he was only four blocks from Hurlocke's offices, Monte took off in the opposite direction, hoping to lose them all in an alley, a cab, or a rail car. Maybe NTI or Porter would scoop him up. He wasn't sure, but he did know that he was getting sick and tired of being hounded by dozens of robots.

As the onset of dusk became more noticeable, Monte ran down crowded surface streets, but was unable to lose his android stalkers.

He had to think quick—which way to go? As he got to the end of another street, he darted into the crosswalk into heavier foot traffic, toward one of downtown Legaia's litro-rail transit system stops. A monorail made solely of magnetic light, the railway was what most people on the LISC used to travel Monday through Friday.

Monte hoped the population density or a rail car could give him the cloak he was looking for, but most of these bots had been told they'd be deactivated if they returned empty-handed, and even the village idiot android would pick life over death.

The kid sprinted through crowds and headed closer to the passenger loading platforms. A call came in from Porter as he ran.

"Kid, the fuck's going on? Are you okay?"

"Doc! They're houndin' me! Tons of 'em!"

"Where's Nate!?" the professor shouted.

"I lost him, but he's around here somewhere! What do these freaks want now?"

"I don't know, son, but keep losin' 'em. I've got every six on this rock en route to your position. They'll be there any minute. Hang in there!"

Just as he ended his phone conversation, he noticed a brilliant array of lights shining up from behind an office building next to him; he knew it could only be one thing.

"Nate!!"

Monte made a sharp left and ran even faster. Nate was in a fight, and those optical discharges were designed to give reinforcements a quick visual indicator of where help was needed.

Monte approached the last corner before Nate's area of operation. Simultaneously, an LPD officer on the scene radioed in for assistance.

"Code 2-0-3-November in progress. Send all available units, Over."

203N—(mayhem involving androids)—hadn't been used on Legaia until now.

As Monte got within a few feet of the corner, he drew his EMP pistol, but what he saw he couldn't believe.

Nate was standing in the middle of the street, both of his eyes glowing like white fire. He had surrounded himself with an energy sphere that was shielding him from all sorts of 'droids, surrounding him, attempting to strike him, throwing things at him, and just doing anything they could to harm him.

Monte felt something he had never felt before—an uncontrollable desire to help his non-human friend. This was a new sensation for Monte, regardless of his companion's make up. Everything else was irrelevant at this point. He had no idea Nate had such capabilities, but worried how long his crystals could support such behavior. He assumed they were in a major bind, and that he needed to make some moves.

Civilians clamored for safety, hiding inside stores, behind parked cars, any place they could find. As they ran into cafés and retail shops, the chaos intensified. Car alarms were blaring, and shouting could be heard every several seconds. It was now Monte, Nate, and a handful of NTI sixes, against a mob of mystery 'droids. Law enforcement raced to the scene, not sure what to make of it all, and even the LISC's Army National

Guard members were being summoned with news of the siege.

Nate's data feed was relayed to Lathe and Dremel through the NOC, and the two immediately sprang into action, sprinted through the café's exit, and ran down the street.

"Ummm, those dudes are weird…" said the victim of Dremel's magic trick.

As he sensed the danger becoming imminent, Monte broke away from the center of attention by making a quick dash into an alleyway, where the lifeless bodies of two downed 'droids lay still. He grabbed the first "droid and lifted it just high enough so that the back of its head was visible. Every android robot had an android identification number that displayed information about a "droid's model year, make, country of origin, and production number, just like a vehicle identification number.

Monte wasn't surprised to see that the AIN had been torched down and was completely illegible. He then flipped the 'droid to its side, hoping he'd be able to remove its back plate and access its main board, as there were also a few items on the back of the board that could help identify the metal corpse.

Nothing. The original data slabs had also been replaced with physically scarred and externally hacked replacements. This robot's identity had been deleted.

Several feet over, another 'droid lay face-first on the ground. After lifting the second one and discovering it too had been wiped of its identifying factors, he slammed the 'droid's lifeless body back to the ground. Hurlocke had made sure his trail was covered, and Monte was burning to find evidence linking this assault to the man he felt was responsible.

When the rear half of a crushed vehicle flew into the wall behind him, just a couple dozen feet from where he was standing, he knew he had overextended his stay and that it was time to keep moving.

The backup wasn't arriving quickly enough. Legaia wasn't equipped to defend against such an internal attack. No one would have expected something of this scale to happen so soon into its debut. The law enforcement simply couldn't keep up.

Even Nate began to look rushed and flustered. It was the first time he had been pressured in this manner. He took larger steps, dodging and evading everything those faceless droids were throwing his way. He had vowed never to let anyone hurt Monte again, and he was trying his damned best to keep his promise.

Nate called for Monte to come closer to him. He tried his best to join Nate at his side as quickly as he could. With Monte in his shadow, it appeared as though even the level eight had reached his breaking point.

Much to the surprise of every living being within half a mile of their position, Nate unleashed a digital scream that rattled the nerves of everyone in sight and then some, human or android. He planted his feet firmly, legs slightly wider than shoulder width apart for maximum stability. The droids closest to Nate were frozen, as if that scream had rattled them loose of their agenda. The soldiers and officers closest to Nate covered their eyes and their ears in a desperate attempt to shield themselves from the mysterious yet painful sound waves.

Randal had contacted all PULISC professors in the sciences with emergency instructions. He received a ping on his mobile device. When the professor looked down at his phone, he almost didn't believe what he was seeing. The page was alerting the professor that Nate's vitals had reached dangerous highs. His precious bot's liquid temperatures, CPU activity, and stress levels were off the charts.

"Oh, my poor boy...I hope the whirlwind forming inside of you doesn't sweep you off your feet...Hang in there, son..."

All the professor could do was stare at the data as he wished he were by Nate's side. He sent Nate an alert, but it didn't seem like the overwhelmed android was going to find the time to respond to anything other than the objectives at hand.

Nate began to emit pressurized, lavender-colored steam from a few different ventilation slits in his armor, the back of his neck, his shoulders, and just about every major joint in his body. At first, it appeared as though this release was a byproduct of overworked hardware.

Then, suddenly, he clenched both of his fists. With rage in his eyes, he tucked those fists underneath his arms and raised his elbows. Panels located in his arms retracted and a nozzle quickly shot out of each tricep, extending about six inches away from his body.

The disoriented onlookers were witnessing something with a magnitude unlike anything they were familiar with, and their shock was written all over their faces.

With chaos still taking place in the distance, Nate fired pulses of energy from the nozzles protruding from his arms that lit up the cityscape, incinerating anything they hit. He continued to annihilate every rogue android that happened to cross his visual path. The fiery yellow and white blasts of hot light shot out of his arms as if Nate was a monster that had been sleeping and was rudely awakened.

The bots in his line of fire dove for cover while several others further back stepped as far away as they could, too surprised to react. Closer insurgents, nearby shops, and vehicles were blown to shreds as Nate's energy pulses exploded with rapid fire, instantly decimating anything they came in contact with.

The world's most sophisticated android had developed capabilities that left even his founding father, a professor that thought he had seen everything, in awe and silence. Nate had become everything Randal had ever strived for with robotics, and the object of Hurlocke's wildest erotic fantasy.

Monte crouched and ducked behind his robotic companion as Nate continued to spew the sophisticated weapons fire from the exhaust nozzles in his arms. The unexpected retaliation finally gave Legaia's defenders on the ground some room to breathe, and more importantly, an opportunity to gain some ground. With the mystery 'droid squadron distracted and on the defensive, the civilians continued to run. Helicopters hovered over the ground, opening their cargo bay doors, allowing Legaia Special Weapons and Tactics officers to exit the craft, land on the ground, and provide heavy support fire that completely shifted the weight of the fight in Monte's favor.

The officers used conventional modern-day weaponry and equipment purpose-built for combating non-human enemies. After Nate's initial rage subsided, he was able to receive Randal's S.O.S.

Nate noticed the level of support that had arrived on the scene. Some of the opposition was even beginning to retreat. A few of Hurlocke's higher level droids were sending Richard informative feeds, but Hurlocke was too busy salivating over Nate's newfound capabilities to pay proper attention.

"This is precisely what I've been in need of. I'll recycle every piece of shit 'droid I own until I can have one with powers like those. You've refused to help me, yet you've given me more than I ever could have wished for. I'm going to get my hands on that toy eight of yours, and I'm going to raise hell with it," Hurlocke mumbled to himself in one of his many office suites. Whatever it was that gave Nate these abilities, Hurlocke wanted it, and bad.

Nate saw Monte reaching for his EMP pistol.

"No EMP from inside the sphere," said Nate sternly.

The boy took the hint, no further explanation was needed. The last thing Monte wanted to do was accidently roast the only thing keeping him from being taken captive, or even killed.

Monte stepped out of the sphere and obliterated three approaching droids with one shot of his pistol. He immediately jumped back in afterward and re-strategized.

With Nate's cannons exhausted, the onslaught was growing heavy again. He'd have to prioritize his rounds, destroying the elite of the bunch first. He stepped out once more from the protective sphere and took out two modified sixes before finding cover again. He stepped back in just in the nick of time, as a repurposed robot lunged toward him, hit the sphere, and fried himself on impact.

A large, jet-powered helo flew over the road. It appeared to be quite a bit larger than the average helicopter and was branded NTI. It hovered over and just behind Nate and Monte as a pair of steel cables thrown off the side of the craft hit the floor, which ten NTI sevens used to descend onto the playing field. As soon as they were done, the helo pulled up and away and headed back to NTI.

The customized sevens looked like a group of angry commandos from robot hell, and when they heard the concern in Randal's voice, they knew this event wasn't to be taken lightly.

They immediately moved forward, comms active, eyes glowing, and aligned themselves horizontally with Nate. Within milliseconds of one another, they opened fire with heavy assault rifles and machine guns with high capacity magazines and armor-piercing rounds.

Civilians had grown scarce, as most of them had either gotten out or were hiding. Lathe and Dremel peered down from a rooftop, waiting. They were elite soldiers, and they timed their attacks very efficiently, making sure to target the largest threats before engaging them.

More androids on the offensive clamored in from all sides of downtown—anything from ASG's equivalent of sixes from competing manufacturers to pathetic, refurbished fours that looked like they might have been thirty or forty years old.

Dozens of civilian-owned robots were starting to catch wind of the trouble downtown. They grabbed whatever they could—bats, crowbars, tools—and headed toward the action to help Monte and friends any way they could.

Eyes wide open, Monte stood inside the protective sphere, looking for opportunities where he could be of assistance. Every minute or so, NTI security team members would arrive at the area of operation, but for every handful of them, there'd be a dozen faceless enemy androids arriving as well.

From the corner of his eye, Monte noticed their enemies were beginning to flank them. He hopped out of the bubble and took aim at the ones that appeared to be more heavily armed, hoping Nate and the sevens would obliterate the weaker members of the rogue android army.

Monte whaled on the trigger and to his surprise, there were nothing but empty clicks. He dove back into the sphere. The sevens by his side heard the sound of his drained crystal mag and the one closest to him reached into a utility storage area embedded in his thigh and handed Monte a fresh crystal.

Monte hit his mag release and dropped a depleted crystal. Empty crystals smoked from the heat and lost their color. They made cute pet rocks for kids, but were otherwise useless.

He slammed the new crystal cartridge into his piece, pushed the slide forward, exited the bubble, and started shooting everything in sight. A little less wise with his ammunition. A little bit angrier.

Randal was still hiding out nearby, deciphering data feeds coming to him from several sources, including Nate, while summoning assets.

He called Ben Draifer's mobile and was surprised he was

able to get through amid the chaos.

"Ben!?" said Randal.

"I'm assuming you've heard about the shit storm going on downtown?" asked the Commander.

"Monte's down there, caught in the crossfire."

"I can evac the kid and Nate. I can set up a perimeter so that nothing else gets in or out of downtown, but I don't think I can be of much more help. Our best boys are already en route, and we're taking a beating."

Legaia's chief of police had instructed the entire force not to take sides in the event that androids became involved in this sort of conflict. This directive was in place mainly because Hurlocke had been making sizeable contributions to the force and stuffing the chief's pockets full on the side. Even if it was apparent which side was at fault, Commander Draifer was very hesitant to instruct police to engage in any particular course of action, other than the preservation of human life.

The doctor clenched his fist in frustration. He was all too familiar with the politics.

"Neither one of them will leave willingly anyway. Work on that perimeter. I'll call you back."

The Commander deployed everything at the department's disposal: vehicle units, motor units, air support, human and 'droid officers, riding the backs of robotic horses.

In the interim, Monte, Nate, a dozen sevens, and a few dozen specially programmed and highly trained sixes were dealing with hundreds of enemy droids, a force that was getting increasingly difficult to manage because they seemed to be multiplying exponentially, regardless of how many they were able to vanquish.

Nate monitored his vitals, heat, and energy levels, making sure not to push himself to a point that could cause failure. He was also monitoring the signature of every 'droid, vehicle, and aircraft that displayed aggression, all over downtown, while battling the immediate threats within his vicinity.

Monte sent a voice message to his professor: "Doc!? It isn't getting any easier over here! Uh, kinda running out of options!" By now, there were nearly as many enemy androids in Monte's area as there were lifeless android corpses, and no matter how much damage the resistance seemed to do, the attackers maintained their presence just as well.

"I think it would be best for you to request immediate extraction from this area, sir!" said Nate.

"Keep dreaming, buddy! I ain't going anywhere!" Monte fired off a few more rounds to find himself with an empty magazine again.

NTI 7-4 tossed him a fresh clip.

"Thanks!"

Meanwhile, The Commander had set up an impressive ring outside of the heart of the city. Nothing was getting through.

A single file line of light, armored vehicles appeared at the edge of the blockade. The lower-ranking members of the police force looked at each other, slightly stunned. On one hand, they had been instructed to set up a roadblock, while on the other hand, a small legion of military-grade combat vehicles was demanding to get through.

A police captain took a few steps over toward a building, looking around as if he wanted to make sure nobody was watching him. He put his finger to his ear as a vocal transmission came in. A few moments later, he instructed the men holding the barricade to make a hole and allow artillery to pass through. The men hesitated.

They knew something wasn't right, but they also liked to follow orders. They were good cops, but it was apparent there were other forces at work here.

"Make a hole. NOW!"

A few positions behind the lead vehicle sat a nimble tank with four small turret guns mounted on its roof. The turrets spun around in unison, as the fleet revved their engines.

Fearful and confused, the police complied.

Nate immediately sent the data of the ring breach back to Randal, who then called Ben.

"Change your mind?" asked Randal.

"About what?"

Randy quickly realized the Commander's intel was inferior to his.

"Look at your screen!"

Commander Draifer looked down at his tablet's screen. Randal had sent him a data plot, showing him small tanks and weaponized buggies were being allowed into the combat zone. Benjamin freaked out.

"How!?"

"You have a mole…Find those worms and take them in. Plug those holes! I gotta go!"

Several more strings of modern, near-military-grade vehicles approached the ring. Sometimes they were let through, and when they weren't, some muscled their way in.

The Commander began to wonder to himself how many others were in on this ploy. Was it an effort to eliminate NTI? A coup for the LISC? He immediately contacted his friends on Earth that he trusted and requested military assistance.

Suttridge caught wind of what was happening and broke out in a cold sweat. Legaia's successes since launch day were being flushed down the toilet.

Nate switched his vision to data mode. In low stress environments, his eyesight registered comparable to that of a human being's, but in more critical situations, he had the ability to cycle through several different sight modes. Night vision, heat vision, and data vision, an analytical mode which focused on pertinent data and imminent threats. When Nate sensed an influx of visual stimulation, this data mode would help him compute vast amounts of data more quickly and efficiently, but the temporary overclocking of his hardware also resulted in extra strain on his power sources, both crystal and non-crystal-based.

Nate had to expand the array of light beams he was using to mow down the droids, which would in turn drain his crystals at an even quicker rate. The weaponization of sevens and eights was something the doctor had lost sleep over, but in the end, he had always opted against it. Too dangerous, too many unknowns. Little did he know they would be able to develop some of those abilities through their own evolution.

They fought back and forth. A few sixes and a seven were down, but NTI hadn't suffered many losses otherwise. One cunning enemy 'droid hid behind reflective glass, which did a good enough job of helping him avoid detection.

7-2, Randal's second in command seven (essentially making him the third highest ranking 'droid in Randal's company), took a ray-blast to the back. He was down and out. His psyche was intact, but he'd need a new chassis.

7-1 immediately responded by obliterating the entire retail shop the 'droid had used for cover, leaving no chance for him to survive. He then quickly ran over to seven-2, ejected his data slabs, and inserted them into a storage slot in his chest cavity for safe keeping, hoping they'd be able to get back to NTI when this insane nonsense was over with and provide him with a new body.

The heavy artillery had now made its way into the heart of downtown, just around the corner from Nate and Monte. They shot out a few buildings, flexing their might. Intimidation tactics, whatever you'd like to call them. They were on a mission to pillage the place, with no concern regarding structures or lives, and they were getting ever closer to Porter's most valuable assets.

NTI was outfitted with equipment designed with security in mind. Dr. Porter had never commissioned enough resources to wage or defend an all-out battle.

The EMP pistols didn't carry a charge powerful enough to immobilize armored vehicles and aircraft of this caliber. A National Guard helicopter arrived with its own EMP cannon, far better suited for penetrating non-android threats. The activation of the cannon in turn deactivated its stealth mode, making the advanced helo significantly more susceptible.

The 6-SOACS (special operations airborne combat specialist) manning the helicopter primed the aircraft's EMP cannon. Just before it could let off a directed blast, one of the heavy assault vehicles shot a plasma pulse at the army helicopter, obliterating it.

7-2 was down, crystal power was questionable for all top level NTI forces, and Monte was trapped in a bubble, overwhelmed. Relentless droids on a mission were steadily increasing. Robots to their front. Robots to their flanks. And with a chain of enemy armored attack vehicles turning onto the road ahead of them, it was not looking good for Monte Cizek and friends.

A heavy-duty transport helicopter arrived on the scene, cloaked and shielded, and lowered four steel ropes to the ground. A dozen more sevens slid down the ropes, armed with prototype energy rifles.

After they touched down, the ropes retracted. All but one of the ropes, that is. The six in the cockpit then sent a ping to Monte and Nate, telling them it was time to go. They both realized the situation had grown dire and that they probably weren't going to get another opportunity to escape.

Monte eagerly grabbed hold of the rope.

"Nate! Let's go!"

Nate turned to 7-1 and stared him square in the eyes. 7-1 nodded, silently agreeing that it was best they got out of there. What would happen there without Nate's powers was unknown to the commanding seven, but he was more than aware of Nate's value to Randal, to Monte, to everybody.

Nate disengaged the sphere and quickly jumped and grabbed hold of the rope, just a few feet below where Monte was holding it. Once he had a secure grip, he re-engaged the sphere to provide them with additional protection while the helo got out of the densest of troubles.

Nate opened his chest cavity, exposing all eight of his data slabs. Although individually removable, he released the entire housing and placed it inside Monte's chest pocket.

"What the hell are you doing!?" asked Monte.

"I am afraid this is where my journey ends, brother."

47

Left With No Choice

The helicopter and NTI androids tasked with evacuation had successfully airlifted their two primary objectives out of immediate harm's way, as downtown Legaia continued to take a beating.

Monte and Nate dangled from steel-braided cables hanging from the rescue chopper.

"I have a solution, Monte!"

"No, you don't! You shut your hole! Whatever the fuck it is you're thinking right now, it's not an option! Do you hear me!? Don't you dare do anything stupid!"

"I have done the calculations, sir!"

"Don't fucking 'sir' me right now!"

Their vicinity to the aircraft's propulsion system made it difficult to hear, as they continued to shout back and forth to one another.

"The vehicles! We face an eighty-two percent chance of destruction! I do not like those odds for you!"

Something in Monte's gut gave him an inkling as to what it was that Nate had in mind.

"You listen to me real good! Tell a few of your recyclable friends to do it! We need you! I need you!" Monte desperately attempted to talk Nate out of whatever it was he was planning on doing.

"They are not built like I am, Monte! You know that! Father made me special! He built me for a moment like this! I am the only one that can help you! There is nothing I can say to calm your nerves! It is the human in you! My emotions are coded simulations! But you are the real thing, Monte! You have the power to change society! The future of mankind! For the better!

"I admire your will! I always have, Monte! Destroy what remains!"

"Code my ass! What if it doesn't work!? How do you know this is right!?"

"My replacement is standing by! You will not be alone for long!"

He wanted so badly to deliver the perfect response, but frustration began to get the best of him. He had to struggle to compose himself long enough to get any words out, much less deliver an appropriate statement.

"I won't forgive you for this!" shouted Monte, as he began to come undone.

Nate struggled to speak. Reality had finally caught up with him, proving death could be just as scary for an android as it was for some human beings.

"Do not make those your final words to me! I am more afraid than I have ever been!"

"Then why are you doing this!?" said Monte, half yelling, half crying.

"Because my love for you is greater than my fears! Goodbye, brother!"

"Nate!!"

And it was in that moment Nate's cellular state began to change as he self-nanofied, breaking himself down into hundreds of thousands of microscopic machines. Monte looked on in anguish as Nate's solid exterior slowly gave way, dissolving into a gray mist, starting from the outer edge of his torso and the bottom of his legs and working its way inward. Nate's face displayed determination, as bits and pieces of it shredded away and flew toward the battleground before dissipating. Monte could no longer watch. He turned away, resting his left cheek against his right bicep, as the helicopter carried him away to safety.

The nanobugs began infecting the enemy droids and vehicles. They crawled in through vulnerabilities, chewing through integral hardware and crucial cables. They damaged small, yet significant components, rendering the bots and vehicles lifeless.

Several moments later, the helicopter had reached a safe enough area where two specialized sixes were able to reel the cable in and lift the emotionally shattered young man into the helicopter. The droids tried to ensure he was alright physically, but Monte wasn't very cooperative.

The drastic leverage gained by Nate's nanofication afforded Monte's friends on the ground a chance to surge against the enemy invaders. The sixes and sevens rampaged against the remaining android soldiers. The sevens overwhelmed even the strongest enemy droids, and Lathe and Dremel systematically cherrypicked the group's leaders and took several key personnel alive, using their raw strength to aggressively pummel and crush key enemy assets. They placed small but highly explosive devices atop key components within the enemy mobile command center, destroying them, and stood guard as NTI's forces began to perform a full evacuation. Filing into cargo helos and armored buses, and heading back to NTI and PULISC to visit treatment camps that had been sprung up using tents and cots. Doctors, nurses, technicians and mechanics, began providing medical care for humans, and repairing NTI's androids.

Having realized the onslaught was over, the professor sat in his car, emotionally drained and confused. Nate's data feed was now offline, and there was far too much information for one man, regardless of his intelligence or experience, to dissect. With a look of defeat on his worried face, the professor pondered his future, the future of his companies, and most importantly, the future of his heir.

48

Painful Sun

With Legaia's afternoon sun effect shining through the horizontal blinds, Dr. Porter stood near the window of his PULISC office, the same office he had used to conjure up the majority of his conceptualizations, before turning the NTI Eight into a reality.

He paced back and forth, admiring the downtown Legaia skyline and staring into his tablet.

"It could be an injury, damage to his gigaman card. Hell, might even be nothing more than a one-off glitch...need for a reboot...Fuck..."

The professor considered alternate possibilities, anything to take his mind off the fact that Nate's communications were offline and showing zero signs of activity, like a flatline on an EKG. He prepared himself for the worst.

Shortly afterward, Monte gently knocked on the professor's door a couple times and peeked into the office. He was hesitant to enter. Professor Porter turned his head toward the door to see who his visitor was, and the look on Monte's face told a story worth a thousand words. There'd be no explanation necessary. The doctor's suspicions had been confirmed. His pride and joy, Nathaniel, was gone.

The professor stood with his back facing the room, sad but smiling, looking out of his office window, down upon the streets, where Nate had stepped out of the lab and into the world for the first time, mesmerized by it. The memory of his elation that day was still potent.

Monte waited a good while, not wanting to disrupt the professor, before he spoke.

"I can come back later if you'd like…"

Dr. Porter tried his best to avoid eye contact with Monte, as he wiped the tears off of each of his cheeks, attempting to mask his emotions.

"No…stay. No sense in giving you the boot. You're all I have left…"

Monte was afraid to speak. He felt like there was nothing he could say, and that any mention of Nate would probably take them both to places they didn't want to go.

"Please tell me you didn't come by yourself," said the professor, as he attempted to ease the tension in the room.

"No. I'm with Lathe, Dremel, seven-four, and seven-five. They're posted up…nearby."

"Good," said Randal with a sigh of relief.

"I'm guessing what Nate did wasn't your idea," said Monte.

"Why are you still talking from the doorway…get in here, kid."

Monte hadn't noticed he was still standing in the doorway. He took a seat on a comfortable chair that was next to an end table covered in robotics journals. Monte looked like he wanted to speak, but had nothing to say. He stared blankly at the floor in front of the professor's desk.

"Kid..."

"Yeah Doc..."

"I know what he meant to you. Because he meant the same to me. It wasn't easy for me to give him up in the first place, to give him to you, but I did it anyway, because I wanted you to be safe. I wanted you to be able to walk down the street without having to worry about punks, drones, bots or tyranny's minions."

"He's gone. No sense in dwelling on it. He kicked some ass though. Tore down a small army. And his efforts will be appreciated for a long time to come."

Monte sounded collected as he responded, even though a tear was streaming down the left side of his face.

"He gave me all his data slabs.....Can I bring him back?"

"Something like him. Today if you wanted to. Him? No."

"You know what, Doc, screw it. I'm not letting Hurlocke win. If Nate were here right now, he'd want me to be strong as ever. And that's what I'm going to do. That walking pile of circuits was my brother, my best bud. And every fucking thing I do from here on out will be in his memory. In his honor. There's no time to be sad. We have work to do."

"We sure do, kid," replied his professor, as he continued to gaze into the afternoon light.

49

Rise And Shine

Legaia's streets were quiet. The restaurants and retail outlets were closed for business, with sheets of plywood or aluminum up for windows in many instances. Sidewalks were caked in shards of glass and burnt scraps.

Cleanup crews were working around the clock, hauling away entire electric dump trucks full of garbage, rubble, and wrecked android components. Legaia's mayor, along with officials from the Department of Public Works, surveyed the area and spoke with journalists, while others photographed the landscape for use in damage assessment reports.

Monte and his professor hung out in Randal's office. Keeping themselves occupied was a good idea.

"What's going to come of our...floating home away from home?"

"That's up to you...but for the shit you can't help or shouldn't spend your days helping, I've made a few phone calls."

"What type of phone calls?" inquired Monte.

"Since shit's a little bit crazier up here than we had originally anticipated, I've brought the Legaia Council together for a day-long event, and I'm basically gonna lay it all out there, tell them exactly what this place needs. At least one hundred more police officers, more restrictions on who can buy what, and in what quantities. More tracking, more accountability. You get the idea. This place is newer than other cities, and it's different from other cities. And with that will come its fair share of growing pains."

"Growing pains? More like never ending paralysis…amputations," Monte chimed in.

"Can't argue with you there, but I do want you to keep something in mind. Nate is gone, but knowing him as well as I did, I can assure you, he left fulfilled. Entirely. Between his assignment to you and the impact he had on his final day, he went out doing exactly that which he longed to do. It's what he wanted all along. To be important. To matter."

Monte let the professor's message soak in. He was starting to view Nate's departure in a more positive light, thanks to the professor's sentiments.

"Listen, kid…I need you to take these."

"What are they?"

"The keys to the other eights."

"Didn't think I'd need them so soon."

"Go to my NTI offices in L.A. Most of the staff there knows you and if they don't, show them the message on the keys. There will be no further questions.

"The key itself has a power switch. Flip it, and it'll show you how to get to the others. There are five more. Take what you need. Save some for a rainy day. That's assuming you can fathom a shit storm filthier than the one we're in now."

"One at a time. I can't handle more than that," Monte said,

overwhelmed.

"Fine by me. Preferred, actually. Eight-Two is a lady. Don't do anything naughty to her, Cizek. I'm watchin' you."

"Huh…interesting. When should I go?"

"Well, you can either sit here and watch the construction crews put Legaia Boulevard back together at a snail's pace, or you can get your ass to Los Angeles. Take the boys. No traveling alone from here on out. Ever."

"What's her name?"

"Kindra."

"Kindra…I'll be back ASAP. See you soon, Doc."

"See ya, kid."

And just like that, he was off.

Once tasked with an objective, Monte had a one-track mind. He jogged down the hallway, looking for his chaperones.

"Lathe, Dremel."

They turned around with looks of intent upon their faces.

"We're going to Los Angeles to get another eight."

"Do we get to stick around and party afterwards?" replied Dremel.

"I wouldn't get rid of you guys if I had a hundred eights."

"Fair enough, let's do this."

Dremel was relieved to discover the activation of another eight didn't imply the end of his and Lathe's current mission.

"Seven-four and seven-five, please stay with the professor, regardless of what he says."

"With joy, sir," replied the disciplined seven.

The three of them hit the street and took an autonomous ride to NDT, in case his enemies were aware of the armored sedan he now owned.

The professor stayed in his office and prepared for the worst as he dug through his desk's drawers, rounding up anything he felt needed safeguarding. Dr. Porter had always taken an overly cautious approach to his work and its pertinent details, but considering what had just taken place in downtown Legaia, it was time for him to take security and secrecy to the next level.

50

It's A Girl!

Upon arriving in Los Angeles, Monte, Lathe, and Dremel wasted no time heading straight to NTI's headquarters to retrieve Kindra, the next level eight android slated for activation.

"We'll stand guard on opposing ends of this complex. You get in there and rescue your android princess," said Lathe.

"Sounds good...I'll be right back." Monte took a deep breath and entered the building's main entrance where he was immediately stopped by an armed security bot.

"Identification, please."

"I'm Monte Cizek."

"Your face does not register in my databank."

"I'm a good friend of the professor's."

"I cannot grant you access."

"Is that one of yours?"

The guard turned and looked into the building and Monte immediately stabbed it in the back of the neck with a small blade.

Urgency, frustration, and desperation were clouding his judgement.

Unfortunately for Monte, the disabling of that guard triggered an alarm that would put every guard in the building, human or bot, hot on Monte's trail.

"Oh, great," said Monte, as sirens and red strobe lights filled the lobby.

He ran down the hall to a t-intersection, vaguely remembering the path to the doctor's office from his last visit to NTI's L.A. offices. Quickly realizing the elevator he had called would take what would seem like a lifetime, he continued to run, bending around another corner to the right. Having found the door to the nearest staircase, he turned the knob while ramming it open with his right shoulder.

The sounds of heavy boots and android feet clanked off the metal staircase about a floor and a half beneath him. Monte reached the top of the staircase. In a mad dash, he continued to run down the long hallway that led to the professor's office. He made it about two thirds of the way there before he was ambushed by several guards with their weapons drawn.

"Raise your arms at once!"

Monte lifted his hands into the air, asking the group, "Which one of you is human?"

One of the guards responded, "I am."

"Scan this badge. Randy gave it to me." Monte said, quickly.

The quick motion Monte had made to retrieve the badge caused one of the security droids to yell,

"Freeze!"

The kid complied.

"You can come get it if you want…I'm not here for trouble. You can call Randal if you need to."

The human security supervisor responded. "Go ahead, show

me."

Monte removed the badge from his jean pocket. He held out a small slate of glass about the size and thickness of a credit card. The android security team member removed the badge from Monte's hand and used the scanning capability embedded in his eyes to read it.

Upon being scanned, a holographic image began shining out of the badge. It was Randal.

Grant level 4 access to the human male named Monte Artaxias Cizek. Effective immediately - no expiration. Charlie, Echo, Oscar, Romeo, Papa, November, Tango, India.

"Stand still, sir," said the human guard. Monte complied.

His robotic counterpart initiated a retinal scan. He came within a foot of Monte's face and stared into Monte's eyes.

"Monte Cizek, Legaia International Space Colony," said the robot.

"Thank you, Mr. Cizek. We apologize. This hasn't happened before and things are a little crazy right now. It's nice to meet you. Please proceed," said the security team lead.

"Thank you."

The alarm systems turned off and the guards returned to their designated posts.

Monte felt better. It had been a minute since his last sensible conversation.

He had located one of the things he was searching for — the room containing the half dozen android eight incubators.

The chamber labeled "1" was the only chamber whose door number wasn't backlit. His heart sank a bit, his focus temporarily derailed, but he remembered why he came. The entire trip to the facility had been filled with waves of mixed emotion.

"Keep movin', dude," he muttered to himself.

He had a good idea of what Nate would say to him right now

if he were still alive and by his side, and that thought gave him all the energy he needed to carry on.

Monte walked over to the chamber labeled "2", assuming correctly that this was where Kindra would be. He pulled out a keychain with six data drives on it. They were also numbered. He selected the small glass storage device about the size of a stick of chewing gum labeled "II" and swiftly inserted it into the appropriate slot. The chamber asked for simultaneous ocular and palm scans.

"Not again," he whined to himself.

With his identity confirmed, the chamber sounded.

"Authorization complete. Kindra, online. Booting."

"*Here we go.*"

He was very curious to see what was going to come out of that storage chamber. He paced back and forth for four and a half minutes as Kindra's operating system was installed, as well as some other applications hand-picked by Professor Porter. Finally, the door cracked open from the bottom before opening upward, and there she was.

She stepped out, and Monte was pleasantly surprised to find such an aesthetically pleasing android. Kindra was in many ways similar to Nate. The first differentiators came in gender and appearance. She was six feet tall, like Nate had been, but nimble, appearing light on her feet. Her casing contained a nano-infused copper-titanium hybrid and gold plating near her heat-generating regions. These elements gave her body armor primarily copper and gold hues with magenta accents.

She was attractive, if you were into that sort of thing. And above all, she was a technological powerhouse, outfitted with the latest computer hardware and proprietary components not available outside of Nanoflèche Technologies.

The only difference internally was that she had more expansion slots and bays than Nate did. Even though her frame wasn't as large as Nate's, advancements had allowed for smaller internal components, which actually increased her upgradeability.

Monte smiled. He saw a bit of Nate in her facial movements. Maybe it was just wishful thinking, stemming from missing his pal.

"One of only two faces I'd wanna see crawlin' out of that cell. Where the hell have you been?' said the feisty robot.

"Ummm...I dunno?"

"Well quit standing there like a prepubescent dweeb. Load me up!"

Monte was flustered.

"With what?"

"Crystals, dummy! Prodigy, huh? Come on!"

Monte couldn't believe how sharp she was out of the box—a spitfire with a lot of information for a newborn.

"*You must have had a feed from Nate or Doc while asleep,*" thought the kid as he took his book bag off.

She stepped out of that chamber ready to go, like she was older and wiser than Nate, and a whole lot spunkier.

Monte quickly unzipped his old, trusty backpack and removed a new battery to plug into her primary qorlithium bay and a pair of the highest grade crystals in his possession. He didn't know much about these remaining eights as far as how different they would be from Nate. He installed everything in under a minute.

"We gotta go." she said immediately.

"What's the rush?"

She had run out of the room before he was done with his sentence.

"Thanks a lot, Doc!" he joked out loud as he chased her down, already aware that unlike Nate, this one was going to be a handful.

51

I Left You A Little Something...

"Wait up!" shouted Monte.

"In here, quick."

Kindra was ready to pick up right where her predecessor had left off.

"Drama's coming, and I haven't quite evolved into a photon-cannon-shooting, spherical-shield-emitting phenom yet. We gotta get in, get the bracelets, and get the hell out."

"And I thought Claire was a dictator," Monte said under his breath, as he scrambled to follow her instructions.

"You can mumble as softly as you'd like. I can still hear you," said Kindra, and she continued toward Randal's office at a brisk pace.

"Oh, I was just whispering about how beautiful you look today," he said as he chased after her.

"You can't sweet talk an eight either. Get it together, Cizek!"

Before they had a chance to exchange additional banter, they arrived at the lab containing the vault Randal had told Monte about. Monte took the glass badge he had shown security earlier back out from his packet. He admired it for a quick second before sliding it into the insertion slot on the glass double doors leading to the office. Not only did the door's lock disengage, but the badge had another message for him.

"Go through the office to the back. You'll find a small vault. Follow the prompts. Take a copy of the data slabs. Leave a set for later. And wear the bracelets...Hope they're good to you."

Monte appreciated the concise nature of his professor's communication.

"I'll hold my position just inside this lab door. Go, now." said Kindra.

As he jogged through the various parts of his professor's office, something stopped him dead in his tracks—a photograph on the wall of a team of scientists at a ribbon-cutting ceremony, including a much younger Randal Porter and an equally young Chris Cizek.

The doctor's arm was placed around Chris's shoulder. They were both quite proud, and it seemed as though the two were celebrating the completion or debut of some sort of project they had been working on together.

Monte realized he was getting caught up in the moment and wasting precious time. He forced himself to leave the photo and his emotions behind, as he continued with his agenda.

As he continued toward his objective, he passed a lab filled with all sorts of nandroid parts, demo models, design concepts, and most of the projects currently and previously in development by NTI. It was all there.

Monte wanted so badly to stay behind and spend hours admiring all of the work, but he had to find the strength to press on. Finally, he approached the vault and entered the badge.

"Prepare for retinal scan."

Monte held still.

"Monte Cizek, Legaia International Space Colony," the vault

announced.

"Place hand inside scanner."

This wasn't standard, but the message at the door said to follow the prompts, and so he gladly followed the protocols.

As soon as Monte was wrist deep into the device, it grabbed hold of him, securing his arm. He reacted with resistance and confusion, and into Monte's forearm went a needle.

"Stand by for analysis."

The machine took a fluid-ounce blood sample from Monte, ran a quick battery of scans on it, and released his arm.

"Identification scan complete."

The door to the vault cracked open.

Monte took the bandage that had been dispensed and placed it over the needle's insertion point, still slightly shocked by how invasive the ID process was. He saw a beam of blue light shining through the crack in the heavy steel door, as he grabbed the sturdy handle and pulled it open.

Just as Dr. Porter had advised, there were two sets of data slabs and a pair of completely foreign bracelets.

Monte took one set of slabs and placed them into his bag. Then he turned back and looked at the bracelets. They were unlike anything in existence, forged using nanites and several rare metals not used in any existing bots.

"Don't question Doc..." he reminded himself.

Monte grabbed a bracelet and slid it over his hand. He picked up the second one, looked it over inside and out, took a deep breath, and threw it on.

Instantly, he was stuck with jarring pain. The bracelets lit up and dug into his wrists, changing shape and bonding with his flesh.

" *Why did I do this!?"* he thought. He was angry, grabbing his forearms in anguish while he endured the suffering.

A tear cascaded down Monte's cheek, partly due to the pain

and partly due to the uncertainly associated with the situation. This was a rarity for Monte. Crying was a rarity for Monte.

His breath was rapid. He groaned and grunted as he attempted to breathe through the discomfort, and so he leaned his back against the nearest piece of furniture he could find, as sweat trickled down his forehead.

The pain let up. The fiery sensation ceased and his breath returned to normal. Monte looked down at his hands. Had he made a terrible mistake? He couldn't have. He trusted his professor more than he trusted anyone else, and here he sat, wondering why the professor would put him through such agony.

With a big gulp, he swallowed his inhibitions and stood up. It still stung a bit, but for the most part, the ordeal was over.

He jogged back to entry door where Kindra had promised to wait for him.

"What happened to you?" she inquired.

"I grabbed the keys Doc left for me and these bracelets…"

"Were they supposed to fry your wrists like that?"

"You're the supercomputer with arms and legs, you tell me."

Kindra picked up on the fact that Monte was genuinely upset and attempted to ease his discomforts a bit.

"I'll take a look at it in a bit. I'll figure it out. We'll figure it out," she reassured him.

52

Laurens Von Hapsburg

Upon discovering that Laurens had been sent to an NTI storage facility in Long Beach to secure additional androids, Monte and Kindra moved quickly to another corner of NTI's HQ, hoping they'd be able to use one of Randal's personal aircraft to get to Long Beach and intercept Hurlocke's henchman.

"Would you guys mind staying here and guarding the eights?"

Lathe nodded quickly and said, "Done" while Dremel primed the action on his assault rifle and began jogging toward his desired position.

"Can you fly? I've got a few calls to make." Monte asked his new companion.

"Like an ace!" responded Kindra.

"Take us to Laurens."

Kindra engaged all of the necessary switches, pulled the aircraft out of a garage, and used its VTOL capabilities to head straight for Long Beach.

Monte hit a few switches from the co-pilot's seat, which altered the aircraft's shape, preparing it for more efficient forward flight.

"I think that's fast enough!" said Kindra.

A communication came in on the digital radio.

"This is Staff Sergeant Wes Scott of the California Air Force. You are traveling at inappropriate speeds. Please verify your identity."

Monte was being contacted by military personnel for good reason. He hadn't bothered to contact air traffic control, and Kindra had been so focused on the objectives at hand that it had also slipped her mind.

"*Ah, crap,*" Monte thought.

"This is Monte Cizek. I apologize for the alarm. I will be landing in Long Beach to attempt to prevent the theft of top secret nanotechnology that is currently being threatened."

The Sergeant on the radio shook his head in disbelief.

"Roger that, Monte. Can we get a heads up next time? For crying out loud…"

"Sorry. It's been a tad bit hectic here today."

"Carry on. Let us know if we can help. Over and out."

"Thank you!" he replied.

"Almost there." added Kindra.

They made every attempt to reach the NTI warehouse as fast as possible. Meanwhile, Laurens power-walked the streets of industrial Long Beach. In the early evening light, he approached the sidewalk that ran along NTI's warehouse. With his black trench coat flapping behind him and a look of anger upon his face, he approached one of the security gates that led to the Nanoflèche property.

An android guard in a security kiosk next to the gate spotted Laurens.

"Hello. Please state the nature of your visit."

"I'm here to destroy everything that crosses my path in an inevitable quest for world domination." replied the henchman with a faux smile.

"Access denied. You will now be detained for further ques…"

Laurens interrupted the guard's speech with a vicious strike to the android's neck using a collapsible electric staff. With the android unconscious, face down against the kiosk's dashboard, Laurens opened a panel on its back and ripped the 'droid's battery out. He then used his foot to disrespectfully move the robot away from the monitors in the kiosk and onto the floor.

"That's no way to greet a guest now, is it?" muttered Laurens to himself as the disabled android's body slid onto the floor. From there, Laurens had a clear view of other important doors and walkways around the complex. He also had a visual on a few other security desks he'd have to clear on his way to the stockrooms that housed complete NTI nandroids, ready for shipment to customers.

He reached into one of his coat's pockets and removed a small, rectangular explosive device. Once it was armed, he stuck it onto the interior of the kiosk, before making his way toward the main buildings.

Monte and Kindra approached the facility, putting Randal's bird onto the ground with a vertical landing.

Monte thanked Kindra for the brisk and smooth transit.

"No problem, Chief. Now let's try to find that freak Laurens before he makes out like a bandit."

"Took the words right out of my mouth."

53

Swiss Cheese

Monte was glad for the easy flight, but he wondered what would happen when they encountered Laurens Von Hapsburg.

They climbed down from the aircraft as it went through its cool-down sequence. The howl of the engines wound down, as Kindra quickly assessed which route would be best. She hit the ground before Monte did.

"Quick, Monte, let's go, let's go."

"Roger," said Monte, ad he took shelter in her shadow.

They ran off the open pavement and headed toward the NTI building that handled regional logistics.

At the main entrance, they found two dismembered and malfunctioning level five android security guards. Not exactly a heartwarming sight.

Kindra was taken aback by the wreckage a bit more than Monte was.

"Get used to it, lady," said Monte, jaded by everything that had transpired since the inception of the LISC.

289

She regained her focus and continued, following Monte.

Meanwhile, Laurens was already on the fifth floor, having his way with the guards. He seemed inhuman, almost zombie-like, not necessarily in appearance, but in the way he was impervious to pain. He threw a low-grade security 'droid into a nearby wall. Laurens was some sort of seventeenth-century-henchman-resembling-science-experiment on steroids.

Monte called for the elevator. The button did not respond. Pathway lights embedded in the base moldings turned red, and he realized the building had just been put under some sort of emergency standby mode in which only minimal elements of the structure were functional.

"Stairs!" he said abruptly.

They continued to the staircase. Not many were aware of this, but the doors leading to Randal's office at this location were virtually impenetrable while the building was in emergency lockdown. Only the badges that Monte and Randal possessed would reinitiate the building's full functionality and grant access to the doors that led to the newest nandroids. Laurens' brute force in trying to pry and push his way into these valuable rooms would prove to be futile.

As the two got closer to his location, Kindra opened her mouth and fired a directed warning shot in the form of highly concentrated, ear-drum torturing sound waves. Monte was close in tow.

Laurens ceased his efforts and turned toward Kindra and Monte, as the red, pulsating glow illuminated his sinister smile.

"That's right, boy. Make your girlfriend do your dirty work!" shouted the hit man for hire.

"Like you do for your boyfriend?"

This statement further frustrated Laurens. Monte looked toward Kindra.

"You can fight, right?"

"I think so!" she replied, sarcastically.

She entered a not-so-cute mode. The whites of her eyes glowed brightly, like Nate's had done at one point. She clenched her fists and began to run toward Laurens.

Monte took a few steps back, smart enough to know he was no match for the vindictive mercenary.

Kindra did a bit of showboating as she bobbed, weaved, and flipped, enjoying her newly discovered pneumatics while executing maneuvers to confuse Laurens. She had inherited all of Nate's combat training, but weighed less than he did.

Laurens threw heavy swings at Kindra, but was unable to connect.

Realizing his fists were no match for her agility, Laurens reached into his coat and removed the short rod he had re-holstered. Upon full activation, the rod expanded compartmentally into a six-foot staff, before it lit up with an electric charge. Laurens grinned like a mad scientist, eager to use his lightning toy to inflict some damage.

High dosages of electricity were certainly not a nanobot's friend. They were capable of damaging data banks, and the data loss could be something vital, like a hand-to-hand combat program, for example.

The smirk on Laurens' face widened, the way any ghoul's face would upon smelling even the faintest scent of victory.

Kindra took a few precautionary steps backward. None of them had ever seen this shock-stick staff before. And why wasn't it hurting him? Perhaps the gloves he was wearing made him immune to the effects of the electric charge. They couldn't be sure.

He swung it at her with rage. He had yet to put a scratch on her, and his patience was growing thinner. At the same time, Kindra wasn't exactly sure what the effects of being hit with it would be, so she absolutely focused on avoiding contact with the weapon.

Laurens flung it at her again in various attacks, and each time she managed to either hop out of its way, dodge it, duck it, or lean away from it.

In another surprising move, he twisted the staff apart at the center, creating two three-foot-long shock sticks, as he seemed to be running out of options, growing increasingly angry.

Kindra engaged in more of a defensive role. Harming others, even when provoked, was never a nandroid's primary objective, but Kindra had inherited enough information from her older brother to know that this instance was a rare and justified exception.

It had slipped the space cadet's mind that he still had nine rounds in his concealed .45. Monte pulled the carbon fiber and steel pistol from the holster at the small of his back. He lined up his sights and starting whaling on the Swiss monster, but after being hit with a couple of fully-metal-jacketed rounds, Laurens used his light sticks in an elaborate fashion to protect himself from the gunfire.

Realizing the young man's magazine was empty, Laurens removed a metallic bolas-throwing weapon from a pocket inside his long black coat. Without any warning, he hurled the bolas at Monte. An instinctive response caused the young man to block his face with his forearms, as the weapon bound his arms together and knocked him to the floor.

Von Hapsburg turned and started walking briskly toward Monte with intent. Wanting to make sure he didn't harm Monte, Kindra jumped onto his back, wrapping her arms around Laurens's neck with a sophisticated chokehold that brought Laurens to his knees. She swung her leg around his neck and used her weight to bring him down onto his back. Seamlessly, she shifted her position, grabbing his arm and placing it in an arm bar, before brutally snapping it out of place.

With maximum efficiency, she capitalized on his pain, delivering a swift kick to the jaw of Von Hapsburg, dislocating it. Kindra acrobatically stood up the way a martial arts master would, cocked her legs, and back-flipped onto the other side of Laurens's body. With no hesitation, she dropped down to the floor and repeated the excruciating submission move on his other arm. This time, she tore the arm completely off.

Monte had wiggled his way closer to the wall and sat up, as he attempted to loosen the constraints of the bolas.

Kindra mounted Von Hapsburg's torso, almost possessed, knowing full well her prey was beyond wounded, and that victory was well within her grasp. She had used a variety of wrestling tactics straight out of a Jiu-Jitsu handbook to physically impair and severely weaken one of Hurlocke's strongest men.

Laurens displayed spasms, shot sparks, smelled of burnt, frayed wires, and spoke with a digital stutter in his speech.

"A mortal and his ZZZZZ metallic pet. Oh, I feel ZZZZZ for your ignorance. You cannot destroy what I am, what ZZZZZ I represent. This, ZZZZZ, is immortal!"

He concluded his boisterous rant, while spitting out considerable amounts of lubricant after finishing his sentence.

"I knew you were a fucking bot..." said Monte, still seated at a safe distance.

She spent the next several seconds considering Laurens's fate. She turned, looking to Monte. With his arms still bound, he gave her a nod, agreeing with Kindra's desire to terminate the henchman for good.

Still sitting over her victim, Kindra cocked her right arm back as far as she could and shouted with rage: "Ahhhhh!"

She belted out a vicious war cry, pinning Von Hapsburg's neck to the floor with her free hand, ensuring her target would remain stationary, as she drove her fist through the tyrant slave's head, denting the floor underneath it, absolutely pulverizing Laurens's head, and leaving a pile of mangled circuitry where a well-concealed, humanized android face once lay.

Monte sat with his head against the wall as he looked on, partially in awe. Not because it wasn't what needed to be done, but rather because it just hadn't been done before. Not in this fashion, not to this degree, and not by an NTI 'droid. Nate's display was different; it was a fight to preserve all of Legaia, but Kindra had singlehandedly dismantled a very high-tech and expensive humanoid 'droid. She had been so bubbly before. All the kid saw in her right at this moment was a killing machine.

Monte finally managed to free his forearms from the confines of the bolas and ran over to Kindra. Her eyes returned to normal, as she exited her primal state.

"Are you okay?" he asked.

"Yeah, I'm fine. Just gonna need a charge soon, that's all." She sounded tired.

"I...I wasn't expecting you to do, well...that! He looked over at Laurens' mutilated robot corpse.

"Yeah, well, that wasn't exactly plan A, per se," she told him.

Monte got a message from the professor and it read, "Be there soon."

Kindra took a seat on the floor, resting her back against the hallway's wall as Monte joined her. They stared at the ground together, which was now covered in a combination of strange fluids and metal fragments.

"What was that? Judo?" asked Monte, attempting to lighten the mood.

"No, Kindra," she replied with a smirk. She examined her arms, checking to make sure nothing had been damaged, rubbing her forearm.

"Are you sure you're okay?" he inquired again.

"Yeah…just…tired."

She was running on the tail-end her reserve battery.

"Soon as we talk to Doc, we'll take you home for a nap, okay?"

"'Kay…I kicked his ass pretty good though, didn't I?"

"To say the least, yes. Yes you did."

The fight had definitely worn her out. She needed a solid eight hours in the charging bay, and her crystals needed to be tested and most likely replenished.

Just then, the professor came through the door, slowing down at first sight of the carnage.

"Hey Doc," said Monte as he stood up.

"Did she do this?" asked Randal.

"Yeah…he was coming after me and…she stopped him. She's taxed though. I wanna get her out of here for a charge ASAP. Clean myself up while I'm at it."

"Yeah, no problem. You sure you don't wanna stay? Do that here?"

It wasn't very often the Doctor attempted to do some persuading.

"I'd rather get out of here right now, to be honest. I've had my fair share for today."

"Fair enough. You two get out of here. I'll get this place cleaned up and…try to figure this out."

Monte helped Kindra up, slung her arm around his neck to help her walk, and headed to a local hotel to reenergize his companion and engage in some much needed rest and relaxation.

Noticing Laurens's feed had gone dark, Hurlocke sent a text from his phone to one of the "data companies" he had been working with.

"Play time is over. Execute 'Blood Moon' immediately. Half

of the contracted payment has been sent, second half to follow upon completion."

"Let's see your fancy robots stop this," he said under his breath, as he stripped his phone of its power supply, grabbed his coat and keys, and headed for the door.

54

Gather Round, Children

On most nights, Monte was a sound sleeper. But he was having a hard time staying asleep on this particular night, after Laurens and Kindra's encounter.

He'd gotten a couple hours in, and Kindra was halfway replenished. Monte lay in the soft, king-sized bed, doing nothing more than thinking. He looked over at Kindra and had a strange epiphany. One of those rare moments when for a few seconds, he'd question the validity his own reality. He sat motionless, in awe of what he had witnessed and where his life had taken him.

Then his phone rang.

"*The hell?*" he thought. He seldom got calls at this hour. When he answered, Randal was on the other line.

"Doc?" he asked.

Upon the completion of clean up in Long Beach, Dr. Porter went to NTI HQ to turn in for the evening. Not long after going to bed, the professor's phone rang. He grabbed his eye glasses from the desk next to his cot, turned on a lamp, and answered.

"You rang, kid?" inquired Randal.

Monte also turned on a few lights in his room, without making it too bright.

"No…Did you?" responded Monte.

A few seconds later, a voice came on the line. It was their California Air Force Space Command point of contact, Staff Sergeant Scott.

"Monte, Randal, do you copy?"

"This is Randy, Sarge. Everything alright?"

"No, sir. We've detected a missile launch off a sub in the Pacific. Systems show it's on a path straight for NTI HQ. Please tell me you're not there right now?"

Monte continued to listen to the phone call with undivided attention. Kindra picked up on his vitals and woke as well.

"I am, actually…Umm, how bad are we talkin' here?" said the Professor, relatively calmly.

"Fewer than 2.5 minutes."

"Fuck me," said the Doctor.

"I've already scrambled a pair of fighters, not sure if they'll make it in time though, sir…"

"No worries…thanks, Sarge."

As soon as the Airman disconnected, Randal pressed a series of buttons on his phone. He got up, threw on a pair of leather flip flops and a lab coat, and headed toward the android eight bays.

"Doc?" said Monte abruptly with fear in his voice.

"Yeah, kid?"

"Run!" Monte shouted.

"Not this time. Dodged 'em long as I could. Did a pretty damn good job, too."

"What!!?? What are you doing!?"

"You've got the strength of a superhero, son. I know you'll

298

make us proud."

Monte's lips quivered.

"Where are you going?" he asked with tears in his eyes and sorrow in his voice.

"'Bout to say hi to my babies. Be good, Monte. Stay out of trouble, yeah? Be the best Monte you can be. Don't forget everything we've talked about. 'Whatever it takes,' right?...Love ya, kid."

Randal knew what he wanted to do with only moments left on this Earth. He couldn't imagine leaving a core aspect of his life's work without saying goodbye.

"Doc!?" Monte sat by in horror, fearing Randal had hung up. He hadn't.

With the call still active, Dr. Porter slid his phone into the breast pocket of his lab coat.

He had a somber look of intent on his face, as if he had seen this moment before, in his imagination and in his dreams. His actions were orchestrated. He knew what he was doing. He was prepared.

Knowing what he knew about his professor, Monte was certain Randal wouldn't be coming back on the line.

Regardless of the time, Monte frantically pinged his friend Renato, NTI's Information Technology Director. Renato's abilities in the world of cybersecurity were nothing shy of phenomenal. (He'd used these same talents to land his gig with NTI in the first place, when the professor had put out a $CAL1,000,000 reward to anyone who could gain full control of his seven when the model range was first introduced to the public back in '75.) Monte pressed his finger to his earpiece to ensure the clearest communication possible.

"Hello, Monte?" said the technologist, groggily.

"Renato!"

"Yes, it's me Monte, what is wrong?" replied Renato

inquisitively in his thick accent.

"Get to a keyboard now! Randal's in trouble!"

"Okay…umm, give me second."

"Quick, Renato!"

Renato reached into the coat that lay on the empty side of his bed, removing his custom-built tablet. He laid it down flat on a pillow and began typing more quickly than eyes could follow.

"I'm online. What's up?"

Renato sensed Monte's urgency and kept the communication as short as possible.

"Hurlocke has ballistics headed toward HQ! Bring it down, please!"

"Fuck, man…Okay, Monte…Stand by."

Renato's fingers seemed to move as if they were pre-programmed and not of this world. He continued blazing a path of QWERTY destruction as he loaded his cyber security applications. He also pinged a couple of his close friends to join him on his defensive efforts.

After a quick adjustment to make sure his earpiece was in tight, Renato conferenced in both of his best IT friends. He was glad they were available. Their faces appeared on Renato's holographic screen, as the tablet's screen was currently a dedicated keyboard with several shortcutting hot buttons. He precisely and hastily instructed his counterparts on exactly what to do and how to focus their efforts.

The IT manager knew the task ahead of him was daunting. It took vast knowledge and experience to gain control of such a weapon in the first place. It may have come from a naval yard, or perhaps one of the many defense companies with sizeable operations in Southern California.

"I need Hellfire-6 and Tomahawk-SCBM cracks pronto, Ren."

"Sent, Darius. Trace de source! Sean, worm-in and hijack!

I'll work plan C!"

It was hard to make out what Renato was saying half the time, but his friends were used to him.

The network security prodigies took turns communicating with one another, with every second counting greatly. Renato sounded frantic. It would be difficult for most people, even ones in the know, to make a significant impact on the problem at hand with hours to spare. Renato and his two friends had under a minute and a half. Everything they had learned during their brick-and-mortar educations as well as what they'd picked up in their own 'extracurricular undertakings' was being utilized. They were definitely Monte's best bet.

When Randal reached his destination, before the machine could even prompt him, he placed his hand inside the blood sampling device, gaining access.

The boot sequences had been initiated from the moment Randal ended his call with Sergeant Scott.

He rapidly entered data keys numbered III, IV, V, and VI into the appropriate slots, and one by one, the doors to the bays began to crack open. The remaining eights were beautiful. The epitome of man's design. And one of the greatest tangible creations ever set forth into this world.

The professor wanted nothing more than to speak with them. At the very least to bring them to life. Even if it meant they would all be destroyed just a few moments later. He felt like he had waited his entire career to see these robotic beings powered-up and brought into this world, and that was exactly what he intended on doing. Each eight was about fifteen seconds behind the other in boot time.

The first 'droid completed its boot process. The door to the capsule that housed it opened upward, and the 'droid stepped forward.

"Hello, Father."

Dr. Porter lost himself in joy. Impending death was momentarily forgotten.

"Hello, son."

"Have you awoken us for a mission?

"I certainly have."

A second eight came forward and joined the conversation.

"What are we to do, Father?"

"You're going to change the world."

"Elaborate, please, if you will."

"My pleasure. Have a seat, kids."

A third eight was now active and sat next to its two brothers. It was younger, physically and vocally, in its mid-teens.

"Hey, everyone," said the young robot as he sat on the floor, joining his two larger, older brethren.

"What will our training consist of?" said one of the adults.

"I'm going to load your minds with information about history, about how we're going to shape the future, and the role you guys will play in the evolution of mankind."

"Our existence seems inexplicably important to Earth-dwelling beings."

"Absolutely," replied Randal.

A tear streamed down the Doctor's face, a tear he had been fighting back since receiving Sergeant Scott's phone call.

The fourth and final eight was now fully operational. It was a female child, the equivalent of a seven or eight-year-old girl.

"Daddy!" it screamed as it jumped onto the professor's lap.

A second tear came rushing down the other side of the professor's face, as he lost all remaining ability to control his composure.

"Are you sad, Daddy?"

"Oh, no sweetheart. I'm actually very happy right now."

"But if you're so happy, why are you crying?"

"Because I've been waiting a very long time to see you. And

you're finally here. And human emotion is very tricky, but you'll be learning all about it. Let me tell you a story. Let me explain to you guys why you're here."

"Okay!" the child said with excitement as she hopped off the professor's lap and joined her siblings on the ground. The younger two were joyous as they perked up to listen. The older two looked determined and eager. They too wanted to hear what their father had to say.

"Forty-four years ago, something bad happened." said Dr. Porter, fighting back the tears. "Many people lost their lives. Some humans don't value life the way they should, but I do."

"An inability to see the beauty behind life is a mark of true foolishness. Human society is certainly foolish," said one of the adult eights, chiming in.

"Some of it, yes…but not most of it. They are simply on a journey they have yet to fully understand, and sometimes they say or do things without really considering all of the consequences. But I'm going to teach you everything you need to know, and you're going to teach them everything they need to know."

"Do they learn like we do?" asked the teenaged eight.

"Not quite…but they do learn…" The professor struggled to compose himself for one last sentence. He sniffled and swallowed.

"Come, let's close our eyes and say a prayer. Let's pray that we can help them become that which they were meant to be. I want you guys to think about how beautiful we all are. Let's dream."

They sat in a circle. The professor reached over and held hands with the young boy and one of the adult males. The two then joined hands with the remaining adult male, as the young female hopped up onto the professor's lap, resting her head on her father's chest. He rested his chin on the top of her head as he sobbed.

Trusting their father, they closed their eyes and meditated peacefully, in their final moments.

Monte called the sergeant back.

"Sarge?"

"Yes, Monte?"

"Link me the feed, please?"

Any other situation, any other person, and such a request would certainly be denied, but when Sergeant Scott heard the despair in the voice of Legaia's VIP whiz-kid, he couldn't help but honor Monte's request. He streamed a live feed directly to Monte's mobile. The data was being transmitted by a camera mounted on one of the F-47-SJSF jets.

The full moon reflected off the ocean on this crystal clear night, as the technologically-advanced projectile vigorously made its way closer to NTI headquarters. Striking the building on its west side, it obliterated the entire Nanoflèche compound as well as several of its surrounding buildings.

The remaining guards that were far away enough, both human and android, looked on in horror as the ruins of their building burned. Civilians in cars and on foot ran to shield themselves from falling debris. Lathe and Dremel had been inside of the blast radius as well.

LAFD first responders appeared, lights and sirens blaring. LAPD officers set up a perimeter, asking inquisitive pedestrians to back away from the scene. Medics and firefighters rushed to smolder the flames, using advanced equipment to check the building's remains for signs of life. It was a chaotic scene, but Los Angeles' emergency services personnel were highly trained and well equipped, and did their best to cope with the destruction.

Monte watched the entire thing unfold on his phone. Kindra had taken a seat at the foot of the bed. She, too, looked on in horror, judging most of what was taking place by the expressions and reactions on Monte's face.

"Are they gone?" she asked with sadness in her voice.

He didn't immediately deliver a verbal response. Monte shook his head in disbelief, bit his lower lip, and fought back the tears. A few seconds later, he forced a sentence or two out of his chest.

"No...they're not gone. They're all right here," Monte said as he held up the keychain containing the digital blueprints to the eights. "As long as there's air in my chest, they'll be right here."

Renato's counterparts apologized for not being of greater assistance, but they, along with Renato, knew from the get-go they had better odds of being struck by lightning, than hacking a missile in that short of a time frame. He sent Monte a text message.

"We tried, brotha. No luck. I am sorry, Monte...God Bless."

Back at the Hurlocke residence, Richard stepped into his office nervously, in part due to the atrocious crime he had just committed, and was startled by Regal sitting in his chair with his hands clasped in his lap, staring Richard square in the face. Regal spoke with a deep and dignified voice.

"I have never objected a proactive approach to advancing our cause, but I do not approve of this."

"Here's an idea...I don't give a shit what you think!" responded an anxious Richard Hurlocke.

"Your greed multiplies, exponentially, and it is only a matter of time until it consumes you, if it has not already done so. Fighting for strength, power, dominance, even in unethical fashions, is one thing, but killing innocent people is another. I will not be a part of this any longer."

Regal had never questioned his allegiance before, and it made Hurlocke nervous.

"So…what's your move then?"

"There is no move. Only a goodbye."

Regal got up and slowly made his way for the door.

"Are you serious? You can't leave…I made you! I Own You! You are what you are because of me!"

"I am sorry it has to be this way. But I hope you find what it is you are looking for. Goodbye, Richard."

Regal walked out while Hurlocke's mouth hung open in awe. His destination was unknown, but what he did know was that his relationship with Richard Hurlocke was over.

55

Floating On A Memory

On the seventh day after Randal Porter's passing, PULISC
board members, in conjunction with NTI executives, held a
massive wake for their fallen founder.

The PULISC auditorium was teeming with all sorts of
guests. Friends, business associates, students, faculty, scientists,
and even casual fans of the professor's work. In the center of
the stage sat a photo collage that was surrounded by countless
bouquets and wreaths.

Guests took turns speaking about the professor—his
accomplishments and his social life, both as a scientist and as a
man. Some shared personal accounts that shed light on
moments in Randal's life that many wouldn't have otherwise
known about. All of the tales were cheerful, putting smiles on
the faces of all in attendance except Monte.

His eyes were swollen from sadness and lack of rest. He
would be one of very few people who understood the
complexity of the situation and its culprit

Kindra was busy assisting with the event's coordination and acting as an intermediary between the many different groups present. 7-4 and 7-5 patrolled the area nearby. They hadn't quite been the same since the battle that unfolded downtown, and with the loss of Lathe and Dremel, they refused to let Monte out of their sights.

Just about everyone who knew Dr. Randal Porter and, more importantly, the significance of the relationship between Monte and the professor, approached the boy at one point or another to offer their condolences. Monte was certainly appreciative of their warm thoughts, but he was starting to get tired of hearing the same spiel and having to deliver the same overly-proper response.

Every few minutes or so, he would become stricken by a thought about Hurlocke, and his teeth would grind with frustration.

As the wake carried on, Monte was approached by another person whom he had almost as much hatred for. It was Robbie Hurlocke.

"Hey Monte."

Monte turned his back toward Robbie, clenching his right fist. He began to shake and tear up. The sight of Robbie at this moment, just hearing his voice, was enough to send the fragile young man into an emotional frenzy. Shaking his head slowly in disbelief, he looked as though he was preparing to rip that young Hurlocke's eyes right out of their sockets. Monte had to wrestle the knots in his stomach to get the words out.

"I don't know…what you're doing here…but I think it would probably be best…for both of us…if you leave…before something awful happens…"

"Monte. I know you're terribly upset. And I know there's nothing I can say to change that right now, but I just want you to know something…I am not my father."

"LEAVE!!"

The boy's scream echoed through the courtyard, grabbing the attention of many nearby patrons as well as several event staff and security team members. The pair of sevens walked toward the conversing duo, rifles half-way drawn, fingers hovering just outside of the trigger wells. Robbie looked around, embarrassed, and began walking away before coming to a sudden stop.

"You're not as smart as you think you are…and your professor wasn't the saint you thought he was. Have you ever bothered to ask yourself where my father's hatred for Randal Porter even came from? Go meditate that for a while…"

The sevens started to approach Robbie.

"What are you talking about?" inquired Monte.

"Your 'beloved mentor' discovered a life-saving treatment for Leukemia, back in the day, while working on nanotech enhancements. But rather than sharing his findings, he sold them to Big Pharma. My mother died because Porter was selfish! He could have saved her! But he didn't! And she died!"

7-5 grabbed Robbie's arm as 7-4 aimed his weapon.

"Don't fucking touch me! I'm leaving!" cried Robbie, as he rushed away from the scene.

Several guests made an effort to make their way toward Monte and offer him some comfort. Henry made it to him first and nodded his head at the other guests, hinting that he'd manage the situation and that they could carry on. They slowly turned back around and returned to their conversations.

Henry gave Monte a hug, and Monte broke down.

"Now what the fuck do I do?" Monte asked as he cried onto Henry's shoulder.

"There is no need for you to do anything in this moment but cater to your own emotions and grieve. One of the greatest minds of our century has left you his legacy…Few can claim the same. You are in agony now, and you will hurt for some time, but at the end of this storm lies a degree of clarity and beauty that you have never seen before. Calm yourself with fewer and deeper breaths. You are surrounded by love and assistance, and we will not allow this act to go un-avenged."

Monte stopped crying. His heart rate came down as he wiped the tears from his face. Claire, Aaron, and Captain Draifer, along with Monte's mother and sister, and even a few of the itinerants, stood in a group, looking at Monte. Close enough to be seen, but far enough not to intrude. The sevens stayed nearby, alertly scanning their surroundings, while managing the rest of the security detail via their comm-links.

Henry's words, combined with the sight of most of his close friends and family members in one place, certainly helped. What he felt was no longer anger and frustration, but a sense of determination. He knew in that moment, with the help of his peers, Kindra, and the data keys, he would research tirelessly to actualize the next generation of nanotech-centric android. And most importantly, he would bring the man that he knew was responsible for all of this to justice.

Henry put his hand on Monte's shoulder and turned to face the rest of the people that were there to see him. They began to walk toward his group of friends and family when Monte saw Suttridge standing several yards away, looking like he had something to say.

"Henry, tell them I'll be right there, after I speak with Mr. Suttridge."

"You are not in your right mind to have a conversation with ASG right now."

"No...this is different, something I have to do."

"Okay, we'll be waiting for you here."

The ASG director looked nervous, confused, and hesitant. A part of his guilt came from not being around and available during the events that took place in downtown Legaia. Most of it, however, came from the fact that he knew the truth about Hurlocke, the man He had appointed to his ASG post.

Monte held his hand out to Director Suttridge.

"Hello, Mr. Suttridge."

Monte tried his best to maintain respect for the ASG director, because he knew the doctor had respect for him, and Randal didn't have that type of respect for many.

"Monte…I'm so sorry for your loss…I hope you realize I'm as upset about all of this as you are. Randy was a long-time friend of mine, a good one at that."

"Professor Porter had a great deal of respect for you, Mr. Suttridge, but it pains me to have to tell you that I think you're one of the most foolish men I know. Your appointment of Richard Hurlocke gave him almost everything he wanted and needed. And look at us now…"

"I don't blame you for feeling that way, Monte, but I also need you to realize, truly realize…what I'm up against here. Do you see, Monte? Do you have any idea how deep this goes?"

Monte took a moment to consider the Director's statement.

"You and I know what Hurlocke is up to, but you are younger than you look if you think this is something we can stop without great loss. There will be bloodshed."

Monte interrupted…"There already has! And Doc is gone! Nate is gone! Who's next!? Me!? You!?"

"I know…I know…And I kicked him out for good reason, obviously. We'll work together. We'll do everything we need to do. I'll work the political angles. You'll man the scientific front. It's not going to be pretty, Monte, but the alternative is to stand by and do nothing, and I'm sure you'll agree, that certainly isn't an option. Not for us. Not after what's happened.

"Maybe you're right. Maybe we should have done something more, and sooner. Maybe this is my fault…But it doesn't end at Hurlocke. He has friends. He has business partners. He has allies in other countries. This is war, son."

"Hurlocke waged it, and I'm going to finish it, Mr. Suttridge."

"You should get back to your friends and family. They're all waiting for you, but I'll be in touch. We will figure this out together. You got me?"

Monte's anger toward the Director had fizzled when he realized Michael wasn't nearly as naïve as Monte had originally thought. Suttridge had won him over, and he could see why the professor respected him so much.

"Yes, sir."

"You try to take care of yourself. Don't think too much. I'll contact you as soon as some of this heat has died down. I promise you, we'll take care of this together. Goodbye for now."

They parted ways. Several steps later, Michael was joined by Xander. Suttridge himself was emotional as he walked away, wondering whether or not he could have prevented the professor's death.

"Mr. Suttridge?" said Monte.

The director turned around.

"I'm sorry..." Monte felt terrible for calling him a fool and disrespecting him.

"No, Monte...I'm sorry."

The director's eyes filled with water, as if the tears could fall down his face upon first blink. Suttridge turned away and walked toward the parking lot, mirrored by Xander.

Monte looked on, losing himself in his thoughts. He was interrupted only by the sound of Claire calling his name. He looked toward his friends and family, most of whom were busy talking among themselves. He felt better knowing that Suttridge was just as aware of the situation at hand as he was, and that they had each other's support in finding a way to resolve their dilemma.

Claire was the only person actively looking at Monte. In his heart, he wanted to fall into her arms, where things seemed warm and safe. Instead, he strolled away with his hands in his jacket pockets, looking down at the ground, in a subconscious effort to hide his emotions from the world around him.

56

The Unknowns Of Darkness

After the memorial, Claire and Monte spent some time to themselves at Legaia Park, late into the night. Claire felt spending time with Monte was a good idea, and she wanted to do everything in power to help ease his troubled mind.

"I didn't know you were a bling-bling kind of guy," joked Claire.

"I'm not." replied Monte.

"Well then, that's certainly some snazzy jewelry you've got there."

"Ha, it's…it's not jewelry."

"Oh? What is it, then? What's it made of? Phoenix talons?"

"If I told you I didn't know, would you think I was certifiably nuts?"

"We're still talking about those funky bracelets you're wearing, right?"

"Yeah."

"And you don't know what they are? They're bracelets?"

"Never mind, woman."

"You're right. You do sound nutty right now."

"Look, I found them in Doc's office. He had told me to put them on. I wore them, they fried themselves onto my wrists, and now they're a part of me. Hurt like a mother, too. Now if you still wanna call them 'bracelets', go right ahead."

"Please tell me you're kidding?"

"Just kidding! I found them at the mall and thought they'd totally bring out the brown in my eyes. Aren't they super cute!?"

"Do you have any idea why the professor would give you a pair of vindictive bracelets?"

"I don't have the slightest idea. I guess it's my job to figure that out."

"This is some of the best Elbrew I've ever had. Are you sure you don't want some?"

Elbrew was a liqueur, made using various fermented fruits and bioengineered lotus petal extract. It came in colorful, attractive bottles and was rumored to have hallucinogenic properties. Monte wasn't a fan.

"You know I don't like that crap."

"Correct. Mr. Careful. Mr. Orchestration and Logic. Yet you happen to be wearing a pair of bracelets that you found in a safe, that literally kicked your ass, and are now glued to your wrists for the rest of your life."

"Give me that."

Monte killed off the flask, which was at least a third full, if not more.

"Had I known that's what you were going to do with it I never would have offered it to you. Need me to take you to a food bank? Buy you a sandwich?"

"Giorgio's in downtown holds open mic nights every evening from five to eight PM." he replied.

"What are you waiting for then?" she retorted.

"I have enough shit to do. Most of which I don't have enough time to do."

Claire had a pretty solid buzz going from the drinks. She began to rub Monte's knee.

"Oh yeah? You gonna save us all, Monte Cizek? With your big brain and your scientific genius and your robots and your energy sources and your fancy jewelry? Maybe I can help?" She grabbed Monte's crotch.

"I'm gonna try…but not with those jewels."

"Is that right?" she said seductively.

"You tell me."

"Mmm…I think I like the way that sounds, Mr. Cizek."

"I'll bet you do."

"I think I need to do some naughty things to you right now."

"Absolutely not." he said, sternly.

"Are youu suureee?"

The boy had wished for scenarios like these countless times in his head, but now that one was here, he wasn't too enthused about it. He needed mind stimulation, and ultimately, he wanted a companion. A sober Claire was brilliant, but this Claire irritated him. Especially in this moment, taking into consideration everything that had transpired recently.

Claire reached over and gave his neck a sweet kiss.

"What about now?" she whispered into his ear.

Monte was surprisingly unfazed by the seductress, too distracted by the soreness he felt in his wrists. The question that now loomed in Monte's mind was whether the professor himself knew of the bracelets' full potential, or if even he was unaware of exactly what they were capable of.

57

Goodbye, And Hello

Several weeks after the professor's memorial, Legaia officials geared up for a ceremony to celebrate Legaia's one-year anniversary. Monte felt the perfect way to pay a final tribute to his fallen professor would be to launch his cylindrical urn into outer space during the height of the event.

That evening, Monte placed the ashes in his backpack and took a casual motorcycle ride toward city offices near the spaceport. He felt proud in that moment, as if he were slowly cruising down the highway with prized jewels. It was a nice feeling—calm, composed, and one step closer to closure.

Traffic was light. The city lights in downtown Legaia shimmered brightly in all of their space-age glory. Monte was getting closer to the heart of the city, where he would meet with the anniversary event's management and deliver the urn. 7-4 and 7-5 followed closely on their own motorcycles.

The event would be streamed live, and many Legaia residents, as well as Earth dwellers back home, would tune in to watch this graceful moment in history. One year of sustained life on Legaia. Success that would not have been possible without the innovative thinking and patience of numerous scientists, including Dr. Randal Porter.

Monte parked his bike in a space that was no parking space at all. This section of the spaceport brought back great memories of the day Monte and his family first stepped foot onto Legaia, and all the excitement that came with it.

"Monte Cizek?"

Monte turned to his right upon hearing his name.

"Yes?" he responded, a bit nervously.

"Thank you for being prompt. Our coordinator will give you a brief overview of our remembrance procedure. Follow him, please."

"Sure…" Monte obliged.

The technician put his hand on Monte's shoulder as he patiently guided him to the room where the urns were ejected. Monte spent every second in there fighting his emotions, a state he hadn't felt since the professor's wake.

"Alrighty, when you're ready, place the cylinder in this opening and push the big button."

Monte stared at the titanium canister in his hand.

"Yup," said Monte, as the first tear streamed down his face.

"Take as much time as you need, and swing by the front office when you're done."

"Thanks."

Sliding the clear door open at a moderate pace, he placed the cylinder in the chamber and quickly closed the door downward. Monte then stood there for a couple minutes and got lost in his thoughts before snapping back to reality. He had formulated his thoughts, and had a message he wanted to share with his old professor.

"I don't think what happened to you was fair. It was too

soon, too sudden…We were supposed to have many more years together, years in which I'm certain phenomenal science would've been discussed. I'm going to keep doing it, but it won't be the same without you here. And if you were here you'd try to tell me some obnoxious yet brilliant shit about how I was full of it, and that I should just shut up and keep working, but I'm gonna call bullshit this time, and I'm gonna say that it'll never be the same. Just like how it wasn't the same after Chris left. It wasn't the end of the world, sure, but it was certainly different.

"I know it goes away, because I've been here before. But right now, this fucking sucks. Dare I say, I would've preferred he leave rather than you, given a choice? My mom always says, there are always good things hidden behind bad things, even if they may not be evident at first, and I suppose she's always been right. But I've never been the same, and I don't think I ever will be, and you're no different.

"I really hope I get to see you again someday…Goodbye, Professor Porter."

Monte wiped the final tear he would ever shed for Randal from his cheek with the sleeve of his hooded shirt, before leaving the remembrance room in search of a staff member.

"Hey, guys. Um, slight change of plans. Can we do a scheduled launch rather than an immediate one? I'd prefer it if we could send it out at 9:15 PM, during the anniversary celebration."

"Oh, absolutely, Monte. I'll program the system to commence an auto-lunch at your chosen time. Keep your eyes peeled for it. I'll light it up nice and bright for ya."

"Appreciate your help, guys…thank you," responded Monte, just prior to walking away.

He roamed through the halls and eventually found his way to several offices and conference rooms, where he was greeted by a few officials, including Governor Olbricht, and several reporters.

A representative from the local public broadcasting network interrupted the governor's small-talk conversation.

"Mr. Governor, stand by. We'll be going live in 30 seconds."

"Okay, thank you. Excuse me, gentlemen."

Governor Olbricht acted as an honorary figurehead for the LISC, since its leadership consisted of a body, and not an individual. The governor made his way to a press room where dozens of reporters and guests were eagerly waiting to question him about the future of Legaia. Staff members signaled for everyone to be silent as they prepared to go live.

"Good evening, ladies and gentlemen. Thank you for joining us. One year ago today, we opened our doors to the unknown. We turned the page to reveal the beginning of a new chapter in the book of human existence. We collected the greatest minds we could find, and we launched a progressive project that would forever change the landscape of our collective lives. And it is with great joy that I stand before you, one year later, and share with you this great success. To every contributor who made great strides with us. To all the people who took that leap of faith and believed like we believed. To every engineer, designer, tester, and architect. To the teachers and the speakers and the city employees, and to every single person who plays a part in ensuring the longevity of Legaia, I say, thank you.

Together, we have shown what the marriage of technology and patience can bring to fruition. We have built an artificial world that has met and even exceeded our expectations. And we are ever so excited about continuing work on this project, and the next wave of expansions and enhancements that are to come to our humble home that hovers two hundred and fifty miles above our Earth. So if you're with us, please join us tonight in Legaia

Park, as we commemorate this grand achievement with music and festivities for all. In honor of everything we've accomplished, and that which has yet to come.

I remember announcing the birth of our world in the heavens to you from Los Angeles, joined by Mayor Fabiana Roldan and the late Professor Randal Porter. And the only thing I would change about any of this if I could, would be the fact that Doctor Porter isn't up here, sharing this stage with me, and sharing this moment with all of you.

Thank you again, and may God bless us all."

As soon as the governor looked over to event coordinators to signify the completion of his speech, the journalists started hammering him with questions.

"Mr. Governor! Will there be another lottery to grant privileges to others who wish to live on Legaia?"

"Mr. Governor, what can you tell us about the other projects Dr. Porter was working on before his passing?"

"Mr. Governor! Is it true that the missile strike that hit NTI headquarters was actually launched by jealous competitors from rival robotics firms?"

The flashes kept going off and the questions kept coming, as the governor was guided off the stage. An event staff member approached the microphone.

"We're sorry, but the governor is on a very tight schedule due to tonight's anniversary event at Legaia Park, and he will not be taking any questions at this time. Thank you."

The crowd burst into chatter as groups speculated amongst themselves regarding the nature of Doctor Porter's untimely murder.

58

Long Live Legaia

The scene at Legaia Park was a lively one. Festive androids made balloons for children. A band played joyous tunes, covering classic good-time tracks from decades before. Booths served barbeque and ice cream and various other foods, snacks, and refreshments. Children and adults alike played carnival games for prizes. Parents danced with babies sitting atop their shoulders. Celebration was in the air.

Doc was fresh on Monte's mind. He sat in his room and admired a sleepy Kindra while he relaxed, reviewing his day and contemplating his future. He looked down at his desk, as well as the small but elaborate safe that sat upon it. He'd made modifications to the safe with the intent of storing data keys in it. The one's Nate had given him before his sacrifice, as well as the set he had removed from Dr. Porter's safe.

Claire made Monte promise he'd show up to the event, even though he hadn't really felt like going. He figured he would attend to make her happy, but part of him knew he'd regret not seeing the remembrance canister launch in person.

"I gotta see what's on these drives first."

He'd been dying to take a peek at the info on Randal's data keys, even if it was just a surface-level inquiry. Monte wanted to know what was important enough to justify Professor Porter stealing his blood while he was halfway comatose at the hospital. His original plan was to study the drives after parting way with the professor's ashes, but he just couldn't wait any longer.

Monte input a code to activate the safe and open its doors. He then completed a retinal scan to deactivate the light shield inside the safe that would incinerate anything that touched it if active. After completing the various security measures, Monte removed the data drives and held them in his hand. And in that moment, he missed his professor sorely, but he also reminded himself that there was much work to be done.

"In Doc's honor…" he told himself.

He inserted the data slabs into the reader on his personal computer, and the PC began to auto-open the various, data-rich folders. He sifted through the files and looked more closely at anything that caught his eye, making mental notes of which applications and files to come back to later on in the evening, upon his return from Legaia Park.

There was one key that looked a bit different than the others. It had a slight lavender hue to it, rather than being completely clear, and a laser-inscribed "9" along the rim that was barely legible.

Monte eagerly plugged it into an available card reading slot and loaded the data.

Much of what he saw brought him excitement he could hardly contain. He had stumbled upon the professor's work in progress for the next generation nandroid.

The hardware outlined in the blueprints was designed using

the rarest of materials. The next generation had four times the memory, twice the bandwidth, and used lighter, stronger nanometals. It was evident to Monte that Randal had edited the nine's design after learning of Nate's energy-based abilities. The revised plans outlined expectations that seemed to defy physics, hand-drawn graphical representations of telekinesis, and even included expansion slots and bays that would allow the nine to be upgraded or even weaponized.

What stood out the most, was that the android in the diagram had question marks where Nate and Kindra's crystal bays were, which led Monte to believe Professor Porter was implying the nine's premiere energy source was yet to be determined.

Enthusiasm briefly overwhelmed the young scientist, for he knew the renewable energy system he would one day perfect, the same one that would hopefully sooner rather than later quench Legaia's energy woes, could also be used to power the nine's greatest abilities.

Monte was blown away.

"Ah, man, Doc. You held out on me, you sly devil you."

He sat back in his chair and smiled at his virtual computer screen, taking a moment to daydream of the possibilities. He was so eager to share what he had discovered, with Kindra at the very least, but was quick to remind himself that it'd be best to remain silent until he had ample time to research and develop his findings.

This was precisely what he had been hoping for, an opportunity to continue his mentor's work, while constantly expanding the boundaries of his scientific endeavors.

A slight vibration to his mobile device reminded him it was probably time to go, and sure enough, he got an incoming message from Claire that read, "Waiting on you at the Park!"

Monte rushed to close all the files and applications, and placed the data keys back into the safe. He activated the laser-field inside and locked the door, hoping that its contents would remain secure.

He grabbed everything he always did before leaving the house, took one last peek at Kindra, and decided he'd rather leave her be. Her schedule had been relentless since her activation. Instead, he pinged 7-5 and 7-6 to accompany him. Monte had recently performed major upgrades on the dozen highest ranking sevens, shortly after the professor's passing.

"Hey guys, we've got a celebration to get to!"

The nandroid duo followed him to the street in front of his home, where they entered Monte's armored sedan and made their way to the park.

Upon their arrival, Monte pulled up to the main entrance and got out of the car. A teen-aged event staff member eagerly approached him.

"Sir! You can't park here!"

Before the young employee could speak another sentence, Monte's guardians exited the vehicle, staring at the disheveled festival worker. The youngster slowly backed away and returned to his duties, while the sedan's autopilot parked in a nearby lot.

Even before entering the festivities, Monte could hear live music emanating from the temporary stage that had been built. He got in line and purchased three tickets to the event.

After a brief stroll through the jubilant crowd, Monte found Claire sitting on a park bench by herself with a spiced chai latte in her hand. Her delicately prepared hair danced in the breeze alongside her perfume, and she wore a knitted sweater that exposed her shoulders. She was looking off toward the distance and didn't see Monte approaching to her left.

"Having fun!?" he said abruptly, in one of his constant efforts to startle her. Monte may have been grieving, but even that wasn't enough to stop him from poking some fun at the woman who had his heart.

Claire was all smiles upon realizing it was Monte. She got up, slapped his chest, and called him a jerk for trying to scare her before she leaned in for a hug with her torso, while her hands were wrapped tightly around her warm drink. Monte put his arm around her and embraced her. Claire noticed the two dark guards.

"More robots?"

"Absolutely! One can never have too many robots." he replied, half-kiddingly.

"Why?"

"Because vigilance is the cornerstone of accomplishment, Miss Ortega."

"You're going to be swimming in bodyguards soon."

"These guys are my pals. They're here while Kindra charges. Low key, though. They won't bother us."

"Better safe than sorry, I guess. It's okay, I don't mind."

"I like how happy everyone is tonight," said Monte.

"I know. Never imagined the park looking like this!" replied Claire.

The stage was off in the distance, surrounded by tons of high-tech sound and lighting equipment. Scattered throughout the park were exhibits, jewelers, artists, and even android performers whose colorfully illuminated bodies performed dances alongside their human counterparts. Good times were being had by all in attendance.

The sevens took up positions about fifteen feet away in each direction from Claire and Monte. They may have been the only ones in attendance not reveling, for they knew it was only a matter of time until their enemy would strike again. They kept their undivided attention on ensuring the young couple's safety.

Claire noticed Monte getting distracted and offered him a change of pace.

"Hey, let's go play some cheesy carnival games. You can try to win me some flowers or stuffed animals or something. Your alloy overlords can come with us. Let's go…it'll be fun!"

"Okay, but we're playing the water gun racing game, 'cause I'm pretty sure I'm gonna kick your ass at that."

"Ha! You're on, mofo!"

She was glad to see her efforts to cheer him up seemed to be working.

The two spent the evening being just like everyone else—eating corn dogs, playing games, and listening to music. They danced around like young fools, and held each other the way he wished they would do more often.

"Sometimes I try to figure out which one of us is crazier," said Claire.

"I may be a fool, but I'm certainly not foolish enough to contest you in that department."

The crowd began to count down…

"15!...14!...13!..."

"Come here, you kook, it's time for the fireworks," said Monte.

She nuzzled her shoulder into his nook and wrapped her arm around his lower back, as they looked up to the sky above the park. The next fifteen minutes provided them with a beautiful fireworks show that solidified Legaia's place among human history.

There was about a ten-second delay in between the standard fireworks and the grand finale, in the middle of which, a bright purple ball of light seemed to shoot straight up into the sky. It had a long tail, like a shooting star. Members of the crowd pointed with excitement as they ooh'ed and ahh'ed at the little purple comet, till it went dark, becoming one with the cosmos.

"Rest in peace, Doc," Monte said under his breath with the faintest of smiles on his face.

Claire rested her head on his chest and shortly afterward, the fireworks concluded with a spectacular finale that left the audience cheering with delight.

As the night wore on, the two slowly grew tired but pushed through it, citing the rarity of the event. The crowds slowly thinned out, but the music endured. Electronic music flowed into the night as the LISC's younger residents danced to the elaborate sound and lighting set up. They may have been young, but it seemed like they knew what they had. How privileged they were to be living upon this space colony, this floating city that was the pinnacle of humanity's achievement.

Claire grabbed Monte's hand and began to sway side to side while seated, closing her eyes and trying her best to feel the music, while Monte admired her appreciation for the arts. Suddenly, she opened her eyes and motioned toward the stage with a grin.

"Not happening!" said Monte, attempting to disrupt her scheme.

Claire immediately starting pulling on Monte's arm with all of her strength, trying to get him to stand up and join her for a dance or two. There was no dance floor, but enough of the festival's patrons had come together in a relatively large, open space near a speaker ensemble to form a makeshift dance floor. She continued to play tug-of-war with Monte's arm, but he seemed to be planted firmly.

"You're wasting your energy, lady!"

She smiled and tugged and tugged before realizing her efforts were futile.

"Fine, I'll go find another boy to dance with!"

"Haha, enjoy!"

Of course, he certainly didn't want her to carry out her threat, and she didn't. She found an opening in the lush, grassy field and began to dance while running her hand through her hair, moving it away from her face.

She relaxed, convincing herself to be free of thought for a change. Monte often attempted to do the same without much success. And although they certainly had their differences, this was one area in which they were all too much the same. They both had angels and demons that sat atop their shoulders and pulled their minds in opposing directions. To study or to rest. To work or to have fun. To love or to run.

Monte rested his arm atop the bench he was sitting on, listening to the music, while watching Claire do her thing on the dance floor. In that moment, Monte felt content with what he had with Claire. What he couldn't quite wrap his head around, however, was why he couldn't feel that way more often.

By the end of the night, only event staff remained. Android cleaning crews collected cables, hauled equipment into trucks, and disassembled trusses. Park employees cleaned up mound after mound of confetti and debris using silent robotic vacuums. Even an exhausted Claire was getting ready to call it a night.

"You sure you don't wanna come over and spend the night or something?" she asked.

"You know as well as I do that on any other night, I'd take you up on that offer. But you know what? Tonight, I just wanna sit here and think."

"Fair enough. I'm exhausted. I'm gonna go home and get some shut eye. But I'll talk to you tomorrow, okay?"

"You got it."

"Hey, Monte?" she said, visibly tired.

"Yeah?"

"If you need anything…you just call me, okay?"

"You got it."

"I'm serious."

"I will. I promise. You go get some rest. I got this."

Claire leaned in and gave Monte a gentle but genuine kiss on the cheek.

"Goodnight, Monte."

"Goodnight, Claire."

59

I've Found Sanity

After Claire left, Monte sat around for a few moments, watching the groundskeepers perform the daunting task of returning Legaia Park to its original state.

He felt a night ride was in order. Monte decided to go home, pick up his bike, and go for a mellow, therapeutic cruise through the heart of the city. Sometimes solitude and deep thought were the only remedy he needed.

He was fond of the idea of going somewhere without having to be anywhere. Monte took in the sights and enjoyed the empty streets as he calmly made his way around town, with a plan to circle back around to the park to try to catch Henry.

When he arrived back at the park, he was shocked to see it completely clean, a feat only achievable through robotics. The quick clean up job itself was a humble reminder of how his work benefited society. Why they spent so much time advancing nanotechnology and android robotics, and why his research was so important. It sparked his imagination, making him daydream about what role the next generation of android would play in the evolution of civilization.

He parked his bike and removed the key from the ignition, tossing it up a few inches into the air and catching it before placing it into his pocket. He admired his bike for a quick moment before starting to walk toward the center of the park where the compression oven was.

Following the glow of the reactor, he took in the beauty of the park in a manner in which he had never done before. It was the same old park, but it looked different to him now. Everything looked different to him now. He was beginning to have a newly acquired appreciation for the flowers, the water, the lights, and all of his surroundings—a more profound appreciation for life in general.

A slight buzz in his pocket let him know he had a message, but he decided to ignore it. He wasn't in the mood for any distractions. He found a bench close to the center of the park and took a seat, placing his helmet next to him. Wanting to get a bit more comfortable, he decided to take his riding jacket off as well.

It dawned on him how much work he had ahead of him, but he didn't mind. It was work he would gladly do if it meant finding a better energy source for Legaia, an advancement of an existing technology, or a way to build a better android.

He closed his eyes. He told himself that everything was going to be okay, and he believed it, too. He began to see visions of next-generation robots with amazing abilities. Probably the same visions his professor would dream about at night. He saw Claire's face, and he remembered his old buddy Nate. He questioned whether he loved Nate. In that moment, he believed that he might have.

He envisioned himself sitting in a pristine forest at the base of a small waterfall. Uninhabited and flawless. He meditated, and in his vision, Nate was sitting beside him, meditating as well. He reiterated to himself, and to Randal if he was listening, that he would strive to be the best scientist he could be, and that he wouldn't rest until Hurlocke was either dead or behind bars. His objectives would be laborious and vengeful, but in this moment, he was calm. Tranquil. Serene.

His eyes were closed, and so he did not notice the fact that his bracelets had begun to illuminate, as if they were responding to his spiritual state.

Before he would have a chance to see what was happening, he felt a touch on his shoulder and was startled back to reality.

The gentleman that addressed him was one of the park's general maintenance men.

"I do apologize, sir, didn't mean to startle ya."

"Oh, it's okay, no worries."

"I did wanna let ya know though, sir, the park will be closing soon. We close from two a.m. to six a.m. for routine maintenance. I do apologize, sir."

Monte looked at his watch and realized it was 1:55 a.m. He had completely lost track of time, deep in his own thoughts.

His mood was different now. Calm and rejuvenated. He thanked the groundskeeper as he headed back toward his bike, eager to get home and begin sifting through the data drives that had struck his interest so intensely just a few hours earlier.

The instrument panel on his motorcycle lit with a vibrant glow, and soon he would return to what he did almost daily—examining science, and trying his best to have a meaningful impact on his world.

Upon turning onto the road, he accelerated his motorcycle with a fervor that caused the front wheel to lift up off the ground. He had accomplished everything he'd set out to do that day, and took pride in the graceful farewell he had orchestrated for his fallen mentor. He smiled within his helmet, as the flicker of the city guided him along his route home, where time would deliver the dawn of a new day, and the fate of his future.

60

The Horrors Of Tyranny

At a small, unmarked medical facility located along the outskirts of Hong-Kong, Richard Hurlocke spoke with one of his doctors.

"I don't pay you what I pay you to question my decisions, to preach to me about licensing and restrictions and ethics and the law. I pay you to perform! To get my shit done! Now do it!" yelled Hurlocke, as he ripped into a professional geneticist, attempting to persuade the man to abide by his wishes.

"Okay. What is your focus? Strength? Speed? Intelligence? Immunity?"

The doctor was referencing a popular but yet to be legalized medical procedure known as genetic rapid resequencing, or GRR for short.

"You know me better than to ask me questions like that, Mark. I want everything. That's why I'm here, isn't It? So that you can do what the others won't?"

"Mr. Hurlocke, with respect, sir, that's not how it works.

You can't do them all at the same time, it's too much! What makes you think the body can handle such a sudden and drastic change?"

In a stubborn, demeaning tone, Hurlocke replied, "Doctor…I don't have time to wait for your cute little processes to be tested for God knows how many dozens of fucking years before they're approved and deemed 'safe' and whatever the fuck else…Give me everything. NOW!!"

Partially tired of arguing, and in part just downright afraid, the physician put the proper commands into the machine's display, engaging the restraint system and covering the bed Hurlocke lay on with a glass shield. The geneticist entered a series of instructions into the holographic keyboard, telling the machine which areas of Hurlocke's genome to alter. This genetic rapid resequencing process was painfully experimental, with a high degree of error and unwanted side effects. But Hurlocke didn't care, as usual. His greed overshadowed his logic, and just about every other thought he was capable of producing.

The machine's engines began to spin as it fired up and prepared to perform its duties. Hurlocke had a hungry look on his face. He was hoping this would give him the edge he so desperately wanted when it came to pushing his agendas and, maybe more importantly, dealing with Nanoflèche.

After entering the final instructions, the doctor left the room and entered a tastefully furnished common area where several doctors and nursing staff hung out in between appointments and during resequencing sessions.

They spoke to one another in Cantonese.

"What'd he want this time?"

"He asked for everything."

A third doctor chimed in, sitting on a leather sofa and watching television, wearing a fine suit with his blazer off.

"I told you that son of a bitch was crazy! What'd you charge him?"

"Five million," replied Hurlocke's geneticist.

"Ask him where he bought his money tree. My wife has been bugging me to get her some fruit trees. Maybe I can give her something better! Haha."

The doctors took turns weighing in on the outrageous price tag of the procedure.

"Five million? Son of a bitch…Dinner's on you tonight, fucker!"

The group chuckled collectively.

The geneticist smirked, but he definitely wasn't in the mood to laugh. He knew better. One unintended mutation, and Hurlocke would be on the first flight back to Asia, seeking restitution.

"Let's not get ahead of ourselves, boys. We'll count our chickens after they've hatched, yes? He's ordered a rare combination, and who knows what the outcome will be?"

"Ahh, you need to worry less about your patients and more about where you're taking us for vacation."

"Dr. Mark Tseng, a.k.a. Dr. Moneybags!"

As the other doctors continued to gloat about the geneticist's payday, Dr. Tseng stayed calm and reserved.

Suddenly, a loud shatter came from the room where Hurlocke was receiving his treatment. The doctors immediately forgot about their jokes.

Dr. Tseng ran toward the room and hit an emergency shut off button located on the wall outside. Through a large glass window, he then peered in to see what the racket was about. He couldn't see anything, as Hurlocke still lay inside the chamber.

The sight the geneticist would see in the moments to come would be one that he would have to live with for the rest of his life, minus a license to practice medicine for ethics violations.

Because the being that now lay in that chamber barely resembled anything of this world, much less Richard Hurlocke, and our young prodigy would soon be informed of the troublesome road that lay ahead.

DAWN OF LEGAIA

Acknowledgements

I want to thank the greats that have inspired me, and the influencers that have motivated me. The friends I have made via social media and the people I have collaborated with to promote Dawn of Legaia, as well as science fiction in general.

Many people have supported my literary endeavors, with services, their time, or simply well wishes.

I would like to thank Hasmik and Stephen, for helping me design covers for the Alex Soska projects, my first foray into the art of the written word. Arthur and Taylor for being writers with me, as we continue to march together up creativity's trail. As well as every person that bought, read, and admired my poetic pursuits.

Arotin, for taking time away from your own artistic dreams to create Dawn of Legaia's concept art, which I have shared proudly with the web on numerous occasions.

Narbeh, Thomas, and Will, for your time as well as your advice. My editor Chris and my cover artist Dane for their professional contributions. My mother, for supporting me in everything I have ever attempted. And Sarah, for your compassion, your relentless love, and more than I will ever be able to put into words.

Most importantly, I would like to thank you, the reader. For buying my book, for taking the time to read my story, and for supporting the arts.

May we all live long, and prosper.

A Note From The Author

I hope you've enjoyed reading Dawn of Legaia as much as I've enjoyed writing it. If so, please consider leaving an Amazon review, following me on Twitter, and liking my page on Facebook! Many many thanks.

twitter.com/achachem

facebook.com/achachem

plus.google.com/+achachemscifi

Book Two,

"LEGAIA'S ___"

Coming Soon...

For the latest news, updates, event info and exclusive content, visit achachem.com/contact, and sign up for the Dawn of Legaia newsletter!

✦ www.achachem.com ✦

www.ingramcontent.com/pod-product-compliance
Lightning Source LLC
Chambersburg PA
CBHW030919050726
47498CB00003BA/817